A Noxian Sunrise

ISBN 978-1-7370726-2-1

Dedication

For my parents, Charles and Pennie, who always encouraged my imagination

For my daughters, Brinley and Noelle, whose curiosity inspired this book with a single question: "How does a seed know when to grow?"

For my husband, Clay, who patiently shared me with my fictional characters as I wrote my way through anxiety late into the night

For my niece, Ellie (Elbert), who lugged the big binder version of this book to school with her every day so she could join the adventure!

Quick Reference Guide

The Florenci System

Oro

Quamir

Phirun

Noxia

Eudora

Asa-en-Darah*

Traveriss*

* Synthetic Planets

Botanicle Brotherhood

Ranunculus

Bindweed

Lamium

Aster

Lisianthus

Stephanotis

Galax

Rue

Prologue

The explosions reverberated throughout the planetary system, spewing debris and hot gases into space, as the dying sun-star engorged itself on surrounding planets. Somehow, the primitive seedpod escaped the sun-star's ingestion and the resultant dust cloud as it was propelled into space, destined for a journey far beyond what the imagination of its lone passenger. The seedpod would sense what it was searching for only when it was found. Until then, it would safely encase its precious sleeping cargo, shielding her from danger, as they traveled through time and space. Days turned into weeks, weeks into months, months into years, and years into centuries.

At last, the long dormant seedpod sensed the time was at hand as it was drawn into a new planetary system. A sun-star welcomed the new arrival with the intensity of its rays as the seedpod drifted passed five planets, until finally entering the orbit of the outermost planet – a planet different than any other the seedpod had encountered. Circling twice prior to entering the atmosphere, the seedpod slowly sacrificed itself for the singular life form it had been safeguarding as the heat of entry consumed it layer by layer. The protective pod's purpose had been accomplished. Now, its occupant was in the hands of the inhabitants of the planet.

Chapter One
A Trespasser

"What is it?"

"Where did it come from?"

"Why did you bring it in here?"

"This was a bad idea, Ranunculus. You should have destroyed it when it came through the atmosphere."

"That's the whole point. It shouldn't have been able to penetrate the outer shield to make it into the atmosphere."

Something wasn't right. Something had gone wrong, terribly wrong. What were these strange sounds she was hearing, growling back and forth at each other? She tried to breathe, but the air wasn't right. She tried to see, but found only darkness. She didn't understand what was happening. Her seedpod should have only opened when the three sun-stars aligned in the sky. Then she should have sunk her roots deep into the soil to begin the growing cycle. Her roots! She panicked. She couldn't feel her roots. She couldn't feel the soil around her. She thrashed. She was exposed. She would die. A slow numbness began creeping over her. Then silence.

She became aware of her consciousness again. How long had she been asleep, trapped in that horrible nightmare? Her eyes were closed, but she squeezed them more tightly shut as she sensed a bright light overhead. Slowly, she allowed them to flutter open, though at first, she could see nothing in the brightness of the light. Gradually, her eyes adjusted, and she could make out seven blurry figures standing in a semi-circle around her. She heard a unified gasp from the crowd.

She had been awakened from a sleep of infancy and transformed into a fully-developed, functioning, and thinking female with no time to learn or grow on her own accord. One moment she existed only as a preserved portion of a forgotten race with no ability to think or speak, completely unaware of her surroundings only to be faced in the next moment with this cacophony of sights, sounds, and sensations that made her feel alien in her own body – or what used to be her own body.

"Betony?" A tall figure stepped toward her. *Yes, Betony was her name, but who was this? Not father. Not mother.* His face came into focus as he spoke again, but this time he was speaking to the others.

"The speech serum takes a few moments to take effect, but I'm sure her comprehension is fully functioning." He turned toward her again. She could see him clearly now. His wilted face was framed with wild orange hair splayed in all directions. The long tuft of hair that clung to his chin was woven with deep green vines. His skin pigmentation was off, only emitting a dim cast of green, but his dark brown eyes were kind.

"Betony. I know your name because it was imprinted in your seedpod, which crash landed on our planet. Please shake your head if you understand me." She shook her head slowly.

3

"My name is Ranunculus. I am a friend. We are friends," he continued while gesturing to the group, which maintained its distance. They were still mesmerized by her appearance. Deep red hair flowed to the floor with hundreds of tiny bright yellow braids woven together like a delicate tiara encircling the top of her head. Shoots of white spikes protruded in a circular pattern within the braids. Her large green eyes, wide with fear, were sparkling gems lined with long, lush, green eyelashes. Her pale green skin was shimmering in the growing lights. Her body was clothed in a flowing green gown several shades darker than her skin tone, overlaid with a sheer green layer that glimmered as she sat up. As she studied the life forms gawking at her, her skin pricked uncomfortably with panic as she realized that these beings were not like her.

"Where am I?" Her voice was raspy from nonuse, but her audience drew in another astonished breath in unison as the beautiful melody of sound danced into their ears. Ranunculus alone seemed unaffected.

"You are on the planet Traveriss in the Florenci System."

"I do not know this place," she whispered.

"I daresay you don't. When your pod was sent into space, this planet did not even exist, and the rest of the planetary system was most likely in its infancy. You see, while it's hard to say for sure exactly how long you've been floating in space, my best guess would be thousands of years. You, my dear, are what we call an Ancient." It was her turn to gasp at Ranunculus's preposterous words. It couldn't be true, and yet when she probed her mind, she could not recollect anything of what had been. There was no past – just a sense of urgency to find soil and sun-stars.

"I don't understand. My seedpod should have only opened when the three

4

sun-stars aligned in the sky." She was on the verge of tears, but not sure why.

"Ah. It is as I feared. You have crossed through the Barren Shield in your travels, and your memory has been veiled." This time, Betony wasn't the only one wallowing in a sea of confusion and disbelief.

"But how?" An eighth man entered the room. His face was shadowed by a white wide-brimmed hat. He wore a long, dark robe that swished as he walked. Large black orbs were anchored to the center of the white of his eyes, and he was leering sinisterly at her as he spoke. "How could it have arrived unscathed?"

"Bindweed, that is no way to treat our guest," Ranunculus chided.

"Guest? Is that what you're calling misplaced and unwanted life forms these days? Too many strange occurrences of late. Too many foreigners breaching supposedly impenetrable shields. Even you must agree with that, Ranunculus. Don't let your inquisitiveness blur your sense of security, my friend," Bindweed spat out the last word as though it left a bitter taste in his mouth.

"He's right." A man with frizzy red hair stepped forward. "First the insect, then the Transparencies, and now an Ancient?" A murmur of agreement passed among the group.

"Mere coincidence, Aster," Ranunculus assured them.

"Or a very clever trap," a tall man with long white hair streaked with purple spoke up. "For a nonexistent enemy, that is."

"Good point, Lamium," Ranunculus supported the opinion. "We have no enemies."

"What you're suggesting, Bindweed, is that there has been some sort of a breach?" Lamium's voice again echoed in the spacious silver room.

"If there has been a breach, he is among us." It was Aster again. Eyes narrowed as they searched each other's faces, unwilling to believe a traitor could exist in their midst.

"Stop this nonsense at once. Suspicion breeds only disunity and distrust. Without trust, the Brotherhood would be dissolved. These matters can be discussed at Council, not here. Rue," Ranunculus called out to a younger man, whose hair was arranged in pink spikes. He was not actually in the semi-circular group but several paces behind and to the left. He had not participated in the speculation, rather he watched and listened closely and carefully. He now stepped forward.

"Please escort our guest to her quarters," Ranunculus instructed, and then turning to Betony, he added, "I'll be along shortly to explain matters in more detail. Please forgive my brothers of their little outburst. Most impolite."

Betony had been sitting on a large table in the center of the room during the entire exchange. She now understood that she was to stand and walk with this 'Rue' to some destination. Rue was waiting by her side as she rose to her feet, but her legs buckled. She didn't know of these legs. She knew of roots, growing and stretching in the soil. Mobility must not have been a necessity from wherever she had come. Rue's quick reflexes saved her from crumpling to the ground in a useless heap.

"Dear me," Ranunculus said. "I've completely forgotten that you don't know how to walk. Not to worry. Not to worry. Rue here will help you along." Rue's face paled by several shades at the request as though he'd been asked to escort an aphid to a plant nursery.

"Go on, my boy," Ranunculus encouraged. Rue seemed to come to grips with whatever had momentarily overcome him. He put his arm around

Betony's waist and firmly gripped her arm as he supported her feathery weight. She winced with pain as she drew in a sharp breath. He perceptively loosened his grip and uttered a barely audible apology. He didn't speak again as he helped her step by step out of the room, down a long corridor, and into a smaller room, where he gently eased her onto a bed. He abruptly exited the room, leaving Betony alone in a strange place, confusion and worry burrowing into her mind.

She sat on the bed, which was a far cry from the flower bed of soil she had been expecting. Then again, she no longer had roots to anchor herself to the soil either. Instead, she was stuck with these mobile sticks. She had been reduced to nothing more than an insect. She moved her legs and wiggled her toes trying to familiarize herself with her new body. A few moments later, a knock came at the door, and Ranunculus let himself in, his face beaming at her with a bright smile.

"I'm sure you're still more than a little disoriented, you poor thing. What a journey you've had!" She could think of nothing to say in response for she didn't remember the journey nor was she about to thank him for turning her into a mutant like himself. When Betony remained silent, Ranunculus continued.

"Well, I suppose I'll try to enlighten you about your situation. Your seedpod has traveled for a very long time as I mentioned before. While you were encapsulated in your pod, your mind was dormant, waiting to be awakened when your pod opened. At some point, you crossed what we refer to as the Barren Shield, where your mind was veiled. We aren't exactly sure why, but anyone who has ever passed the Barren Shield has had memory disruptions. Sometimes the memories are merely veiled, sometimes erased.

Because your seedpod was quite remarkably unscathed, I have every reason to believe your memories are intact. You see, your memories were encased in your seedpod, set to be transferred to you upon your awakening. It is very important that we try to recover these memories because they will be the key to finding out who you are, where you came from, and why you were launched into space alone. Furthermore, they are the key to unlocking all your abilities."

"But I can speak and think," Betony interrupted. "I have my abilities." Ranunculus shook his head patiently.

"No. You can speak only because I administered a speech serum. I manually woke up parts of your brain so you could interact with us. I was only able to open your seedpod by experimenting to find its trigger point, which in your case happened to be exposure to intense light. When the seedpod opened, I realized you were special indeed – an Ancient. I've only met one other Ancient in my lifetime. You've also noticed that I had to adapt your body to this planetary system, so you wouldn't die. I do apologize, but I really had no choice in the matter. We can't necessarily send you back, now, can we?"

"You mean I must remain here – in this place? I cannot go to my own kind?" Betony had never imagined being trapped in this dreary place forever.

"I'm afraid so. Of course, you won't live here on Traveriss. This is a synthetic planet I created with my own hands. It is home only to the members of the Botanical Brotherhood. We are elite scientists with expertise in a wide spectrum of areas from phytopathology to astrophysics, paleobotany to phytochemistry. We've devoted our lives to science. It's an extraordinary place to be – my life's dream coming to fruition, but not a place for one like you." Ranunculus was clearly passionate about his work with the Brotherhood, and Betony had no interest in staying in this dark place with a team of strange scientists. Besides, the only light was artificial, which was less than regenerating. No, this was not the place for her.

"Where will I go?" she asked glumly. Was there a home somewhere in this planetary system for her?

"Ah, don't fret about that, Ancient One. One step at a time. One foot in front of the other. I have a plan, and we'll discuss it at Council tomorrow." Betony felt better knowing Ranunculus was looking out for her. For some reason, she trusted this stranger. A loud noise ripped her from her thoughts as the device implanted in Ranunculus's arm, which flashed every few seconds indicating its functionality, turned red and began emitting a high-pitched chirp every two seconds. Betony clapped her hands over her ears to muffle the noise. It lasted for only a few terrifying moments before the light changed to a steady blue, and the sound ceased, though its echo was reverberating in her head.

"Drats. Pesky things, anyway," Ranunculus muttered. Betony was shaking, and he reached out his hand to pat her awkwardly on the leg to calm her.

"What was that?" she asked weakly.

"It seems a new pest species, the Transparencies, has infiltrated our planet, threatening to wipe us out if we don't eradicate it first. But it's a tricky endeavor because they're invisible and faster than you can imagine. They feed on our life force, you see, slowly draining it from us until we die. We created this implant that detects them when they've entered our bodies, immediately releasing an inoculation into our circulatory system that kills them but leaves us unharmed. The ten rapid beeps you heard at the end signal the death and dissolution of the Transparency. Brilliant idea for Traveriss, but not so easily mass-produced for the rest of the planetary system."

"Am I in danger then?" Betony's eyes showed her alarm.

"No. This room has been specially protected by a detector shield. Those Transparencies must have entered my life force before I entered the room. Yet another reason to remove you from Traveriss, though. The sooner the better." Ranunculus patted her leg again. "Don't worry. Try to get some rest, won't you? It's best to leave the growing light on to help you regain some strength. I've intensified the rays just for you. Hydrate yourself frequently as well. Your system won't be ready for any food yet, so I'll prepare a vitamin and mineral supplement for you to take in the morning." He rose to leave.

"Thank you," Betony whispered, somewhat reluctantly since she was still debating whether she had been rescued or imprisoned for life. Ranunculus turned and smiled at her. When the door was securely closed behind him, Betony hugged her knees to her chest and curled up on the soft surface of the bed, silently wishing she was still asleep in the familiar confines of her seedpod with its comforting smell and sound-proof exterior. This place smelled of sterility and lifelessness. She could hear distant sounds: a faint tapping, an inaudible voice, a clank, a laugh.

Her greatest struggle, however, was silencing the thousand voices in her head that were demanding answers she could not provide. Who was she? Where was she from? Why had she been abandoned in space? The last question lingered, forcing new, more haunting questions to the front stage of her mind. What if Ranunculus was wrong about her? What if she was just a pawn in a terrible plot to destroy Traveriss? Maybe not knowing the details of her hidden past would be better after all. Were some secrets better left buried?

As she tried to calm herself, her body trembled at the thought of her fate being decided by a Brotherhood of scientific strangers only a few short hours from now. She also knew, however, that she would abide by whatever decision they made. She was, after all, nothing more than a trespasser in their land, however welcomed Ranunculus had tried to make her feel. A trespasser – she quivered at the thought and closed her eyes again.

Chapter Two
A Destination

Betony must have nodded off sometime during the night because she was awakened by a soft knocking at her door. A beautiful female popped her head in, her curly yellow hair bouncing as she entered.

"Hello, there. I'm Tansy. Ranunculus asked me to bring in your vitamin supplement." Betony rubbed her eyes as she sat up.

"Are you part of the Brotherhood?" Betony asked, but Tansy only laughed in response.

"Oh, no. I'm a traveling guardian. Every two years, Ranunculus recruits two individuals to observe operations at Traveriss and to travel around to the other planets with him or one of the Brothers as the need arises. He calls us traveling guardians because in a sense we become guardians of the history we have recorded while we're here. I've only got a few months left before I rotate back to my home planet with Valerian," Tansy explained.

"Valerian?" Betony queried.

"He's the other traveling guardian. There are always two."

"How did you come to be a traveling guardian?" Betony was trying to understand why anyone would choose to live on Traveriss.

"Valerian and I were exploring one day on our planet. We come from Phirun, which is one of the most beautiful planets in the planetary system I might add, now that I've seen the others. Anyway, we were hiking near the recharge station. I bet you don't know what that is, do you?" Betony shook her head.

"Well, when we fly pods in space, they de-energize, so Ranunculus asked permission from each of the planet heads to install recharging stations for his pods, so they could re-energize. His space monitors, which are basically research robots that collect data throughout the planetary system, also re-energize using the charging stations."

"That makes sense. Please continue," Betony urged, understanding the need to recharge.

"While Valerian and I were near the recharging station, Ranunculus landed in a pod. We had never seen a pod in person before. We'd only heard tales of them because our people are planet-bound. We don't have the technological capability of flying to other planets. We were fascinated by the pod, and we were seeking some adventure. Of course, everyone in the planetary system knows who Ranunculus is, so we were equally astounded by our luck in having run into him. We asked Ranunculus if there was any way he could take us for a ride in his pod, and he offered us something far better, traveling guardianships."

"And you like it here?"

"Yeah, Traveriss is okay. We really like when we get to accompany the Brotherhood on flight missions though. That's where the real adventures are. Not much happens here from day to day that would excite an ordinary Phirunite like me. We aren't very science-oriented," she chuckled, and Betony found herself laughing for the first time too.

"Me neither," she agreed. "And I could use a few more sun-stars."

"There aren't many of those in this planetary system, I'm afraid," Tansy informed her, crushing Betony's hope as the words hammered her dire circumstances into her brain with force. Tansy noticed Betony's downcast look but couldn't retract the words.

"Sorry. Maybe this will help," she said as she offered Betony a glass filled with a brown liquid. Betony drank the nasty concoction, choking on the last gulp.

"Ranunculus isn't known for his culinary skills. Taste means little to him. It's all about substance," Tansy explained as Betony wiped her mouth with her hand.

"I've been asked to escort you to Council this morning as well, whenever you're ready. And there's plenty of time for a little tour of the facility if you'd like." Tansy helped Betony to her feet, and they practiced walking around the room until Betony was able to balance on her own two feet. She wanted to walk to Council unassisted.

Tansy first showed Betony to the Florenci System Room. The only light in the room was coming from a scaled replica of a sun-star that was free-floating in the center of the room at eye level. Betony soon realized that this room contained a 3-D replica of the Florenci System. The planets, moons, and stars were accurate right down to the minutest detail. The planets were hovering in the air in their own orbital paths. She noted a black planet, a golden planet, a white cloud-covered planet, two blue and green planets, and a semi-transparent planet Betony could barely make out. That must be Traveriss. There were even miniature replicas of the space monitors positioned exactly where they were at that moment in space. As she watched them in fascination, she could see that they were all moving, slowly and steadily toward different locations. She was mesmerized by the sight, and as she turned to leave, she caught a glimpse of a comet entering the planetary system at top-notch speed.

The next room Tansy showed her was the Botanical Room, so named because it housed an array of exotic plants and vegetation, all apparently genetically engineered. The room resembled a large green house with a stagnant smell, despite the re-circulating air. The adjoining room was the Paleobotany Room, which was Ranunculus's pet project. Fossilized plants adorned the walls and excavated plant remains, which had been procured from other galaxies, were displayed in glass cases. There were hundreds of them, each with detailed descriptions as to their origins, dates of existence, functions, and every other possible fact that had been uncovered about them.

Another room was filled with prototypes of a menagerie of equipment and devises from odd-looking space monitors to communication devises resembling some kind of insect to synthetic nebulas floating aimlessly about the room, which were captivating to watch even if they served no other purpose. Betony nearly tripped over a discarded food synthesizer, which Tansy assured her had been a big failure. Far too soon, the time for the touring came to an abrupt halt at the top of the hour when Council was scheduled to begin. Tansy rushed her down the corridor.

The Council Room was circular with an ornate round table in the center. The walls were painted with extravagantly detailed images of what Betony knew now to be the planet surfaces of all the planets in the planetary system. Just as she noted in the Florenci System Room, each was different but beautiful in its own right, except the last one, which was depicted as a black circle and nothing more. Eight men sat in the circle – no one was distinguished above another. Betony had supposed Ranunculus to be the leader, but in Council at least, they appeared to be equals. She was surprised to see Rue seated among them. He had not been in the semi-circle at the initial meeting, and he seemed different from the rest of them. Betony had assumed him to be an apprentice because he was the youngest by decades and didn't dress as the others did. The older men all wore robes of various colors, while Rue wore loose brown fabric and leather pants, and a white collared shirt with a brown leather jacket. He certainly didn't look the part of the Brotherhood in Betony's opinion.

"Welcome, Betony," Ranunculus said cheerily as Tansy seated her next to him.

"Welcome," the other seven men repeated in low, monotone voices. Betony bowed her head in acknowledgement. She wondered if that was a form of greeting from her own planet because she had done it instinctively.

"I trust you are well?" Ranunculus swiveled in his chair to face her. She scanned the room slowly before answering, fully aware that the thunderhead of tension was looming in the air ready to unleash its downpour at any moment.

"As well as can be expected." Her eyes drifted toward Rue, but he looked away the instant their eyes met.

"I think introductions should be our first order of business," Ranunculus began. He pointed to the first man on his left, whose hair spiraled into a high lavender cone on his head.

"This is Galax." Ranunculus continued around the room as he introduced Aster, with his frizzy red hair, and Lamium, who looked regal with his white, long silken hair highlighted with deep purple strands. She remembered each of them from yesterday's brief encounter. Next to him was Bindweed, whose hat had been removed, revealing very short gray hair that matched his short goatee. He looked less menacing without the hat shadowing his face, darkening his features into a shade of callousness. Next sat Lisianthus, a short plump man with wispy pink hair. Stephanotis was a tall delicate looking man whose white hair was shaped into five distinct points that stuck straight out from his scalp like a flattened crown. He winked at her as he was introduced. Rue was the last to be introduced, and he only briefly looked in her direction with a slight nod of his head.

"Now that we're all acquainted, we might as well get right down to business. Brothers, I have thought long and hard about what course of action to pursue, and I have a proposal to submit for your approval. Betony must drink the Water of the Cloud to taste of remembering." A hush fell over the room.

"Impossible!" Aster whispered.

"It's madness," Lisianthus concurred.

"I will not allow it," Bindweed bellowed, slamming a fist onto the table. "That location is not to be revealed to anyone under any circumstances, particularly when we don't know of her origin. You know as well as I Ranunculus that there are those who would resort to such trickery to ascertain the location to which you are most unwisely referring."

"Your concerns are duly noted by all," Lamium responded calmly, "but I agree with Ranunculus. We have no other choice. The location need not be revealed but to the one who escorts her. Thus, the secrecy is preserved between you and Ranunculus and the escort since you still don't trust even the rest of us in the Brotherhood enough to disclose the location. Besides, if my understanding is correct, another Ancient resides on that planet. The girl may feel at home there." Sweat was now beading on Bindweed's forehead, evidencing his vehement opposition. Betony's heart raced at the thought of meeting another Ancient like herself.

"You seem to be well informed of the nature of this place," Bindweed snapped.

"Bindweed, good Brother, we have all heard the rumors about this place. They've circulated the planetary system for years. I think Lamium speaks well, but who shall be the escort? Not one of us surely. With this Transparency threat hovering over our planet, we must remain here to resolve the situation," Stephanotis prompted.

"What about Rue?" suggested Lamium. Rue had been silently listening to the exchange among his elders as if he didn't really belong to the group, and yet, he did. His eyes now widened with fear or surprise. Betony couldn't tell which.

"I was about to suggest that myself," Ranunculus agreed, rising to his feet. "Bindweed?"

"My position is unchanged," Bindweed said bitterly.

"I had hoped for a unanimous decision," Ranunculus murmured.

"Let's put it to a vote," Lamium urged.

"All in favor..." Ranunculus called. All hands went up but two, Rue's and Bindweed's. Even Bindweed was visibly shocked at the result.

"Rue?" Ranunculus questioned disapprovingly.

"You might have asked my opinion before putting it to a vote," Rue said in a surprisingly firm tone. He was not quiet after all, merely unassuming unless moved to take a position. He was clearly irritated that Bindweed's concerns had been addressed, but no one had given the slightest thought to address his.

"You have reservations about the proposition?" Ranunculus probed.

"No, I fully concur with the plan. There is no other course to pursue," Rue replied.

"So why did you not vote in favor?" Stephanotis interjected.

"I have reservations about the escort," Rue answered. The room erupted in laughter; even the corners of Bindweed's lips approached the faintest hint of a smile. Rue, however, was not amused. Betony couldn't help but wonder if Rue had something against her. He had looked sick to death yesterday when he had taken her to her quarters. Maybe she was unintentionally emitting a pheromone that repulsed him.

"Why send the least traveled, the least experienced of the Brotherhood?" he inquired. The laughter ceased as Rue revealed his own feelings of inadequacy without embarrassment or shame. He continued, "Would it not be in the best interest of the Ancient to travel with a more experienced and knowledgeable companion?"

"Rue, my boy, you know as much as the rest of us, and more in some cases," Ranunculus subtly shifted his eyes in the direction of Lisianthus. "And this would be an excellent opportunity for you to make your 'maiden' voyage from Traveriss, so to speak." Chuckles again echoed in the room; the double meaning of Ranunculus's carefully chosen phrase was not lost on the adept audience.

"And don't forget, young Rue," Ranunculus added, stroking his long orange beard as he spoke, "you already know the way."

"This is most enlightening," Lamium was enraged. "You tell a mere seedling, and leave us in the dark."

"It is not your secret to know Lamium, although you do seem quite eager and uncharacteristically agitated concerning this topic. Why the sudden interest?" Bindweed seethed.

"Yes, yes, of course it is none of my business. I was out of line. My apologies. Sometimes my curiosity gets the better of me," Lamium apologized, his serene demeanor returning.

"Rue?" Ranunculus turned. "Are you still opposed?"

"I can think of no better alternative," Rue reluctantly agreed.

"Excellent," Ranunculus clapped his hands together contentedly. Betony sat in silence throughout the meeting, oblivious to what had been decided aside from the fact that once again she was to go with Rue to some unknown destination. The Council was adjourned, and the members of the Brotherhood excused themselves one by one, each bowing respectfully toward Betony as he left. Only Rue and Ranunculus remained.

"So, it's settled," Ranunculus said. "You shall leave in the morning in the long-range exploration pod, Rue. Oh, and I think I'll send the traveling guardians along so Betony can have some company. It's a long trip, and they are due to return to Phirun soon anyway as I recall."

"But then they'll know the location," Rue reminded him.

"Clary can take care of that when you get there."

"Sir?" Rue sought an explanation.

"Too many questions, my boy."

"I learned well then," Rue quipped.

"Indeed, you did. Indeed, you did." Ranunculus looked at Rue with the quiet admiration of a scientist applauding his latest discovery. He quickly snapped back to reality, adding, "Now, we have many preparations before your departure." Without disclosing any more information about her destination, Ranunculus escorted Betony to her quarters, advising her to rest. She willingly complied, exhausted from merely listening to eight men argue her fate.

INTERGALACTIC INTERCEPTION #1

Prey yawned as he stared out into the darkness from his pod, five hundred days into his commission from Ranunculus to explore the Southern Cape. Nothing noteworthy to report, except a vast desert of blackness. Prey was on his way home from yet another disappointing, not to mention pointless, waste of his time. What did Ranunculus hope to find anyway? Why did Prey keep accepting his absurd commissions to explore the great beyond? That was an easy question. The answer clung to his mind like the thick, viscous innards of a delectable mealworm stuck to his mouth. Mmm. Mmm. What he wouldn't give for a taste of that at the moment!

But back to the point. The answer had everything to do with being exiled from his own planetary system for attempting to mate with the High Ambassador's daughter. Not the smartest thing he'd ever done, but oh was she worth it! He had been shuttled and strapped to the nearest comet without as much as a last goodbye for his dear mother. The comet, without a navigation system of its own, crashed into a moon not long into the journey, but at the speed of a comet, the distance was incalculable. There would be no returning.

He had been near the point of starvation when a space monitor landed on the moon. With the last of his strength, he had managed to attach himself to the probe before giving way to unconsciousness. When he awoke, he was in

Ranunculus's laboratory. That's right. Old Run-dung, Prey's personal term of endearment for his rescuer, had saved his life and allowed him to live on Traveriss in exchange for his exploration services. It was a fair deal. He was alive, wasn't he?

There was another perk he had forgotten about momentarily that came to his mind as he set his coordinates to return to Traveriss. When he was in space, he didn't have to engage in evasive maneuvers to stay out of the clutches of entomologist-wanna-be Stephanotis, who would stop at nothing short of a dissection to satisfy his rabid curiosity about evolving insects. Prey shuddered as he turned on the communicator to report to Run-dung his impending return. The green indicator light flickered twice and went black. Typical. He had meant to fix that after his last commission. He'd have to move it to the top of his priority list right after his debriefing, which would take about a millisecond since there was nothing to report yet again. He was beginning to suspect these explorations were a farce designed to keep him out of the way of the Brotherhood. He didn't blame Run-Dung, of course. Prey was bred out of mischief; thus, he bred mischief. It was his nature. He couldn't help but get into trouble.

His receptor signal began to buzz, indicating an outgoing message from Traveriss. While his communicator, which allowed him to send messages to Traveriss, was off-line, Prey made quite sure his receptor, which allowed him to receive messages from Traveriss, was always in tip-top shape. In fact, he had tweaked it a bit himself so he could hear all outgoing messages rather than only those from Run-Dung. He had very few sources of entertainment as he floated in space alone all the time. He couldn't help himself. He enjoyed listening in on conversations when he was in range.

Most of it bored him right out of his exoskeleton, but every once in a while, he got a juicy tidbit or two as one of the Brotherhood contacted his home planet. He was secretly hoping for information with which to blackmail Stephanotis into leaving him alone, but his tweaking hadn't been perfected yet. He couldn't hear the voices clearly enough to determine who was speaking, and he hadn't been able to hack into their personal signature codes yet to identify the speaker. Maybe he would move that to the top of his priority list after his debriefing. Who needs a communicator after all? It's not like Rundung and he had any heart-to-heart talks while he was in deep space. He muted the voice in his head to listen to the intergalactic interception.

Voice 1: I'd like to add an addendum to our agreement.

Voice 2: What? Kidnapping the Queen wasn't enough for you?

Voice 1: Quite enough for what you're getting in exchange.

Voice 2: Don't forget you're still the primary beneficiary of that little arrangement too.

It seems all the cards are stacked in your favor for the moment.

Voice 1: This might tip them more toward your direction if you come through.

Voice 2: I'm listening.

Voice 1: Another Ancient has been recovered, and she's on her way to visit your one and only of so long ago.

Voice 2: Two beauties with one stone. What's the price?

Voice 1: I want the escort dead.

Voice 2: I thought you were already taking care of that.

Voice 1: Oh, be assured that I am and quite successfully, but I don't want a slow death for him. I want a sure death this time. I

23

shouldn't have to remind you that he should already be dead. Call this a second chance.

Voice 2: I've taken care of the traitor that ensured his survival the first time. Give me the details.

Voice 1: They will be traveling in a long-range exploration pod, departing in the morning with a party of four: the escort, the Ancient, and two traveling guardians. The Ancient is yours for the taking, only after the escort is confirmed dead.

Voice 2: I can't kill him until he reaches his destination.

Voice 1: Wrong again. His course will be mapped out on his star charts. You need only commandeer the vessel for the location.

Voice 2: And the traveling guardians?

Voice 1: Ignorant Phirunites. Do with them as you please.

Voice 2: (sinister cackling) Always a pleasure working with you, *Brother.*

Static.

Prey's lenses were twitching a thousand different directions, making him dizzy. He took a deep breath to steady himself and checked the frequencies again. The signal had come through a wormhole line Prey had hacked into just yesterday. He had been expecting intergalactic gossip through that line from other galaxies, maybe even his own, certainly not a treacherous plot to kill someone – someone he probably knew. The frequency was in fact emanating from Traveriss.

Prey tracked back through the conversation. An Ancient had come to Traveriss. Prey had no idea what that meant. Traveling guardians changed too frequently for Prey to know any of them personally since he was gone for such long periods of time. An escort. An escort. His mind was whirling. It must be a member of the Brotherhood another member was trying to assassinate. But what was that about a slow death and a kidnapped Queen? If only Prey hadn't been so stupid to procrastinate his communicator repair, he could radio Rundung right now to warn him. Not that the old man would believe him, but now he could do nothing more than gnaw on his foreleg and wait for the next interception. Wait. Wait. Wait. He couldn't just wait around for the next report. He couldn't make the pod go faster either, so he set to work trying to decode the signature encoding in an effort to at least identify the traitor.

Chapter Three _A Journey_

Betony was brought to the pod early the following morning. Although much bigger than her own seed-pod, this pod bore a striking resemblance to its ancestral cousin. It looked like an elongated seed on steroids with a sleek brown outer covering. There were three on-board rooms, each only large enough for a small bed and a metal stand with a drawer. The pod's maximum occupancy was four since someone always stayed in the pilot station. The only other sectioned areas were the pilot station and the Commons, which were also the only areas with windows to the outside. The Commons was an area large enough for all four of them to gather to eat, while the pilot station had room for two.

Betony gripped the sides of her chair with white knuckles as the pod lifted off. She preferred flying better unconscious. A roaring sound permeated the pod as it ascended through the atmosphere, and her stomach rose into her throat. As soon as they were in open space, the vibrations ceased, and she was able to relax, or at least breathe at regular intervals. Rue was piloting the pod with Valerian serving as navigator. Earlier that morning, Betony had met Valerian for the first time. He was an amiable and handsome man with short purple hair knotted tightly to his head. She liked him almost immediately.

"We're in for a long flight," Tansy commented, settling into the chair next to her. "But it's only rough riding when we have to enter or leave a planet's atmosphere. I'll give you plenty of warning before that happens."

"I doubt warning would do much to assuage my anxiety."

"You'll get used to it," Tansy assured her. "How about a bit of Florenci System history to get your mind off it?"

"Since I dare say I'm not leaving the planetary system in my lifetime, I suppose it would be in my best interest to learn as much as I can about my new abode."

"We'll see how much I can remember. They don't teach much about the other planets on Phirun, but I've learned quite a bit as a traveling guardian. The entire planetary system is composed of only five planets plus two synthetic planets created by Ranunculus and Bindweed. The two synthetic planets are Traveriss and Asa-en-Darah, which is our secret destination. I just learned its name in our briefing this morning."

"Why is it such a secret?" Betony wondered.

"To protect the Ancient who lives there. Her name is Clary, and Asa-en-Darah was created as a sanctuary for her and her alone."

"To protect her from what?"

"That I don't know."

"And she lives there all by herself in isolation?"

"I guess. I really don't know that much about it. There's lots of speculation among the Brotherhood as you heard at Council yesterday, but Ranunculus and Bindweed refuse to talk about it. While Bindweed seems like a sketchy character, I know Ranunculus wouldn't force her to stay there alone if she didn't want too. This is the greatest adventure I could have ever hoped for. I'll be the first person outside the Brotherhood to see Asa-en-Darah and meet

Clary," Tansy paused for a moment of introspection before continuing.

"The next planet is Oro, which is known as the land of the golden desert because the entire planet is one giant desert with very little water. Some of the inhabitants are very strange-looking - very tall with bristly hair all over their bodies, but others look just like me. That was one of my favorite stops on flight missions because the planet is completely opposite of mine. Phirun, which is always obscured by cloud cover, is basically a water planet with lots of rain. That's what I miss most about home - the smell of a Phirun rainstorm. Quamir is Ranunculus's home planet. It has the most beautiful four moons you have ever seen, each a different color. And then there's Eudora," Tansy's lip quivered faintly as she mentioned the planet's name, and she had to take a moment to regain her composure before she was able to continue. "Eudora was once the most beautiful planet in the Florenci System from the pictures I've seen of it, anyway."

"What happened to it? Is it not beautiful anymore?"

"I'm sure it's still as beautiful, but it's a ghost planet now."

"A ghost planet? What do you mean?" Betony asked sifting through the vocabulary the speech serum had implanted in her brain. She came up blank.

"The entire population of the planet was wiped out by a plague. Not a single being escaped, but no one even knew about its extinction until much later. There wasn't a trace of Eudora's inhabitants or the plague that exterminated them. It's almost as if they all simply vanished into thin air."

"Did no one come to their aid? How can an entire population cease to exist without anyone noticing?"

"The Florenci System doesn't operate as a unified planetary group. We each operate independently of one another, and there is no trade and no

28

communication. I have heard of some interplanetary travel, but it's limited. Most planets simply don't have the ability or the desire to develop the technology. A few rogue seedlings break out of the mold and try to venture to one of the other planets, but outsiders are not usually welcomed on any planet, aside from Ranunculus."

"That doesn't seem to make sense. What if something happened on your planet? Wouldn't you want someone to help you?"

"Sure, I would, but who? We have no allies. We are independently responsible for what happens to us."

"The plague is surely a great scientific anomaly - something powerful enough to destroy an entire civilization without a trace. Why doesn't Ranunculus do something? He seemed quite anxious to eradicate the Transparencies before they spread to other planets."

"Ranunculus has been gathering information and analyzing it for years, but he can't find anything. He was planning to go to the planet's surface himself soon since all the space monitor reports assure him it's safe, but then the Transparencies showed up. They must be dealt with first."

"What about the last planet?"

"Noxia - the dark planet." Betony remembered the mural in the Council Room that depicted one black circle.

"Is it inhabited?"

"Unfortunately."

"Why do you say it like that? Have you been there?"

"No one in the Brotherhood is allowed to travel to Noxia as part of an embargo Ranunculus imposed."

"But why would Ranunculus ostracize an entire planet?"

"The Noxians aren't exactly kind. Ranunculus has thwarted their efforts twice to invade other planets using his space monitors. Their leader, Tussock, is power hungry. Ranunculus suspects that he wants nothing more than to take over a planet and make the inhabitants his slaves. No one mentions Noxia around Ranunculus. He distrusts anyone who misuses science, which the Noxians frequently do."

"Oh," Betony whispered, her arms erupting in goose bumps at the mention of these Noxian fiends. "Tell me more about Phirun." Betony tried to elude the sensation of uneasiness that had unexpectedly overtaken her. Tansy launched into a long but interesting discussion of Phirun, which is how they passed the long days in the cramped pod traveling across the blackness of space with its flickering freckles of light shimmering from light years away. Rue mostly confined himself to the pilot station. Occasionally, Betony caught him staring at them through the corridor, but he disappeared into the shadows moments later, leaving her to wonder if she had only imagined his appearance.

Valerian, on the other hand, joined them frequently. Betony watched his interaction with Tansy with interest. She had learned that Valerian and Tansy were betrothed, which meant they would form an unbreakable union together and undergo something known as a Grafting Ceremony. The idea of unionizing and Grafting Ceremonies was new to her. She noticed the way Valerian stared at Tansy when she wasn't looking, and Tansy always knew how Valerian seemed to feel by the expression in his voice without seeing his face. She observed that they always held hands as if touching skin to skin brought them the greatest pleasure. They had been together their entire lives, and yet they never tired of being in each other's company. Their laughter filtered through Betony, filling her with a sense of longing that she didn't quite understand.

Ranunculus may have unlocked parts of her brain, but Tansy and Valerian were unlocking parts of her heart she didn't know existed. One day, she rallied the courage to talk to them about it.

"What is it exactly that you two have that I don't?" she asked. Tansy and Valerian gave each other knowing smiles, the kind of smiles that left Betony feeling excluded.

"It's called love," Tansy explained. "It's an emotion or a strong feeling of attachment that I feel for Valerian, and he feels for me. I care very deeply about everything that happens to him, and I want to be a part of his life always."

"This is what it means to be betrothed?"

"Yes," Tansy explained, "it's a promise that two people will one day form a union with each other, and eventually have seedlings of their own."

"And what exactly is a union?"

"A union," Valerian chimed in, "takes place when two people love each other so much they want to be together always – it's a ceremonial way to show that commitment and dedication to the other person."

"And the Grafting Ceremony?"

"That is the ritual that is performed when two people unionize. A small piece of Tansy's skin is grafted onto my chest, and a small part of my skin is grafted onto her chest over the heart to signify that we are now one. I am a part of her, and she is a part of me."

"So, this union and Grafting Ceremony aren't just for reproductive purposes?" Valerian's face flushed red at Betony's unexpected question.

"No, there's more to it than that," Tansy answered.

"Although reproduction is certainly part of it," Valerian added with a sly smile in Tansy's direction.

"Betony, it's really hard to explain, but I guarantee that you'll understand when you feel it for yourself," Tansy assured her.

Betony supposed it must be the same as trying to explain to Tansy what it felt like to have roots. She simply couldn't describe the feeling from any angle that helped Tansy understand it any better. As for this feeling called love that would move two people to exchange skin cells, she was at a complete loss to comprehend. To her, reproduction occurred naturally and didn't require physical contact with another person, which would have proven difficult for root-bound species. Betony let the subject drop since she didn't wish to delve any further into this aspect of her new surroundings. Perhaps she wasn't meant to understand.

The following day after the morning meal, Betony and Tansy were sitting around a table in the Commons. Tansy was eating, although Betony still wasn't ready for the kind of slimy vegetation the other three consumed by the bowlfuls. She rarely joined them at mealtimes since she couldn't stomach the smell of their food. As Tansy slurped her breakfast soup, Betony noticed Rue again, lurking in the corner, just watching.

"Why does he always just stand there watching us?" Betony asked in annoyance.

"He's terrified of females. If I even try to greet him, his face turns as red as Aster's hair. One time I winked at him, and the poor boy nearly passed out. When I tried to steady him on his feet, he started to hyperventilate. I finally just left and sent Valerian to pick up the pieces. He's incredibly shy. I mean, come on – the only people he's been around since he was a seedling was a bunch of withered, stuffy scientists." Betony glanced in his direction again, and he quickly averted his eyes, his face matching the shade of his pink hair for a moment. Betony studied his features. He was quite handsome in a rugged Florenci System sort of way, and even Betony had to admit that nothing she had seen so far could equal his deep blue eyes. He was the only blue-eyed person she had yet seen. She paused to take a sip of her water, only to find that he had disappeared again.

"So, he's been on Traveriss his whole life?" Betony asked.

"It seems so, although I don't know much more than that. He never talks about his past, not even to Valerian. He's not the same as the other members of the Brotherhood. They treat us like intruders interrupting their precious work, but Rue is eager to learn from us – to learn about our planet. Back on Phirun, Valerian is a light marshal. His job is to collect and store the light from the sun-star, so it can be harnessed as energy. Rue has spent hours helping Valerian research and test new techniques and technologies that will help him be a better light marshal – quite possibly the best light marshal Phirun has ever seen. No one else in the Brotherhood would have done that. They think they are superior to us because we're planet-bound, and they equate that with ignorance. But not Rue – never Rue. He's Valerian's best friend, and to me, that's saying quite a lot."

"That's comforting since my entire future is in his hands," Betony admitted. The conversation then turned to a discussion of the sun-star, but Betony felt more at ease as she slept that night knowing that she was in good hands.

Chapter Four
An Incarceration

Betony was awakened the next morning by a knock on her door.

"Better brace yourself for landing," Tansy announced.

"Landing?"

"We've reached Quamir, and we need to recharge. We're only a few minutes from entering the atmosphere," Tansy explained. Betony followed her to the Commons and took a seat, bracing herself for impact. She heard the pod power down when they reached solid ground, but Betony's eyeballs were still vibrating around in her head, and her ears were still ringing.

"We might as well get out and stretch our legs. We'll be here the better part of the day as the pod recharges," Tansy said as she opened the hatch. It appeared to be nearing dawn on Quamir, and Betony was relieved to see a source of natural light for a change. Four moons still hovered in the sky emitting bright glows in brilliant shades of blue, green, red, and orange. Natural vegetation covered the ground near the recharging station, and Betony could see that the land extended far beyond her own sight. For the first time she felt like she could take a deep breath without worrying that it would lead to her eventual suffocation. There were no walls holding her captive here on Quamir.

"What do you think?" Tansy asked with a smile.

"I love it! I could stay here forever," Betony replied, closing her eyes, and twirling around in a wide circle as the air rushed into her lungs and filtered to her extremities. She quickly stopped her revelry when she opened her eyes to find that Rue had emerged from the hatch. He was staring at her again, and she suddenly felt very self-conscious.

"Feel free to explore the area," he said. "But don't go too far from the recharging station."

Tansy, who had visited Quamir on four separate occasions with a member of the Brotherhood, offered to give her a tour of the surrounding area. Betony touched every leaf, bush, and lump of soil. Everything felt so much more alive here than it had on Traveriss. It flourished in its natural environment, and Betony felt that all too familiar longing to anchor herself into the ground with her roots and sway in the slight breeze. After spending the entire day in exploration, Tansy decided it was time to return to the pod for some food, although Betony hardly felt hungry since she had been drinking in the glorious rays from the sun-star and quenching her thirst from the freshwater streams that trickled down the mountainous paths.

As they approached the recharging station, Tansy suddenly stopped, motioning for Betony to do the same. Betony sensed something was wrong when she heard strange voices close by. She hoped they were Quamirians, but Tansy's wide eyes indicated otherwise. They waited for a few seconds, and the voices seemed to drift off into the distance. Tansy signaled to her that they should cautiously walk toward the pod, but before Betony took a step, someone or something grabbed her from behind, locking her arms to her sides.

Her eyes darted around until she saw that Tansy had also been captured by a large man with a thick tuft of golden grass-like hair on his head and face. He wore no shirt, revealing tanned skin with strange markings that reminded

Betony of blackened vines crawling all over his torso and arms. A dark round circle was prominently tattooed on his left arm. There was no question in her mind that these men were not from Quamir - they were clearly Noxians. Sudden fear coursed through her body, immobilizing her as her captor carried her forward without the slightest hint of exertion.

Once they reached the recharging station, the Noxians ushered Betony and Tansy into a circular glass holding tank. Betony screamed when her body touched something, but when she turned to look, she found Valerian staring back at her with Rue standing at his side. They had been ambushed. The holding tank was barely large enough for the four of them to sit down, so they were forced to crouch closely together, which may have been fine for Valerian and Tansy who were seated next to each other, but not for Betony or Rue.

"What's going on?" Tansy whispered to Valerian.

"I don't know. We were examining the pod's outer structure to make sure there was no damage, and these guys came out of nowhere and jumped us." Apparently, Valerian and Rue had put up a fight because both of them were bruised and battered.

"Are they Noxians?" Betony ventured. Rue looked surprised that she had pieced that part of the puzzle together. Maybe he thought Ancients to be unintelligent.

"They appear to be, but they aren't just regular Noxians out on a joyride. The tattoos all over their bodies indicate that they are members of the Guard - the law-keeping force in Noxia. If the black circle was a yellow circle instead, we'd be dealing with Tussock's own personal Elite Guard," Rue explained.

"What do you think they're doing on Quamir?" Valerian inquired, rubbing his hands together nervously.

"Maybe they want to commandeer our pod?" Tansy suggested, but Rue quickly shook his head.

"I don't think so. They would have taken it by now and probably killed us."

"Quiet in there!" one of the Noxians called out, his face full of fury and hatred.

No one dared speak again, so they tuned their ears toward the Noxians to see if they could gather any bits and pieces from their conversation.

"Good work, Dodder," the one with the golden hair congratulated the one with the yellow hair.

"Yes, we will be well rewarded, Sprangletop. As soon as the Elite Guard arrives to transport them, we can finally go back to Noxia. I've had enough of this place and all its moons."

"I alerted High Command. They should be here by daybreak, I'd guess."

"Well, the prisoners aren't going anywhere. Look at them – they look like a bunch of scared seedlings huddled in a crib." The two Noxians guffawed in raspy tones, oblivious to their hideousness.

"Might as well settle in for the night, Sprangletop," Dodder said as he lay down on the grass several feet away from the glass prison.

"This isn't good news," Valerian whispered as soon as sleep had finally overtaken their captors.

"They were expecting us. They've been waiting here for a while, and they know who we are already or else they would have interrogated us," Rue said in hushed tones.

"I suppose they plan on taking us to Noxia," Tansy mused. "That is one place I never wanted to set foot on."

"Don't worry, Tansy. We'll think of something," Valerian tried to reassure her. He put his arm around her, and she cuddled close to him. "I won't let anything happen to you, and that is a promise." Tansy smiled weakly.

"Rue? Any ideas?" Valerian asked expectantly, but Rue just shook his head.

"We have no weapons but our fists, and I'm not necessarily trained in the defensive arts as you clearly saw this afternoon. They surely have weapons, and if they don't, you can be assured that the Elite Guard does, and they won't be afraid to use them. But we do have one thing going for us. Apparently, they want us alive, and that may at least buy us some time until I can come up with some sort of a plan," Rue's eyes sparkled in the rainbow of moonlight as the blackness of night descended upon the planet. Betony comforted herself with the thought that Valerian and Tansy had confidence in Rue, and he would think of some escape plan before they reached Noxia.

Tansy eventually fell asleep nestled next to Valerian, and Betony watched as his eyes too grew heavy and closed. She didn't dare look at Rue, who was sitting by her side. She was wide awake, having basked in the natural light all day. In fact, she felt more awake than she had since she had come to this planetary system. Her mind was toiling over the information she had learned since leaving Traveriss. More questions. Would there ever be any answers? She moved uncomfortably to relieve a cramp in her leg, another side effect of the adaptation. These legs cramped so easily when they couldn't stretch.

"Are you still awake?" she heard Rue whisper.

She thought about pretending to be asleep to avoid any awkward conversation, but Rue wouldn't be in this mess if it weren't for her.

"Yes," she replied softly.

"I'm sorry you're stuck in here. I didn't see this coming."

"Why are you apologizing to me?" she asked, but he didn't respond.

"Rue?"

"Yeah."

"How did they know we were coming?"

"There's only one way: We've been betrayed by a member of the Brotherhood."

"But why?"

"I wish I knew, but I have my suspicions of who it could be," he said, but Betony didn't bother asking to whom he was referring.

"Try to get some sleep. Who knows what tomorrow will bring?" Rue said. The conversation was the longest she had with Rue since they had met, but she was glad she hadn't pretended to be asleep. While she didn't know much about Rue, she knew that he took his responsibility as her escort very seriously. If there was a way out, she was confident he would think of it. She lifted her knees to her chest, rested her arms on them, and then relaxed her forehead onto the soft cushion of her skin to pass the long night.

It was only then that she realized she was shivering as the temperature had dropped several degrees with the disappearance of the sun-star. She felt Rue jostling around next to her, bumping into her several times. Then she felt him draping his jacket over her delicate frame, embracing her with its warmth. For the moment, the dread of the morning light was whisked away as her eyes blinked slowly closed.

Chapter Five
An Escape

A black Noxian pod arrived at dawn, nearly blowing the glass prison over and jarring its occupants cruelly awake. Shouting preceded the four Noxians who disembarked before the pod had even powered down. They, too, were bare-chested, wearing only black pants and boots, and they bore the tattoos of their comrades, although Betony noticed immediately the bright yellow circle that signified their membership in the Elite Guard. There was too much noise to understand anything they were saying, but in just a few moments, Dodder and Sprangletop had lifted off in their own pod and disappeared in the horizon. A large Noxian sporting white spiny hair not unlike Rue's stepped forward. He ordered the other three to position themselves around the container.

"Well. Well. What have we here?" he said in an accented tone. "Two measly Phirunites, an Ancient (now there's a find) and what's this – a member of the royal Brotherhood?" Valerian stared the man down defiantly for insulting his heritage, but the man only laughed and continued, "Now, we're going to let you out of your cage, so don't do anything you might regret later, all right?" Had he just winked at them? Was he patronizing them, or was that some sort of a signal? She glanced at Rue, wondering if he had seen it, but if he had, his face didn't register it. On the count of three, the man pressed a button, and the glass prison collapsed into a flat, hollow sphere encircling them.

No one moved - as if an invisible force field prevented them from even thinking about stepping outside of the circle.

"Now, watch it there. I said no tricky stuff, or you're going to have to pay," the man was now gesturing with his hand as if he were punching himself in the face. Did he want an excuse to fight with them? Valerian and Rue were perplexed, unsure of what to make of this lunatic posing as a member of the feared Elite Guard whose reputation preceded them in planet-lore throughout the planetary system. The Noxian switched tactics to a more effective lure.

"What are you staring at you ignorant Phirunite runt? I didn't realize the Brotherhood had finally come to its senses and joined the slave trade, though we all know Phirunites aren't worth the skin on my pinky finger." The verbal attack was directed at Valerian, who readily took the bait.

"If it's a fight you're looking for, bring it on," Valerian yelled as he lunged at the leader, swinging his fists in fury. His right hand connected with the intended target's face, knocking him backward. Rue was ready to jump in when he noticed that the other three Noxians were scuffling with each other, simultaneously removing their communicators as they wrestled and crushing them into nothing more than metallic dust. With their communicators destroyed, they marched over to Valerian and pulled him off their leader, destroying his communicator in the process. This meant only one thing: certain death. They didn't want Tussock to know that they had killed his prisoners without so much as a tussle.

"What took you so long?" The leader got to his feet, rubbing his jaw. Everyone was utterly confused at this point, eyeing the Noxians warily.

"I promise no harm will come to you at our hands," the man tried to assure them as he reached a hand toward Valerian in a gesture of peace.

Valerian shook the proffered hand hesitantly.

"Crofton's my name. This is Tornillo and Salsola. And that big bag of muscle over there is Pilipiliula, but we just call him Pili."

"And exactly who are you if you aren't members of the Elite Guard?" Rue queried suspiciously.

"Oh, we are clearly members of the Elite Guard, Tussock's most trusted servants and soldiers, but we are also rebels. You know...deviants, miscreants, defectors, traitors, insurgents, mutineers. You get the idea. We prefer to go by the Fraternity for Freedom," Crofton tried to explain.

"We havim own Brotherhood – the Free Frats," Pili echoed as he raised his fists in the air and knocked them together. Crofton, Tornillo, and Salsola then repeated the gesture.

"I don't believe it," Rue said. "There are traitors in the highest ranks of Tussock's Elite Guard?"

"Give us Noxians a little credit, why don't you? We aren't all power-hungry monsters, just because you choose to punish us for our leader's demented aspirations. There are those of us who will defy him at all costs."

"So that little show you put on was just a ruse?" Valerian was keenly interested in the events unfolding before him.

"We must maintain our positions as Elite Guardsman as long as possible, or we lose a valuable facet of information – like the plot to kidnap you. It's much more believable if our communicators are crushed in an unexpected ambush of fists and rebellion rather than a meek surrender."

"Why rescue us?" Rue asked still unconvinced.

"Good question. We figure that if Tussock wants you badly enough to send out the Elite Guard, it is in our best interest to thwart his plans."

"So, you don't know why he wants us?" Rue continued to probe.

"Listen, there is intragalactic warfare brewing here. You're just pawns in a much bigger game."

"Intergalactic warfare?" Rue echoed in disbelief.

"You guys sit out there in your synthetic bubble all in the name of science and advancement, but you're not the only ones with ambitions and the brains to achieve them. We're working on something far more important here. We're trying to save our planetary system. We can't afford to turn a blind eye to pursue our own self-interests. While you're in your neat little laboratories researching, Tussock is infiltrating planets one by one. Eudora ring a bell? Let's just say that was no accidental plague, and our sources tell us that 'natural disaster' was masterminded by someone who is now within your precious Botanical Brotherhood. How do you think we know about you? Although I hope you've got enough brains to have figured that out by now. Tussock has help - inside help," Crofton confirmed resentfully. Rue exchanged glances with Valerian. This was far more serious that Rue had thought, and he was tiring quickly of Crofton's constant bashing of the Brotherhood.

"All right, well what's the plan now?" Valerian finally asked.

"We leave Quamir immediately. I don't want to put any of its inhabitants at risk if Tussock sends someone looking for us, which he might since our communicators are blowing in the wind somewhere," Crofton said. "The pods only hold four, so we'll have to split up: two for two."

"Why can't we just leave together?" Tansy asked, suddenly alarmed at the thought of being separated.

"If we come home empty-handed, Tussock is going to hunt you and kill us. We have to leave the planet as ordered, but I've already got a plan in place so you'll never reach Noxia. You'll be homeward bound, if everything goes off without a hitch."

"What exactly is this plan?" Rue's distrust was surfacing again.

"I don't have time to explain. Our mission was timed precisely. If we aren't in the air in one minute, Tussock will send out the Tracers, and we'll have no choice but to go back to Noxia. We haven't been able to figure out how to out-maneuver a Tracer yet. There are some disadvantages to technological advancement."

"What's a Tracer?" Tansy asked hesitantly.

"A mechanical bug that bores itself into your skin, so your every movement can be tracked by Tussock," Tornillo explained as Betony shuddered at the thought.

"We've got to move," Crofton urged. "Pili you come with me, along with the Phirunite girl and the Ancient in their pod. Salsola and Tornillo, you take the two males with you in our pod."

"No," shrieked Tansy. "I can't be separated from Valerian."

"Fine, fine. You go with them in the Noxian pod and Bubble Boy will come with us," Crofton commanded, his annoyance evident in his tone. Finding no alternative but to trust Crofton, Rue reluctantly climbed aboard the pod after Betony. He took a seat in the Commons, fixing his eyes in the direction of the pilot station – his pilot station, which had been overtaken by a foul and unlikely rescuer who couldn't pass up a chance to throw out an insult whenever the opportunity presented itself. Betony prepared for lift-off, still not accustomed to the noise of the pod.

"We're forty-five seconds late guys," Crofton called from the pilot's seat. "Let's hope Tussock is feeling generous today."

INTERGALACTIC INTERCEPTION #2

Prey knew he should have paid more attention in Flight School during his Deep Space Adventure Simulation Course. He could vaguely recall being taught how to construct hydro-boosters out of common on-board materials. Now, he couldn't remember exactly what he needed because his memory kept returning to Mantila's beautiful buggy eyes - all five of them. His hundreds of lenses had been focused on her thorax shifting from side to side as she walked in front of him. Apparently, her sensuous sway had distracted him from his lessons that day - not even one lens to spare to watch the instructor. No wonder he had failed the course. Well, technically, he had been expelled, but Prey wasn't one to quibble over small details.

He looked around the battered pod. There must be some way to boost his speed. He rummaged under the dash controls. Oh - a candied mealworm! He had dropped that two missions ago. He eyed the green fuzzy mold that now adorned it like a warm winter coat. He shrugged and popped it into his mouth. Not bad. Not bad at all. Now what had he been looking for? Before his train of thought returned, the buzzer sounded, alerting him of another outgoing message. He tensed as the conversation began, focusing his one ear so he could catch every inflection.

Voice 1: I need an update. Surely, you've intercepted the pod by now.

Voice 2: We have. They are in transport with my Elite Guard as we speak. The escort's demise will look like an unfortunate accident just as you wish. I am awaiting confirmation now since I seem to have lost communication temporarily with my ground team. But before I go further, I think it's time I knew what your motivations are since I now seem to have the advantage.

Voice 1: I told you. I have my reasons.

Voice 2: And I'm telling you that I will go no further until I know why. You're a dangerous man, annihilating an entire planet, thinking up a distraction to cover your tracks so the Brotherhood doesn't uncover your trail before they're dead, teaming up with me to accomplish your plans. Why all the trouble? What's in it for you?

Voice 1: Revenge, quite simply. Revenge for the Eudoran monarchy's rejection of my father's right to the throne, which led to his eventual expulsion from the planet.

Voice 2: Revenge – a worthy cause. You are a man after my own heart. But what does the Brotherhood have to do with it?

Voice 1: My quarrel began shortly before Ranunculus formed his precious so-called Brotherhood. He denied my father's requests for help after his expulsion, and he was backed by the rest of his merry little band of research fanatics. Thus, I hold them all accountable for my father's dismal fate. I am, in fact, the true founder of the Brotherhood in a sense. Without the elimination of Eudora, Ranunculus may well still be meddling from the confines of Quamir.

Voice 2: The Brotherhood would deny your father's request, yet embrace my former Chief Guard as their brother - a Noxian traitor? Very interesting indeed. I think I now understand your interest in the escort as well. I will not fail twice.

Voice 1: Be aware, I don't release all my spores in the same wind. You see, even if you don't come through, the escort's expiration draws nigh anyway. Only my impatience drives me to bargain with you. The end result is the same, and I can think of no better way to torture Ranunculus in his dying breaths than to tell him both of his precious Ancients are in your hands.

Voice 2: A man of many means. So, what becomes of you when you've exacted your revenge?

Voice 1: That remains to be seen - maybe a possible retirement to Eudora where I rightfully belong.

Voice 2: Well, I surely hope you shall consider me an ally when my own schemes have come to fruition, and I finally control the Florenci System.

Voice 1: I warn you: do not cross me, or you too will reap the destruction of my wrath. And please note: Eudora is mine. You'll not interfere with that planet.

Voice 2: I don't take well to threats.

Voice 1: Keep to the plan, and there is no threat.

The situation was clearly escalating. The pod had been intercepted. Already one member of the Brotherhood, the escort, was probably dead. Another member of the Brotherhood had engineered the plague that extinguished an entire civilization. Even Prey had heard about Eudora, and he didn't usually pay attention to intragalactic history. Someone was going to take over the Florenci System. It didn't take much to unravel that little mystery. The second voice was clearly Tussock - who else had a Chief Guard or an Elite Guard for that matter? Yes, Prey also knew about Tussock. Ranunculus had told him enough to scare the wings right off him, and he had vowed then and there to steer clear of Noxia and its leader.

If he could figure out which one of the Brotherhood was a Noxian, he could rule him out. He wasn't a cohort with his former employer. That's it! Back to the signature codes. He could figure it out by the process of elimination. He already knew Ranunculus's signature code, so that only left seven to go. He hadn't made much progress since his earlier attempt, but his latest eavesdropping intelligence gave him the extra motivation he needed to rededicate himself to the mind-numbing task. If only someone else would make another transmission off Traveriss besides the traitor.

Chapter Six
An Incineration

Their pod was still hovering low to the ground when Betony heard the explosion. The aftershock from the blast sent everyone in the pod spiraling out of control with Betony banging against every surface of the Commons. Rue had managed to grab onto the water dispensing pole that was anchored to both the ceiling and the floor. He reached for Betony as the impact of her body slamming into the window propelled her across the room in his direction. He was able to catch her by the wrist, pulling her in toward him so he could wrap his arm around her, pinning her against the pole and his own body. The pod continued to career across the planet's surface before coming to a stop. When Rue was sure the pod wasn't moving, he gently released Betony, scrutinizing her for injuries. She appeared to be fine.

"Everyone okay in there?" Crofton scrambled to the Commons from the pilot station, followed by a panting Pili. Miraculously, everyone was not only alive, but also relatively uninjured. Rue kicked opened the hatch and crawled out, helping the other three jump to the planet's surface since the hatch was pointed upward. They scanned the landscape in search of the Noxian pod, which wasn't hard to find.

Flames licked the bark of a splintered tree nearby, eager to devour the blackened mass that had torn it asunder. Betony ran toward the flames, the wind rushing through her ears like a roaring river. The exhilaration of running mixed with the adrenaline surging through her resulted in a burst of energy. She was the first to arrive at the scene of the smoldering pile of rubble. A tongue of the fire was lapping at the sides of the overturned vessel. Valerian, who must have been ejected from the pod before it lay to rest on its own hatch, was struggling to his feet a few feet away. He was badly injured but attempted to limp toward the crash site in desperation. No one else seemed to have escaped the fiery furnace. Betony's eyes found a small circular window at the same time as Valerian's. Two frantic eyes stared back at them, wild with fear, fists pounding on the glass. Tansy was trapped inside.

Valerian scrambled forward, reaching the window, and struggling to break it open. Betony stood frozen, a silent witness to the horror. Valerian was now joined by Rue, Crofton, and Pili. Immediately understanding the dire situation, they rushed around the pod to find another way inside. The Noxian pod was different from the exploration pod in that it had a rear viewspace in addition to the pilot's viewspace. The rear viewspace had been shattered in the blast, which Valerian was the first to notice. Without hesitation, he leaped inside, cutting himself on the sharp shards of reinforced glass as he went. It took only moments for Tansy's face to appear in the same spot in which Valerian had disappeared. Rue, Crofton, and Pili helped her out just as a small explosion rocked the pod.

There may have been shouting for Valerian to get out - to leave Tornillo and Salsola, who were either already dead or unconscious or trapped inside the pilot station. There may have been a lot of commotion and movement Betony neither saw nor heard. She seemed to be witnessing the event from very far away. Another explosion shifted the pod again. Still no Valerian. Betony saw

Tansy's mouth opening and closing as if in slow motion, and she was sure she was screaming Valerian's name repeatedly, although she heard no sound. Her mind was subconsciously muting all noise.

Finally, Betony saw a hint of movement at the rear viewspace – a hand – Valerian's hand, but in the next instant another explosion sent Betony hurtling backward into a tree. She felt the blackness creep over her mind – a dark fog offering to shield her from the horrific scene she had just witnessed, but she forced her eyes to stay open – to focus on the light. Her mind was a blur as she saw images of the pod consumed in flames, of a fiery ball being ejected from the pod – a fiery ball with arms and legs – of Rue, Tansy, Crofton, and Pili flying through the air, of their lifeless bodies heaped upon the ground.

Betony was on her feet again, staggering in the direction the fireball had gone. She half-walked, half-ran as fast as her shaking legs could carry her through the brush, weaving between trees, down an embankment, and finally to a small stream. With a stroke of luck, the stream had extinguished most of the flames, but Valerian was lying face down. She rushed toward him and somehow managed to turn him onto his back, drowning the remaining flames.

She placed her hand on his neck, feeling for the pulse of his life force, and as she did, a strange sensation marched from her fingertip into her hand and up her arm, eventually branching off in all directions until her whole body was tingling. It was a painful sensation that startled her so much she quickly withdrew her fingertips, and just as suddenly, the sensation was gone. She couldn't remember if she had felt Valerian's life force or not, but before she could verify, she heard voices rushing toward her. Soon she was surrounded by a large group of people, gawking at the charred and melted remnants of Valerian and the strange being hunched by his side.

"It's an Ancient," someone cried out. "I recognize her from my Advanced Prehistoric History lessons." The group fell silent, and finally Betony's voice broke free.

"Help me," she said weakly. "Help us. There was an explosion at the recharging station. My friends are still there." Suddenly there was a flurry of activity. Several male Quamirians disappeared into the trees. One withered female withdrew an odd-looking instrument in the shape of a five-point star from her side pouch. She raised it to her cracked lips and blew. An eerie musical sound filled the air, and minutes later a rugged looking vehicle appeared by the stream, driven by a very young seedling. The small shuttle was only big enough to transport one person. The female, her hair an elaborate mass of blue braids, approached Betony.

"We will help, but you must let your friend come with us," she said kindly. Betony nodded, and several people came forward to load Valerian into the shuttle, which rose in the sky and disappeared from view. As Betony rose to her feet, she saw Rue, Crofton, Pili, and Tansy making their way soberly down the embankment toward her. She was relieved to see that they were alive.

They waited in silence for another shuttle to arrive, and the five of them boarded it as directed. They were left alone in the passenger hold. Betony watched as it lifted off the ground, rising higher and higher in the sky. The dispersing crowd below became nothing more than black specks of dust. Betony was sitting by Tansy, who was staring blankly out the window. She could think of nothing to say that would comfort Tansy, so she said nothing at all. Rue was the first to shatter the wall of silence behind which each of them was hiding from reality.

"What was that?" he asked Crofton, who was seated across from him.

"Solar flare," Crofton replied matter-of-factly, his tone void of emotion.

"We're not close enough to the sun-star to get hit by a solar flare, and that would have incinerated the entire planet," Rue countered.

"Spoken like a sheltered scientist," Crofton mocked. Rue tried to ignore the remark. "You have just been an eye witness to Tussock's newest weapon in his ever-expanding arsenal: the synthetic solar flare."

"And is Tussock in the habit of killing members of his own personal Elite Guard as well?" Rue said spitefully.

"If it's in his best interest, he'll do whatever it takes."

"I thought you said you were transporting us to Noxia."

"Well, it looks as though Tussock had other plans that I wasn't privy too, doesn't it?"

"Tussock or you?"

"Why would I rescue you only to kill you moments later? My neck is on the line here, as well as my whole operation that I've spent years organizing. Don't you get it? I just lost two of my best soldiers, not to mention good friends, in that fiery furnace. Don't be making any hasty accusations, Lab Rat."

"So what, Tussock was trying to eliminate witnesses?" Rue prodded, trying to make sense of what had just happened.

"He was trying to eliminate you. My orders were to escort the Ancient and the two traveling guardians back to Noxia personally. Pili, Tornillo, and Salsola were to shuttle you alone in that smoldering pile of rubble. You, Mr. High and Mighty, were supposed to be aboard." Rue fell silent.

"Thatim rightim. Summim be wantim you deadim," Pili added emphatically with his strangely slurred and awkward speech. Betony gasped. She had been so wrapped up in Valerian that she had forgotten about the other two Noxians who never emerged from the pod. *Dead?* She had seen them just this morning, and now they were simply gone? Nonexistent? *Dead.* They had helped her escape. *Dead.* They had been killed by their own leader, who didn't even know of their treachery against him? *Dead.* Was Valerian dead as well? *Dead.* Someone wanted to kill Rue? This had been her first exposure to death, and already it was haunting her, tormenting her with its ghostly roll call echoing in her head. Crofton cast an icy glare in her direction.

"What? The little princess can't handle the real world? Was she imagining long days of basking in the sunlight instead of conspiracy theories and murders? Well, welcome to the real Florenci System, Princess – not the fabricated land of scientific bliss in which Ranunculus lives." There was more pain in his voice than anger. He had lost two friends after all.

"Crofton, just leave her out of this. She had no choice in where she crash-landed. As it turns out, anywhere would have been better than here," Rue lashed back. Silence once again occupied the shuttle until a voice over the intercom announced that they were landing at the best Quamirian medical facility on the planet.

Rue, Crofton, and Pili were ushered to a room to meet with Quamirian leaders who were eager for an explanation of the morning's events. Hopefully, Rue's close connection to Ranunculus, who was a Quamirian himself, would help him plead their case. Tansy, after much begging and even more threatening, was permitted to see Valerian, while Betony was taken to an observatory on the second deck.

The entire facility appeared to be made of glass since constant exposure to natural light was the best source of healing. Betony looked out of her glass window. To the rear, she could see outside of the medical facility into a world where no one knew about the Noxian attack or the life and death battle that was being fought just feet away. To either side, she could see into the other observation rooms, which were empty. Looking in the window directly in front of her, she found that all the observation rooms on the second deck were arranged in a circular pattern overlooking a large room below. There were several beds in a tic-tac-toe formation with barriers of narrow walled hallways, ensuring separation from other patients. There was clearly no privacy, however, since there was no ceiling except the sun-roof located several decks above Betony.

There were few patients, only three in fact, but her eyes settled on the body that occupied the center square. She could see Valerian very clearly, as if the glass magnified the person on whom she focused. When Betony looked at Valerian, she had to choke down the vomit that surfaced in her throat at his repulsive appearance, remembering the smell of his burning flesh as she knelt over him. She suppressed the scream of horror that was creeping its way up her vocal cords. She couldn't bear to look at him and turned away for a moment, ashamed at her retreat. She noted Tansy, her body convulsing with heavy sobs as she hovered over his charred and mutilated body. She herself bore some disfigurement on her right arm.

Betony watched as Tansy eventually quieted her own sobs and tenderly stroked the few remaining patches of hair on Valerian's head. The tears streamed silently down Tansy's cheeks, splashing onto the blanket like the spray of a waterfall. She bent closer to him, whispering in his ear, and then she gently pressed her lips against the melted flesh that used to be his mouth. There was no opening anymore since his face was a pile of mush, hardening into a horrific mask as he lay sedated from the pain.

The anatomists would eventually carve out his features over time, but the carvings would only be a rudimentary replica of his beautiful face. He would forever look like a science project gone terribly wrong, eliciting horrified stares and downcast eyes. He would be outcast by the unintentional reactions of his fellow beings, unable to disguise the terrible price he paid to save his love. Would Tansy be able to bear to look at him, to touch him as she did before? Of course, he would be honored as a hero. He would be revered for his bravery. All would know his story. All would pity his appearance. All would feel compassion, and yet, still, he would be ostracized.

Betony was weeping now. The river of tears was racing down her soft green cheeks. The hope she once had for the future was nothing more than an evaporating dew drop in the late morning sun. She silently wished her seed pod was still floating aimlessly through space, protecting her from this travesty. She felt small, weak, and alone, like a seedling exposed to the elements, barely clinging to life. But for what? Why was she still clinging? Rue's fragrance preceded his physical presence in the room, and Betony successfully dammed the tears from flowing.

"The specialist says Valerian will pull through," the deep timbre of his voice inched slowly toward her fractured heart. So, he would live. Somehow, she had already known that. Her fear was for the quality of life he would live, but she couldn't divulge that nugget of truth to Rue.

"Betony?" He stepped closer. She had still not turned toward him. She could not meet his eyes with fear still swimming about in her own, thrashing to stay alive though she was silently trying to drown it. What if it had been her? She ran her fingers subconsciously through her long red hair, encountering masses of tangles she had yet to comb out. She so desperately wanted to confide in him, to trust him with her weaknesses. Instead, she rallied her strength.

"Good. He'll survive," she echoed. No wave of relief washed over her as she spoke the words. What did it mean to survive? What pain and agony did the word survive hold for him? Would he want to survive if he knew? Would he ever feel normal again, or would he feel like a caged monster imprisoned in his own body? Would he thank them to be alive, or would he curse them for the life sentence of deformity and pain they pressed upon him by rescuing him? Her thoughts kept returning to the unanswered questions, lapping them up as if they were water but consequently causing an unquenchable thirst.

Rue placed his hand on her shoulder, hesitantly. She trembled, the soil of her strength eroding with his gentle touch. She didn't dare move, afraid she would collapse. She raised her hand to gesture for him to leave her, but as her hand brushed her own cheek, she was surprised to feel a fleshy gash oozing. She felt no pain. As she withdrew her hand, the clear liquid of her life force shimmered in the sun lamps. Rue must have seen it as well because his hand tightened on her shoulder, twisting her to face him.

"You're hurt," he noted softly.

"It's nothing," she mumbled, turning away from him again.

"I'll get someone to look at it right away."

"Don't. They have enough to do right now. I'll be just fine, not that I can say the same for my friends." Her lip quivered as she spoke, but her dam held. Rue left the room helplessly, and Betony was alone again - alone with her questions.

Chapter Seven
A Parting

While she enjoyed the constant exposure to the natural light, Betony longed for her privacy. She was constantly looking around with the sudden impression that someone was staring at her, and she was usually correct. No one on Quamir had seen an Ancient before, and they couldn't help but gape at her as they passed. At one point, a group of onlookers gathered in the square outside the medical facility to watch her since the glass walls presented an open invitation for all to see the oddity, prompting Betony to seek refuge elsewhere. Each room had its own lift, which emerged from the floor with the push of a button. Betony pushed the call button and made her escape on the ground floor. She hadn't seen anyone since she had pushed Rue away that morning, and it was late afternoon now. She wandered around the facility, stopping just before rounding a corner when she heard familiar voices.

"Whatim be planim?" Pili asked.

"With our pod blown to bits, we'll have to use the space gliders to get off the planet. The Free Frats always keep a few tucked away on every planet's surface, just in case," Crofton answered.

"But Tussock will be expecting your arrival in the exploration pod," Rue's voice was instantly recognizable.

"I know that, but we can't leave you without transportation, and space gliders are no way to travel for the weary of heart or inexperienced flyers," Crofton replied, the edge in his voice as sharp as ever. The space gliders to which Crofton was referring were single occupancy glass bubbles with two small wings extending from each side. They were difficult to steer even for seasoned veterans, and Betony certainly was not in that category nor was Rue since all he had ever flown were long range exploration pods.

"What about the Tracers?" Rue queried.

"If they haven't shown up by now, I don't think Tussock is going to send them. He must assume we're on our way. It's a five-day flight to Noxia from here, so that will buy us some time while I round up the nearest Free Frats. We'll come up with something. At the moment, we've thwarted whatever it was he had planned, which must have been to stop you from getting to wherever you're going. By the way, where are you going?"

"Can't say," Rue answered.

"It figures. Top secret Brotherhood garbage, I suppose. I put my neck on the line for you and lost two of my best men in the process, so you could at least give me something to go on here. I'll try to keep Tussock off your trail as long as I can, but I can't do that if I don't know where you're going," Crofton did not want Rue and the Ancient falling back into Tussock's hands after losing two of his own Free Frats in their botched rescue attempt. It was hard to double cross a double-crosser who was firing synthetic solar flares from space.

"We're heading in the direction of the Drop-off," Rue reluctantly conceded.

Betony remembered Tansy briefly mentioning the Drop-off as a place where no one ventured because a space anomaly caused strange things to happen to any pods that came within a close proximity - the perfect hiding place for a secret planet.

"I see," Crofton didn't push for any more information.

"The Quamirian government has offered to help repair my pod. In fact, their work crews have been up there all morning. The pod should be flight ready within the hour," Rue explained.

"Well, there's a bit of good information. I doubt they would have lifted a finger to help us anywhere but off the planet strapped to a rocket headed straight for the sun-star." Anger seemed to emanate from Crofton just as heat from a fire. Betony almost felt sorry for him, being stereotyped as an evil Noxian when he was quite the opposite. She owed him her life, and she would never forget that. After all, he was trying to help the Quamirians, whether they realized it or not

"Look," Crofton continued. "I'll alert my men of your intentions as soon as we have a secure signal. They'll be on the lookout for Tracers, so they can lure them in other directions. All I ask in return is that you send word to Ranunculus that Tussock is about to unveil something big, something he is very pleased with himself about, something that only spells trouble for the entire Florenci System. We can use all the help we can get, but I won't be reduced to groveling, if that's what Ranunculus is waiting for."

"With a traitor in the Brotherhood, I can't send word until we reach our destination. I only hope there is a secure communicator where we are going, or I doubt he'll get a message. Anyone willing to go the lengths this traitor has gone to wreak havoc and destruction, will certainly be monitoring all incoming and outgoing communication. And as of right now, I don't want anyone to know I'm still alive," Rue advised.

"Well, for the sake of the Florenci System, I wish you luck," Crofton added.

"The same to you," Rue echoed. "And thank you for your help. I owe you my life." Crofton didn't respond directly to Rue, but Betony admired Rue for expressing his gratitude to someone who despised him and made no point to disguise his hatred.

"Let's go, Pili," Crofton rounded the corner as he gave the command and bumped into Betony. She prepared herself for the verbal bashing that would surely follow, but instead Crofton said simply, "I was out of line on the shuttle when I spoke to you so disrespectfully."

"Thank you," she replied, shocked at the unexpected apology. "And I'm sorry about your friends." He stiffly tipped his head forward and continued his march down the corridor as Betony watched.

"We need to be leaving soon as well," Rue was standing by her side. "We should say our goodbyes to Tansy and Valerian." He headed in the opposite direction as Crofton with Betony closely following.

Tansy was still at Valerian's side when they were finally allowed admittance into his room. Her eyes were swollen and red, and Valerian's disfigurement remained unchanged. He was still heavily sedated until the specialists could figure out which of his injuries to attempt to repair first. Tansy looked up as she heard them enter the cubicle.

"I assume you're coming to say goodbye," she said as she stood up to greet them.

"I'm afraid so," Rue confirmed.

"I'm so sorry about all of this," Betony whispered as she hugged her.

"It's not your fault, Betony. Please don't blame yourself. It's just something that happened, and now we have to deal with it."

"He'll pull through," Rue tried to comfort her by awkwardly patting her on the back before quickly withdrawing his hand.

"I know he will. He always does. He wouldn't dare leave me alone," Tansy managed a faint laugh, and Betony tried to smile, failing miserably.

"This is the best medical facility in the Florenci System. Ranunculus offers nothing but his praises for the astute staff here. In fact, he often refers to it as the Traveriss of Medicine. I wouldn't leave you here if I didn't think it was for the best. The Quamirian government has offered every available service, comfort, and convenience during your stay. We'll find a way to get you back to Phirun when Valerian is well enough. You can count on that," he assured her.

"I'm not worried, Rue. I know you aren't abandoning us, and unfortunately, I think we're safer here than with you," she admitted gravely as if Rue had somehow forgotten that he had a death warrant on his head – as if he had forgotten that he was the intended target who should be lying in Valerian's place.

"Thank you for everything," Betony said. Tansy had introduced her to friendship and love, and she would desperately miss her companionship on the long voyage that lay ahead of her.

"Good luck," Tansy blinked away another tear before it spilled down her cheek. She turned her head back toward Valerian and sat down again, but Betony turned away. She couldn't bear to see his face again. She didn't want the image etched in her mind.

"Do you mind if I have a minute alone with Valerian?" Rue asked hesitantly, avoiding Tansy's eyes.

"Sure," she said. "I need to grab something to eat anyway, and I'd feel better knowing he wasn't alone." She gave Betony another hug before disappearing down the hallway. Betony followed her out the door, leaning against the outer wall to wait for Rue. She tried not to listen but found herself drawn to the sound of Rue's shaky voice. For some reason, she was also eager to know what Rue could possibly have to say to Valerian.

"I don't know if you can hear me or not Valerian – it's me, Rue. I have to get on with my mission now, so I wanted to say goodbye...and that...I'm sorry. That was supposed to be me in that pod, not you, and I don't know if I can ever forgive myself for what's happened to you." His voice cracked, and he paused for a moment to gain control over his emotions. "You know, you are my only friend, and the last two years that you've been on Traveriss have taught me more about life than all the knowledge Ranunculus has drilled into my head since I was a seedling. I only hope that someday I can be half the man you are. You better get well soon. Phirun needs its new light marshal." Several minutes passed before Rue emerged from the room, but he wore his typical business-as-usual expression on his face.

"Did you want to go in?" he asked Betony unexpectedly.

"No...I...didn't know him that well," she declined, but guilt and remorse immediately washed over her. She hadn't lied. She really didn't know him very well, but she felt even more responsible for him lying in that bed than Rue knew. She had saved him from drowning and subjected him to such a bleak future filled with so much pain, and she simply couldn't face him. Rue didn't press her. Instead, he picked up his pace down the hallway. And that was it. A farewell. A goodbye. A departure.

INTERGALACTIC INTERCEPTION #3

Prey had only just settled back into his chair after the last interception when his buzzer announced another outgoing message. He checked the frequency. It was on the normal line, so it must be someone other than the conspirator. He turned up the volume and jotted down the signature code in hopes of the individual identifying himself. The message was going to Quamir.

Voice 3: Hello?

Voice 4: You don't know how good it is to hear your voice, Ixora.

Voice 3: Aster? Is that you? You don't sound like yourself, but then again, it has been a long time since you bothered to contact me.

Voice 4: Yes, dear sister. Things have been...busy here, you might say. Listen, I've been a little under the weather lately, and I think a trip home might be just what I need. Might I intrude upon you as your guest?

Voice 3: Well, of course. You needn't even ask such a question. When will you be coming?

Voice 4: I have yet to make the official arrangements, but soon. I'll be in touch.

What luck! Prey stretched his three pairs of legs. One down, and six to go. The traitor was not Aster! With one or two more calls, he may be able to determine the pattern behind the assignment of the signature codes. But Aster had said he wasn't feeling well. Was he just ill or was the traitor already at work with his death plan?

Chapter Eight
A New Beginning

Betony isolated herself in her chambers when she and Rue returned to the seed-pod. She laid down on her bed, focusing her sun-star simulator directly on herself, waking only for the occasional drink of water. She had difficulty deciphering between night and day except for the fact that every morning, a cup of her vitamin supplement was always waiting for her, compliments of Rue. Each time she woke, she felt as though she hadn't slept at all. Her sleep was an open invitation for nightmares: explosions, Tansy's expression of fear when she was trapped, Valerian's melting face, ambushes, Noxians, and on and on and on. On the third day, Betony couldn't stand it any longer. If she didn't leave her room, she was afraid she would become trapped in her nightmares.

She walked noiselessly through the narrow passageway that led to the pilot's station. She didn't bother knocking. Instead, she opened the door a crack. Star charts and papers were strewn everywhere in the small room, but Rue was sitting in the pilot's chair, alert and attentive, just as she had expected. She opened the door the rest of the way.

"Mind if I join you?" she asked. He jumped in surprise and cleared his throat.

"No...no...not at all," he stammered while clearing star charts out of the extra chair – the chair Valerian had once occupied as navigator. She sat down.

"How did you sleep?" he asked tentatively.

"Oh, is that what I was trying to do? It felt like I was reliving the past few days over and over again from different angles - all horribly distorted," she replied. Betony's true personality was emerging with each passing day. Before she had merely spoken to gather information, but she felt that little by little her own voice was wiping away the dust from her many years in storage - sarcasm being a fairly recent disclosure. Maybe experiencing such a tragedy, such a brush with death herself, had awakened the part of herself that was still slumbering, jolting her into reality all at once instead of steadily adapting.

"I know what you mean," Rue agreed. Only then did she notice the dark circles under his blue eyes.

"I'm sorry," she said. "I've been so selfish. How do you even sleep in here?" On their journey to Quamir, Rue and Valerian had rotating sleeping schedules.

"Auto-pilot and a reclining seat, but I can't seem to get the images out of my head either." Of course, he couldn't. Had she thought because he appeared to be unemotional that he didn't have feelings or nightmares? After all, she had overheard his tender goodbye to his best friend.

"I'm sorry about Valerian," she muttered. "I feel like it's all my fault. None of you would be here if not for me. You should all be back on Traveriss safe and sound."

"We can each try to assume responsibility, but ultimately, it doesn't matter. What's done is done, and there is much more going on here than meets the eye, Betony. They may be after you, but they wanted me eliminated so badly they were willing to murder members of their own Elite Guard. I don't think this is about you at all. You just happen to be an added bonus for Tussock. I think everyone in the Florenci System is pretty much oblivious to the danger we're all in. I had no idea..." his voice trailed off.

"Thank you...for helping me. I know you didn't want to come, but you did," she said, recalling Rue's opposition to being volunteered as her escort.

"It wasn't that I didn't want to come. You must have misunderstood my reluctance. I am honored to be your escort, truly. I just wanted to make sure you were with the most qualified individual...for your own safety. Though I know a lot about the Florenci System, I am not as well traveled as others, but I assure you that I'll do my best to get you to Asa-en-Darah safely, even if I die trying," he rebuffed.

She wondered if he would ever comprehend the great sense of safety and security that those few words conveyed. She felt as though she was basking in the light of three sun-stars, but the light was radiating from Rue, which caught her off guard. She had judged him harshly before, thinking he was weaker than the other members of the Brotherhood because he wasn't as outspoken, but now his quiet confidence quelled her fears. She knew she was safe in his hands – the hands that had so gently wrapped his jacket around her when they were imprisoned, the hands that tried to comfort her when Valerian was nearly incinerated, and the hands that brought her vitamin supplements every morning even though he didn't have to. She couldn't picture another member of the Brotherhood being so perceptive to her every need. She hadn't paid attention to it herself, until now.

"Well, thank you, again," she said.

He looked at her sheepishly and smiled. "You're welcome."

She left him to his piloting then, feeling that she could sleep for the first time since the accident. When she awoke, she was well rested, even happy to be flying to Asa-en-Darah with Rue. It was a new beginning. As she saw her vitamin supplement once again waiting for her, she smiled. After drinking her breakfast, she found herself making her way to the pilot's station. When she opened the door this time, however, she found the station neatly organized and a vessel of water waiting for her.

"Expecting company?" she asked before sitting down.

"I was hoping you might visit again. It gets pretty lonely sitting here for hours on end with no company," he admitted.

"You might come to regret the open invitation," she laughed.

"I seriously doubt that," he objected, looking away from her toward his monitor as he spoke, hoping not to reveal the great anticipation he felt at her arrival.

"I don't know - maybe your first impression will come back to haunt you."

"I don't quite catch your meaning," he said, staring at her quizzically with a furrowed brow.

"You looked sick to death when Ranunculus asked you to take me to my quarters."

"Oh that," his face reddened.

"I thought maybe Ancient Ones emitted a repulsive smell or something equally offensive."

"No, not at all," he looked alarmed. "There is nothing wrong with you. It was me...I...well...I...I might as well just say it already. I have never seen anyone more beautiful than you and I...I...didn't feel comfortable in your presence," his speaking rate had steadily accelerated as he fumbled to reveal his carefully hidden feelings, and he breathed a faint sigh of relief when he was finished, as though a great boulder had suddenly been lifted off his chest. Betony was flattered. She had assumed people were always gawking at her because she was a freak, but Rue had been terrified to talk to her because he thought she was beautiful. It was her turn to blush.

"The most beautiful, huh? You yourself said you didn't get out much, didn't you?" He laughed heartily, finally letting the dandelion puff of his nervousness and self-consciousness float away in the cool breeze of her voice.

"I've been meaning to ask you something that's been on my mind. Ranunculus said back on Traveriss that you already knew the way to Asa-en-Darah. Tansy told me that the planet's location was so top secret that only Ranunculus and Bindweed knew where it was. Some of the Brotherhood seemed quite upset and surprised to find out that you knew when they didn't. How do you know?" Rue shifted uncomfortably in his seat and took so long to answer that Betony wasn't sure he would. Maybe she had crossed some invisible line Rue had placed between them.

"I've been there before," he finally answered. Betony drew in her breath.

"You've seen the other Ancient?" Rue nodded, and Betony waited for him to elaborate, not wanting to push him. He glanced in Betony's direction, reluctant to let his guard down around her too much. He had never spoken about his life to anyone, and the internal turmoil manifested itself quite plainly on his face.

"It's okay, Rue. You don't have to tell me if you don't want to."

"It's not that...it's not you. I mean...I'm just not very good at talking to people about my personal life, that's all. I can lecture you on the four moons of Quamir or the most recent paleobotany excavations in the nearest four galaxies, but unearthing myself is a little bit harder."

"Is that why you keep yourself tucked away in a laboratory on the outer reaches of the Florenci System?" Again, he smiled at her. She seemed to have a gift for easing his discomfort, and he had a disarming smile.

"There's not much to tell really. Like yours, my seed-pod was opened by Ranunculus, although I didn't crash land on Traveriss. Ranunculus found my seed-pod floating in deep space, so he rescued me. Unlike yours, my seed-pod was severely damaged. Ranunculus couldn't get it to respond to any known trigger points, so he had to open it manually. Basically, he pried it open, and it nearly killed me. I spent months in stimulators as he tried to revive me. Eventually, I came around, but my memories were destroyed. He could only decipher my encoded name." Rue paused to adjust his coordinates.

"So, Ranunculus took you to drink of the Water of the Cloud to see if you could recover any of your memories," Betony surmised.

"Yes. That's when I met Clary, the Ancient, but she couldn't help me. I returned to Traveriss with Ranunculus as his charge. He has personally tutored me and taught me everything I know. In some ways, I am nothing more than one of his creations. I will never know who I really am or where I came from or who I was meant to be. I have lived in seclusion on Traveriss ever since then."

"Won't he let you leave?"

"I've never bothered to ask. Where would I go? I don't belong anywhere, and most of the inhabitants don't take kindly to transplants. An occasional visitor is fine, but they don't want just anyone taking up permanent residence." Betony felt tears surfacing on her face, and she wished she had roots to drain them away. Rue had understood all this time exactly how she had been feeling.

"But you don't have to worry about that," he tried to reassure her, sensing her discomposure and trying to differentiate between their fates. "Clary can help you. She'll get your memories back for you, and Ranunculus will find a place for you where you can be happy and safe. Ranunculus is good for that. He'll create a planet for you if he has too, just like he did for himself and for Clary. Asa-en-Darah really is a work of art. You'll love it, even if it is lit by sun-star simulators." She nestled back in her chair watching the blackness through the window as they passed an occasional comet or meteor belt.

"It seems odd to me that the planets here operate so independently that an entire planet can be wiped out like Eudora, and no one knows or cares. Or that some planets have so little protection that the Noxians can test weapons on them with no threat of retaliation because its inhabitants are planet-bound," Betony said thoughtfully.

"It wasn't always like that."

"Really?" she urged him to elaborate.

"A century or so ago, certain visitors came to the Florenci System. These visitors called themselves Thrips. They were a cunning race, much more technologically advanced than our ancestors at the time. They were readily accepted into our societies. At one time the Florenci System was home to ten planets rather than five, and they created communications between all the planets, not to mention spaceways that allowed travel between planets. They weaseled their way into leadership positions and gained the confidence of the top authorities on each planet. The planets appeared to be united and thriving. Florenci System-wide laws were adopted to govern the people – laws about how marriages were performed, about morality, about murder. This had been unheard of before – each planet had its own customs and cultures, yet the changes were met with very little resistance. Years passed before the true intentions of the Thrips were made known, but by then it was too late.

72

"Legions of their kind began relocating to our planetary system. The Thrips we welcomed were an advance party sent to prepare our planetary system for invasion if the time arose that their people required relocation. You see, when they depleted the resources and assimilated all knowledge of one planetary system, they simply overtook another. They were nomadic parasites in effect. Within a month their kind outnumbered ours. Tensions were high, distrust and suspicion abounded. People returned to their home planets in an attempt to drive the Thrips out, but the Thrips controlled all the resources. People were torn. Many had befriended the Thrips, and a betrayal of this magnitude was inconceivable. The Thrips, however, made one fatal miscalculation.

"When they had abandoned their last planetary system, they unknowingly left survivors behind. They were few, but they were fierce and thirsty for revenge even if it cost the extinction of their race. They were determined to stop the Thrips once and for all, and so they pursued them to the Florenci System. A massive war ensued that lasted years. The Florencies were trying to fight the Thrips, the Pursuers as they came to be called, and even each other at times. After five planets had been completely destroyed, the Florencies finally agreed to join forces with the Pursuers to end the war that had devastated the planetary system. The Thrips were annihilated. Not even one was left alive. Though outnumbered, the Pursuers had won because they had advanced weaponry that eventually overpowered the Thrips - weaponry they had been able to keep hidden all those years the Thrips had been assimilating their knowledge.

"Those that remained of the Florencies negotiated a peace agreement with the Pursuers. With the Thrips destroyed and their own planetary system in ruins, they asked only for a planet to inhabit. They were given Noxia as it was too dark to sustain life for Florencies. With all communications and spaceways destroyed, the other planets once again chose to govern themselves independently. They signed a pact maintaining some of the planetary system-wide laws that all would follow, including the Noxians, and they went their separate ways once again to rebuild their planets and cultures.

"The Noxians, in turn, destroyed the weapons they had used in the war as a sign that they wished only to live in peace with and isolation from the rest of the planetary system. No law enforcers were needed because in those days, as it still is today, a vow is virtually unbreakable once signed. You see, the pact was not signed with ink but with the life force of each governing individual. Tussock has broken a very old oath that no one else has dared breach, and there will be consequences. I just hope it doesn't result in a war.

"You know, Ranunculus believes our planetary system needs to be unified again. He often refers to the Great Unifier who will one day bring everyone together again for the greater good of all, although the greater good to which he refers is purely scientific, I'm sure. He always says, 'Rue, my boy, just think of all the scientific and technological advances we could make if we all worked together,'" Rue did an excellent Ranunculus impression, right down to the wide, sweeping hand gestures.

"You make a good Ranunculus," Betony commented with a chuckle.

"No, I make a good puppet," Rue's tone hissed with resentment.

"The idea of a Great Unifier is a good one, Rue. You must admit that. With a more unified system there would be more opportunities, and there would be places for the Free Frats to seek asylum."

"I don't disagree, but it would take millennia to put such a system in place.

Change takes time, and people tend to oppose change, especially after such a dark history. And, I'm not a huge fan of the idea that one person would not only shoulder all the responsibility, but also control all the power. I guess if anyone could do it though, it would be Ranunculus."

"The Free Frats certainly don't like him much."

"They don't seem to like me much either if you hadn't noticed."

"I did notice, and I might add that you handled their insults with nobility. A lesser man wouldn't have dismissed them so easily."

"Not that I had much choice - they were saving our lives, after all. And if what they are telling us about Tussock is true, which I'm quite inclined to believe it is, I'd be more than a little upset with Ranunculus as well for not stepping in to help."

"Do you think Ranunculus has any idea there is a traitor among the Brotherhood?"

"It's hard to say with him. He rarely reveals all he knows, and he often speaks in riddles and puzzles - half of which I never bother to piece together. He has his suspicions about Eudora, but I don't think he would ever suspect anyone in the Brotherhood, or he wouldn't have given him a post on Traveriss. Likewise, if Ranunculus knew who the traitor was, he would have expelled him from the Brotherhood. So, he either doesn't know, or he suspects someone but can't pinpoint the suspect's identity."

"Who do you suspect?"

"One person keeps coming to mind...Bindweed."

"But he was the only one opposed to this mission, besides you, of course."

"A great cover, if you ask me. He's always so contrary to everything, and he seems to know everything there is to know about Noxia. Maybe his zealous interest in the Dark Planet finally turned him or maybe it's his animosity for Ranunculus. I'll never understand why Ranunculus ever started the Brotherhood with him. Here's an interesting little tidbit for you: Bindweed was the first official member after Ranunculus."

"None of this seems to make sense to me."

"That makes two of us, but I think Ranunculus has a little something up his sleeve because he asked me to retrieve an ancient artifact on Asa-en-Darah and bring it back to him."

"This journey just seems to get more and more interesting as it goes, doesn't it?" Rue looked at Betony as she tried to laugh at her assertion in an attempt to cover the sadness that edged toward her heart at the thought of the terrible turn of events on Quamir.

"That's odd," he said, still examining Betony's face.

"What?" Betony inquired, alarmed by the look on Rue's face. He brushed her cheek hesitantly with his hand, causing her skin to prickle.

"Your cheek. It's completely healed – not even a hint of a blemish," Betony reached up to feel her cheek, inadvertently touching his hand as he withdrew it. Their eyes met for a moment before he broke his gaze. Betony felt her face, only to find he was right. There was no scab or scar. Her skin was as smooth as silk.

"I have been sleeping with the sun-star simulator all night and all day at full shine," she offered, but Rue still looked perplexed.

"Maybe it's Ranunculus's vitamins?" she tried again.

"Maybe," he said, unconvinced.

The conversation turned toward an upcoming nebula, and the rest of the day was filled with ceaseless chatter between the two. The following day Rue gave Betony flight lessons. The day after that he taught her how to read star charts and navigate through the Florenci System. Betony was surprised at how quickly she learned and how eager she was to know even more. Rue quite possibly knew everything there was to know, and he was incredibly patient even when she nearly collided with a space monitor. He made a quick course correction, offered advise on how to avoid a collision in the future, and laughed it off. She was more than comfortable with her new traveling companion. Her relationship with him had taken a direct about-face, and she was almost reluctant to reach Asa-en-Darah.

Chapter Nine

A Drink

Betony was sitting in the pilot's station when Rue announced the approach of Asa-en-Darah. She strained her eyes, but could see nothing at all, not even the slightest distortion of space. Rue pushed a button on the control panel, and a dim flash lit up the dark nothingness. Slowly, as if she were blinking it into existence, a small blue planet appeared before them. Rue let go of the controls as the planet slowly drew them inside its protected perimeter. Betony was much more accustomed to entering and leaving atmospheres by now as they had stopped to recharge several times, and she didn't feel the need to cover her ears to muffle the sound.

Upon landing, Rue opened the hatch and helped Betony to the ground. She shielded her eyes with her hand as they adjusted to the brightness of the sun-star simulators. She was amazed at the beautiful sight that unfolded before her. Waterfalls cascaded in every direction with crystal bridges arching above them. To the left of the landing zone, a small cottage was nestled in a menagerie of climbing vines, radiant green bushes, and exotic shimmering trees with a rainbow assortment of flowers woven among them. The terrace of the cottage hovered in the air off an overhang.

A figure emerged from the cottage, gracefully walking up the narrow path toward them as if she were floating in the air. A picture of divine beauty was before them as her pale green skin glittered in the light. A pale violet gown was arranged in flowing tiers as it tapered to the ground, and her silvery white hair was highlighted with a hint of indigo that started at the roots and darkened as it twisted around her head in an intricate weave. Rue bowed respectfully as she approached.

"I'll have none of that nonsense," the woman spoke with a musical voice, her laugh tinkling like chimes in a soft breeze. The woman extended her hand toward Betony. "I am Clary, protectorate of Asa-en-Darah," she introduced herself as Betony clasped her hand. "I am ever so happy to meet you, Betony. And Rue, it's been such a long time. I'm glad you've come again."

"Thank you for your warm welcome," Rue said, completely at ease.

"I'm sorry to learn of your troubled journey here. I send my regards to your friends," she sympathized. Betony was puzzled that Clary knew about Valerian and Tansy, and Clary sensed her consternation. "My child, I have the gift of sight. I *see* things others can't. I sense emotions, and I can see a person's memories – although the subject must be in my presence. Now that you are here, I know all that has happened to you, and even more interesting is that I see it from two completely different perspectives. How fascinating! I must admit I have too few visitors here upon which I can use my gift."

"So, you know from where I have come?" Betony asked expectantly.

"No. You must drink of the Water of the Cloud for that," Clary answered, gesturing toward a waterfall on the far side of the planet that seemed to be originating from a cloud in the sky.

"But how can synthetic water remove the veil?"

"You've been among the scientists too long, young one," Clary laughed. "Always full of questions, that lot, with too few answers. To preserve my gift, I imparted a portion of it to the cloud where it is in a more concentrated form. While a gift is not tangible, the aura of my gift gravitates toward that particular waterfall. When you drink the water, the essence of my gift also enters your life force, unlocking any veiled memories. If it works, you will be given back the sight of your memories. If it doesn't work, you will feel no different." Clary looked sorrowfully at Rue, but he appeared to be lost in his own thoughts as he stared into the distance.

"You've had a long journey on a bleak pod, no doubt. Come and refresh yourselves," Clary offered. Betony and Rue followed her to the cottage where she had prepared a banquet of food: crushed roots in a glaze, an assortment of exotic vegetables, herbed water, and seasoned tubers. Betony hung back tentatively, having eaten no food since her seed-pod had been opened.

"It's okay, Betony," Rue encouraged. "You've had more than enough time to adapt. You might find that you actually like it, and at any rate, it's bound to be better than those smelly vitamins you've been drinking." Rue crinkled his nose in distaste at the thought of the vitamins. He grabbed a plate and filled it with small proportions of each dish for her to sample, and then he held the plate out to her.

"Here. Just try it," he prodded. She eyed the strange food reluctantly as he added, "For me?" For some reason, she found herself taking the plate out of his hands. Now why would she do it for him? Strangely, since their journey together from Quamir, she had the sudden urge to please him, to impress him, to hear him offer her praise as he had done whenever she had mastered a new flight skill. She heard Clary chuckle faintly and suddenly wondered if Clary could read her thoughts too, or if she was just perusing through someone's memories without restraint. She wasn't exactly sure if she liked the gift of sight.

Betony sat down next to Rue and tasted the vegetables. Two platefuls later, Rue commented with a grin, "I guess this means you like it."

"Like it? I love it," she said as she took a sip of herbed water.

"I think you've been starving the poor girl, Rue," Clary added.

"I didn't have anything this delectable to offer," he rebuffed.

"That's right. Ranunculus isn't really into the culinary sciences, is he?" she quipped back.

With a good meal in her stomach and good company, Betony could hardly imagine that her short life had any dark spots at all. Here, the events on Quamir seemed like a distant memory from someone else's life - a temporary fog that was slowly dissipating. All too soon, Clary rose to her feet.

"I do believe it is too late now to go to the waterfall. Why don't you both bed down for the night? We'll go at first light." Clary showed them each to their rooms.

Sleep kept dancing away from Betony - maybe it was the food or the anticipation of what tomorrow held. At any rate, she couldn't toss and turn for another moment. She crept out the door, surprised to find the sky dark. A place as beautiful as this seemed as though it should always be illuminated. Betony walked along a path, suddenly aware that in the brightness of the full moon, the planet had transformed into a scene that looked like a sparkling spider web covered with frost and dew glistening in the light, and yet the night air was warm and refreshing. Each intricate archway and pathway connected in the light, and Betony understood why the darkness was allowed to penetrate the synthetic light. Only in the contrast of nightfall could such beauty be seen.

She was surprised to see the silhouette of a figure leaning against a shimmering railing on a ledge that overlooked the water below. She didn't recognize him until he looked up at her, and then his blue eyes were unmistakable even in the moonlight. He looked back down toward the water as she approached, and they stood side by side in silence for a few moments before she finally spoke.

"How do you like being off of Traveriss?"

"Aside from my attempted murder, I'd say it's a dream come true," he even managed to laugh as he said it.

"You don't like being a member of the Brotherhood, do you?"

"How can I make that determination when it's all I've known? I've never experienced the alternative. Don't get me wrong. The guys in the Brotherhood are a bunch of crazy kooks whom I greatly respect and admire. They are, after all, the only family I've ever known. They've done their best by me for a bunch of old men who've chosen a reclusive life on a planet that shouldn't even exist, but it was their choice to do that. Crofton was right about one thing. I have led a sheltered life, but it wasn't by my own choice. That's why I've always gravitated toward the traveling guardians. They were my idea after all. I had to find some way to access the outside world, and since I couldn't go to them, I found a way to bring them to me. Although, they weren't always exactly what I had in mind, since Ranunculus hand-picked them, but for the most part, they taught me what the others could not."

"Rue, now that I've safely arrived here, will you return to Traveriss?" She wasn't exactly sure why she had asked the question aloud, but she was intensely interested in his answer now that it had been vocalized. She sensed that their time together was drawing to a close, and the thought left her feeling empty inside – a feeling she had never experienced before in that way. It wasn't loneliness, for she knew that feeling well, but rather emptiness as though a part of her would go with him when he left.

"I won't leave you, Betony, if that's what's worrying you. I'm bound by l..." he stopped himself abruptly, so he could substitute a different four-letter word that left his deeply rooted feelings unsaid – feelings that had come upon him so quickly and so unexpectedly that he dared not reveal them, "duty. I'm still bound by duty to protect you."

Betony suddenly felt disappointed, and she wasn't exactly sure why. Had she hoped he felt more about her than a sense of duty? Even if he had said he was bound by friendship – that would have been more satisfying than duty. Clearly, he couldn't feel toward her the same as Valerian did toward Tansy, and that thought was suddenly unsettling. Betony found a sprout of anger take hold of her heart momentarily, which was ridiculous. She pushed the feeling aside, unaware that she had been looking at Rue awkwardly. He was fidgeting with his hands on the railing, having noted the perplexity, uncertainty, and anger at his response.

"That is...unless...you'd rather me not be your escort anymore. Perhaps I was being a bit presumptuous," he mumbled without looking at her. He had misinterpreted her reaction, thinking that she wished to be rid of him or that she had sensed his near slip up that would have pronounced his love for her and was angered that he dared even think such things. She didn't know exactly how to reassure him because she didn't know how to untangle the spectrum of feelings that had suddenly blurred her clarity of thought. She did know, however, that she didn't like the look of misery that had suddenly shadowed his face.

"No. No. Not at all..." she stammered, embarrassed by her ineptness at expressing herself. She reached toward his arm hesitantly in the hope that physical contact might be more effective at easing his uncertainty. She had seen Tansy do this more than once to Valerian, and she also remembered Ranunculus's awkward pat on her leg the day he was trying to offer her comfort. She was relieved when Rue relaxed almost instantaneously at the touch of her fingers on his bare arm. He smiled as she withdrew her hand.

"You've got a big day ahead of you. We'd better head back so you can get some sleep," he said. She nodded in agreement, and they walked back together in silence. Oddly enough, as soon as Betony's head was nestled into the contours of the pillow, she was asleep and dreaming of Rue. The light that streamed through her window just a few hours later was an unwelcome intruder, but she willed herself to get up despite her heart's objections.

"It's time," Clary announced after they had eaten their morning meal. She beckoned for them to follow her as she stepped onto the hovering terrace. As Betony attempted to step up, the terrace shifted slightly under the increasing weight. Rue was quick to catch her hand to steady her, and he didn't release it when she was balanced again. She wondered at the strange emotions and sensations suddenly bubbling within her like an unknown concoction being mixed in a laboratory beaker. She wondered if Rue knew he was conducting the experiment at all. As the terrace floated forward, she gripped his hand tightly, the vice of nervousness tightening its strangling squeeze on her. The touch of his hand seemed to comfort her, just as hers had done for him earlier that morning.

The terrace drifted slowly in the air. Betony noticed that there were tiers of waterfalls spilling down the outer walls of a circular caldera, with all the water collecting in a massive lake of sparkling blue. The iridescent bridges, which appeared to be suspended in the air, were interconnected, arching over the waterfalls and weaving through forest glens of deep green in what could only be described as an elaborate celestial walkway through nature. Asa-en-Darah was the opposite of Traveriss, and Betony could hardly imagine that both planets had been created by the same Ranunculus. The trip took about an hour, but they were so overcome with the beauty surrounding them, neither of them dared speak. Their voices were sure to disrupt the serenity that permeated the very air they breathed.

Finally, the time had come. Clary drew a cup from her pocket – a small cup no bigger than the flower of a bluebell. She carefully filled it with droplets from the spray of the waterfall, offering it to Betony.

"The Water of the Cloud. Drink," Clary instructed, and Betony obeyed. She swallowed the water in one gulp and felt the cold liquid slide down her throat and into her life force. She closed her eyes to wait for the aura to unveil her mind.

In an instant, the entire existence of her planet was flashing through her mind. She saw the birth of her planet – the planet Unn in the Sira planetary system. It orbited three brilliant sun-stars, and her people thrived and evolved as the planet aged. Suddenly, her mind was flooded with Unn's history – indigenous species of life forms, their appearances, their languages. Generations worth of accumulated knowledge was implanted in her mind. She saw the Red Wood, which used to be her home. She saw her father, her mother, brothers, sisters, cousins, and friends. She felt their love, their joy, their sorrow, and then their urgent desperation. The largest of the sun-stars was too close – too close – too close. The memories came swiftly now but in broken bits and pieces. *Can't leave. Can't move. Must anchor in soil. Evacuate seed-pods. Only hope. Launch seed-pods into space. Too late. Fire. One seed-pod left. Hurry. Hurry. Heat is here. Preserve our memory. Survive. Fire. Fire.* Screaming – horrific screaming. The smell of fire and smoke – burning flesh. A dying planet. Sun-star swallowing Unn. Too close. Too close to the light. Death. Death. The word was hissing in her ears. No mother. No father. No brothers. No sisters. No Unn. Darkness. Black. Despair. Silence. Void. The connection broken.

In a matter of moments, she had gained and lost everything – lost everyone. In one moment, she had felt the generational relationships of love that had bound her planet together as if she had been there. She had seen the faces of her family and her people, shared their memories, and experienced their deaths. And now it was all gone. Betony released Rue's hand, her eyes still closed. She felt her heart being broken to pieces with the heavy anvil of reality striking the final devastating blow. The darkness was engulfing her. *You do not belong here,* it whispered. *You cannot escape. I have found you at last.*

Then, it was clear what she must do to silence the voice. She slowly stepped over the edge of the terrace, freefalling into the waterfall. She didn't resist the force of gravity dragging her downward. She plummeted, fully relaxed. One hundred feet. Two hundred feet. Three hundred feet. A thousand feet. What did it matter? If the silent stalker death wanted her that badly, she would not resist. She would relinquish her life to satisfy its demands. It would not haunt her anymore.

Her body hit the pool of water that had once seemed so calm, but had now transformed into a churning bath of death, pulling her under. Pain. Excruciating pain. A small price to pay for her freedom. No air. She needed air. She had triggered her survival mode again. She opened her eyes for an instant in the panic, almost certain she saw Rue's face peering back at her from above the pool of water. Death's last cruel joke. Even so, she reached her hand toward his beautiful blue eyes as a last farewell gesture. Surely, Rue of all people would understand. Then, she let the water fill her lungs, breathing it in deeply. The darkness soon followed to take her home in its black chariot of despair.

Chapter Ten An Artifact

Death was nothing more than a disturbed sleep, Betony kept thinking after the blackness engulfed her. There were still nightmares though, and the ghostly voices of Rue and Clary that were nothing more than faded whispers she couldn't understand. She hadn't expected this. Was there no escape from the torture even now that she was death's prisoner? Voices again. Why was her hand still tingling where Rue's had once held so firmly? Should she still feel his presence here? As the questions crowded in her mind, the black fog returned, once again clouding her consciousness with its thick vapor.

Clary approached Rue, sensing it was time for her to give him the item for which he had been sent. Rue was standing on the bridge that overlooked the waterfall that days before had nearly claimed Betony's life, if not for him. He heard Clary's quiet approach, but he did not turn toward her.

"Rue," she said softly. "It's time."

"I know." He reluctantly shifted his eyes in her direction. She held a strange devise within his reach. Rue looked at it quizzically. The triangular device had four buttons on its outer edge with a teardrop shaped impression directly at its center.

"This isn't an ancient artifact," he observed.

"No," she answered, "but this is." She placed an ancient seed in his hand that matched the impression in the device. "It comes with a message," she whispered. "You are the one."

"What? Why must he always be so cryptic with his riddles and puzzles? What am I supposed to do with this? What does he mean 'I am the one'?" Rue's tone was agitated and weary. Clary offered a smile.

"You already know what it means, young Rue."

"But I'm not the one. I am a nobody – another stray in Ranunculus's exotic collection."

"He's been grooming you for this, educating you, fine-tuning you..."

"But," Rue interrupted, "he's the one. The whole idea of a Great Unifier is his. Everyone knows him and respects him. Everyone will listen to him. Nobody even knows who I am. This is the first time I've ever been allowed off Traveriss since the last time I saw you. Why now? Why me?"

"Ranunculus is well-respected, even well-loved, but he lacks the one quality the Great Unifier needs the most: the ability to love others. There is a stark and defining difference between being well-loved and being able to love well. The only thing Ranunculus has ever been in love with is his research. You, on the other hand, you have demonstrated your ability to love deeply, and that is what will make you the Great Unifier. You are the one, Rue." Rue looked away from her gaze.

"Rue, I know you feel inadequate, but that too will make you a good leader. You aren't seeking for power. It has come to you out of necessity."

Rue didn't want to admit that Clary's gentle appeals somehow made sense to him, and he wasn't one to shirk such a great responsibility. If he was the only one who could do it, he would, and he would perform his duty to the best of his ability. As for the fear that was sprouting in his heart while his trembling fingers encircled the ancient seed, he would learn to stifle its growth or use it to his advantage. For now, he knew he would have to leave Asa-en-Darah, immediately and alone. He had a puzzle to fit together, and he needed a solitary place to sort it out. He had no idea what he was supposed to do with the device, and he knew Ranunculus well enough to understand that he was expected to figure it out on his own. Ranunculus had never intended for him to return to Traveriss after all, but what would become of Betony?

Clary hadn't spoken of Betony's memories to him, though he knew very well that she knew why Betony had tried to drowned herself. He could only guess at the horrific scene she must have witnessed as her memories were unveiled, but he couldn't wait for her to wake up. Not now. Not if the situation was escalating as quickly as the Free Frats had led him to believe. He had been so distracted by Betony's second brush with death that he had forgotten about trying to contact Ranunculus to tell him what had happened on Quamir.

"Clary, do you have a secure means of communicating with Ranunculus? You seemed to be expecting our arrival. Did he somehow send word that we were coming?" he asked.

"Of course, Ranunculus wouldn't leave me stranded here all alone. He communicates with me through microscopic spores. They are truly one of his more ingenious inventions. He can record a message on one of his spores, program it with the correct coordinates, and send it off into space. When it arrives, it implants itself into a special pot of soil I keep in the cottage. Within seconds, it blossoms into a flower. The flower then speaks the message to me.

I do love when I receive those flowers. And he left me with pre-programmed spores so I can send messages to him as well," she explained.

"Would it be possible for me to send a message to Ranunculus?"

"Certainly," she escorted him over the bridges that led back to the cottage, where he recorded his message, detailing all the information he had gathered on his brief encounter with Crofton. He launched his spore into space with the help of a special devise designed solely for that purpose. Rue then packed the food Clary gave him for the journey along with a fresh supply of water and left in the pod to unravel the mystery of the ancient artifact.

Chapter Eleven  A Story

Something was stinging her nostrils and forcing her eyes open at the same time. She tried to keep them closed to delay her introduction to death, but whatever was stinging her nose refused to grant its permission. She finally managed to pry her eyes open, quite surprised to find Clary peering at her from above.

"Yes, it's time to wake up now. You've slept long enough," Clary said, her voice still a symphony of instruments.

"But I thought..."

"You thought you were dead? Come, dear girl, Rue would have never allowed that to happen. He jumped in to save you."

"Rue saved me?" Betony looked around the room to find Rue, but her head was spinning, and her eyes lost focus.

"He stayed until he knew for sure you'd be okay. In fact, he never left your side."

"He feels responsible for me," Betony acknowledged.

"You know better than that, Betony." How could Betony argue with someone who had the gift of sight?

"I knew your memories wouldn't be pleasant. They never are when a pod has been evacuated to space, but I thought with Rue there, you would be strong enough to withstand the darkness. You surrendered to it instead," Clary recalled, deeply disappointed.

"But you saw what I saw. You saw their faces and heard their screams." Betony found herself pleading for exoneration.

"You were lucky that your memories could be retrieved. You now know who you are and where you came from. You know why you were saved, and you can feel the love that your family had for you."

"But they're all gone now. I experienced every one of their deaths, in case you missed that part. I almost think I'd rather not know."

"Be careful for what you wish. In time you will come to see that I am right. You will grieve for your loss, but you will always have the memories with you. There were thousands more good memories than the last few moments of their lives. They wanted you to survive so they wouldn't be forgotten. You are their link to life, and you nearly severed it with that little stunt...and Rue...I don't even want to think about what you did to him," Clary chided, and Betony looked away as the tears welled up in her eyes.

"You don't seem to understand much about Rue. He has none of his memories, and he has no hope of ever retrieving them as you have just done. He'll never have the answers to the questions who, what, where, when, and why. He is alone, and he's lived in isolation on Traveriss his entire life trying to feel acceptance and love from Ranunculus, but Ranunculus doesn't know how to love."

"And how would you know about any of it aside from poking about in people's memories without their permission?" Betony countered defiantly.

"I think it's time I told you my story," Clary said calmly. "I didn't mean to be harsh with you. You've just been given your memories back, and the adjustment can take time. I guess I also feel responsible for what happened to you. I should have warned you. I should have been prepared for such a rash decision, and the only reason I didn't anticipate it is because I was seeing what you were seeing. It was tragic, and something I wish I didn't have to see. My gift can be a burden at times, and I have endured much because of it. I might have done the same thing if I had not been given my memories the instant my pod was opened. You see, my pod crash landed on a planet called Noxia." Betony gasped.

"Yes, it is quite alarming, and you're lucky you were spared my fate for it was Tussock himself who opened my pod. Seeing that I was an Ancient, he immediately sought to form a union with me as a symbol of his power – that even the Ancients came to him and were subject to him. He had heard that all Ancients were bestowed with gifts, and he was desperate to find out what my gift was. When his efforts to unlock my gift were met only with failure, he planned to drain the pigment from my skin as a sign of shame and then make me his personal servant. Throughout this time, however, I was guarded by his Chief Guard. We became friends, and he protected me as much as he could from Tussock's cruelty. When he learned of Tussock's plans, he risked his life to save me. I believe you are acquainted with him. His name was Bindweed." Betony drew in her breath in shock at the unexpected revelation. *Bindweed was a Noxian?* Clary ignored her reaction.

"We fled Noxia together, although even then the Noxians were hated. We sought refuge on Oro and Phirun, but we were not well received. Next, we tried Quamir, where we happened across a young man named Ranunculus, who was well acquainted with Tussock. He immediately took us in and offered to help me find a place of refuge. When nowhere could be agreed upon, he set about to create a place for me with Bindweed's help. They are both so brilliant. Within a year, Asa-en-Darah was created and hidden away. I had the privilege of naming it myself. Asa-en-Darah means born in the morning among the stars. Its creation was fascinating to watch for all of us – a new beginning of sorts. Both Ranunculus and Bindweed took up residence here after the planet was completed.

"As time went on, I fell in love with Ranunculus. He spent all of his time with me, asking questions, getting to know me. He wanted to know everything about where I had come from and what had happened to my planet. He was always very concerned about me, and I found him to be equally fascinating. He had such a passion for knowledge. Looking back, I suppose maybe I had my suspicions about his true intentions, but I let myself believe that he loved me."

"Ranunculus didn't love you?"

"Quite the contrary. He cared for me very deeply. I was young, and I misinterpreted the feeling until much later when I honed my deciphering skills. I was still developing my gift at that point in my life. I came to realize that he loved me for what I was not who I was. To him, I was an extraordinary scientific discovery with special powers. He spent so much time with me because he was studying me, analyzing me. My former planet esteemed love as the highest emotion. It was the premise from which we operated, and I was desperately seeking it. Again, I was young. After Ranunculus had collected all the data he wanted, he left without so much as a goodbye. My heart was broken. The channel of clarity for my sight was disrupted, and for a time I lost my gift. I withdrew in my sadness, neglected Bindweed, and refused to see him or talk to him. I was despondent, and he had no choice but to leave.

"Eventually, I was able to come to love other things: this world they created

95

for me in all its beauty. Ranunculus isn't a bad man. He's quite the opposite – very compassionate, always willing to help someone else, but he's driven by his curiosity – by situations and beings that challenge and test his knowledge and abilities. He's driven by his love for science. It wasn't until it was too late that I recalled and analyzed my own memories to see things as I should have seen then. It was Bindweed who gave me my sight with his love, not Ranunculus. It was Bindweed who saved me from Tussock and the Noxians. It was Bindweed who sacrificed everything he had for me. It was Bindweed whose heart was pure with love. It was Bindweed who stayed to pick up the broken pieces when Ranunculus left. It was Bindweed's breaking heart that caused my sight to blur, not my sadness as I had thought, and it was Bindweed whom I drove away," Clary's voice broke off abruptly.

"So that's why Bindweed dislikes Ranunculus. That's why he didn't want me to come here. He was afraid Tussock was using me to get to you." Betony was beginning to understand. "Bindweed is still protecting you. He still loves you."

"Yes, I know, but I think some heartbreak cannot be undone, and what I did to him cannot be forgiven. I cannot face him. But you, Betony...don't you make the same mistake as I did. Rue is a good man, and he is steady and true, but I'm sensing that you don't need me to tell you that," Betony nodded her head, not wishing to discuss Rue at the moment. Clary helped Betony to her feet, and they walked along the crystal arches until they came to the waterfall coming from the cloud. Betony shuddered as she watched the water cascade into the swirling pool below, remembering her own plummet into the icy waters.

"Do you know why my aura gravitates here?" Clary asked, not waiting for an answer. "Bindweed created this particular waterfall for me after Ranunculus left. It was here that he professed his love to me. It was here that he bid his farewell when I gave him no response. It was here that the purest love I have ever known was freely given, and though I refused it, my aura gathers here on its own to mingle with the synthetic droplets of water created just for me by Bindweed...But that's enough about me. What about your gift?"

"My gift?"

"Yes, Betony. All Ancients have a gift, including you."

"But all I saw was Unn's destruction."

"I know what you saw, Betony, but you must understand that a gift is not something you see. It is something you feel in your heart - in your life force."

"I'm afraid I have no gift then."

"Your gift is there, and you'll discover it when the time is right, I'm sure." She left Betony, continuing to stroll on the archways until she disappeared in the greenery. Betony did not follow her. She had never felt more alone than at that moment. She reached her hand toward the waterfall, feeling the cool mist on her fingers, wishing that Rue was by her side, which he very well might have been if she had been able to cling to his light amidst that swirling darkness that overcame her when Unn was destroyed in her memories. She wondered where Rue had gone. Clary made no mention of why he had left, and she had a sudden and urgent need to know where he was.

She ran back to the cottage, but Clary was not there. She didn't appear to be coming back anytime soon either because the evening meal was set out for her. She realized as she looked at all the food that she was famished. She hadn't eaten since the waterfall incident, so she stuffed herself until she thought she would be sick. Still Clary did not return, and Betony finally retired to her bed, though she could only see Rue's sorrowful face staring at her in her dreams – his blue eyes filled with pain and anger, his mouth straight-lipped and icy. She tried to conjure up more pleasant memories, but his face always rippled through them until they were nothing more than distortions in the background. She tossed and turned, yet he remained – the silent sentinel of her sleep.

INTERGALACTIC INTERCEPTION #4

If he ever made it back to find Ranunculus alive, Prey was resigning his post whether Run-Dung permitted him to or not. The stress was too much for him. He had molted twice already since these interceptions began, and he was long past the molting stage of his development. Not healthful at all. He'd more than done his time for his crime. In the midst of his complaining, the buzzer went off indicating another message. It was coming on the regular frequency again.

Voice 5: Dr. Lantana, please.

Voice 6: You'll be connected momentarily.

Dr. Lantana: Dr. Lantana here.

Voice 5: Yes, doctor. It's Stephanotis.

Dr. Lantana: What can I do for you old friend?

Stephanotis: I've just sent some life force samples to you via a space monitor. I wonder if you might analyze them for me. Treat them as a biohazard though, just as a precaution. I'm not sure exactly what we're dealing with here.

Dr. Lantana: Certainly. Certainly. Everything okay?

Stephanotis: Of course - just a little research we're working on.

Nothing to be alarmed about, but Quamir is better equipped for this analysis.

Dr. Lantana: Anything in particular I'm looking for?

Stephanotis: Run tests for everything you can think of.

Dr. Lantana: While I've got you on the line, you'd be happy to know that your traveling guardian is recovering better than we could have hoped.

Stephanotis: Traveling guardian?

Dr. Lantana: Oh, maybe I shouldn't have...Just forget I said anything, okay?

Stephanotis: What's this about? What's going on there?

Dr. Lantana: Sorry. I've just been paged - medical emergency.

Stephanotis: Sure, there is - darned Ranunculus and all his secrets anyway.

Just thinking of the voice on the other end of the line sent shivers down Prey's exposed interior. Stephanotis. He crossed the name off his list unhappily. Prey would have liked to see that guy roast personally. In fact, he would've been more than happy to load him on the skewer himself. It was just Prey's luck that Stephanotis happened to be the good guy this time. He focused on the list.

Five more to go. No way to know. It could be any of them. Rue was the least likely suspect - the quiet type. Then again, from Prey's experience, the quiet type could be the deadliest. He'd nearly lost his head once to a girl by the name of Antis. He had mistakenly interpreted the nod of her head as a green light to approach, but apparently, she had a nervous twitch. Talk about dodging an incisor just in the nick of time. Phew. He hated to even think about that, so he was grateful for the distraction of adding another signature code. With three, he was sure to be able to spot any patterns.

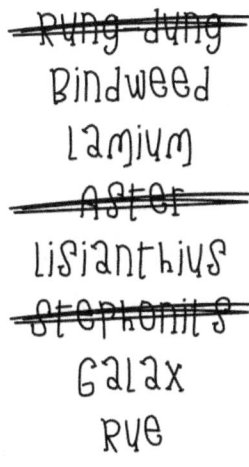

Chapter Twelve
A Reluctant Entourage

The rumbling noise of a landing pod jolted Betony awake the next morning. Her heart raced as she ran to the door of the cottage nearly bumping into Clary in hopes of finding Rue, but she was sorely disappointed.

"You called?" Crofton said as he and Pili approached them.

"You know each other?" Betony looked from Crofton to Pili to Clary in utter disbelief.

"Of course, we know each other. I aid and abet those who are in opposition to tyrannical evil, the epitome of which is Tussock," Clary explained with a smile.

"Two of our space gliders ran out of power near the Drop Off. We thought we were goners when suddenly a small planet materialized right in front of our eyes. We were pulled through the atmosphere by some sort of tractor beam. That's when we met Clary," Crofton added.

"Incredible," Betony whispered under her breath. That's why Crofton hadn't prodded Rue further when he told him they were going to the Drop Off zone. He already knew their destination.

"Betony needs an escort off Asa-en-Darah, and I thought you might be able to help," Clary told Crofton. Betony felt a pang of shame when she heard the word escort.

"It beim pleasure," Pili plastered a grin on his face, which somehow endeared him to Betony.

"Where will we take her?" Crofton asked, his eyes clouding with worry. Clearly the idea was less amenable to him. "It's only a matter of time before Tussock realizes she's not coming."

"You leave Tussock to me, Crofton. I'll buy you some time, but right now you need to find Rue," Clary instructed.

"You mean the Brotherhood is willing to help?" Crofton asked skeptically.

"It appears so," Clary replied.

"Why now? They've never cared before. Did they wait until there was an imminent danger before descending from their glass pedestal to the level of the common people to claim the glory?" Crofton spat out the words bitterly.

"Ranunculus was waiting until his protégé was ready, Crofton. He waited to make his move until all the stars were aligned," Clary tried to diffuse his anger.

"Well, praises be they aligned before we were all enslaved to Tussock."

"Crofton, now is the time. Not a moment too soon, not a moment too late. You know as well as I that the timing is right...now. Had anyone intervened before, there would have been no chance of success."

"A little common courtesy would have been nice. He might have at least answered one of our requests for a meeting, so we could discuss a possible plan with him. Our lives are at stake after all, not his."

"That's not his way. At least he was listening intently."

"Once again, all hail to the Mighty Ranunculus," Crofton remarked sarcastically.

"What does Rue have to do with any of this?" Betony interrupted. She had been listening with interest, but she couldn't contain her curiosity any longer.

"Rue is the Great Unifier," Clary said matter-of-factly. Betony's eyes widened.

"Him?" Pili said, smirking.

"Do not underestimate him. I have seen his heart. I have seen his mind. He is the one we've been waiting for. With him, you may not fail. Without him, you will not win," Clary rebuked sternly.

"But the girl...surely, she would be safer here," Crofton interjected.

"You mean surely I'll get in your way," Betony corrected. Crofton shifted his eyes downward, affirming her assertion.

"No, she must go with you. She has yet to discover her gift. If she can unlock it, she'll be an asset to the cause," Clary urged.

"Don't I get a say in any of this?" Betony asked, suddenly realizing how Rue felt the day in Council meeting when he was chosen as her escort. An awkward silence ensued. Apparently, no one had considered her feelings. She was just another potential weapon in the war against Tussock.

"Well, of course, I'm willing to help. It would just be nice to be acknowledged. I have a brain of my own, you know. I don't need to be coddled by anyone – not anymore, anyway," Betony clarified her position. In reality, she felt she had no choice but to help. Aside from Tansy and Valerian, the only person she cared about in this planetary system was Rue, and if Rue was fighting for the cause as the Great Unifier, she would stand by his side.

"Where do we find Rue?" Crofton asked, relieved that Betony would not have to be taken off the planet by force.

"He didn't say where he was going, but I'd try the third moon of Quamir. He knows of a small research station there," Clary answered.

"Very well," Crofton complied reluctantly. Apparently, none of this had been part of his master plan, and he didn't like the improvisation.

"And Clary," he added before turning to leave, "don't do anything to put yourself at risk."

"I thank you for your concern, Crofton, but I've taken care of myself for a long time now. I think I can handle the situation," Clary assured him as she stared him straight in the eyes. She offered several bags of provisions to Crofton and Pili. As they were loading them into the Noxian pod, she turned to go inside the cottage, but Betony caught her arm.

"Thank you," she said. "Thank you for your help in retrieving my memories, and I'm sorry."

"Don't apologize, my child. It has been my privilege meeting you and finally sharing my story with someone else. I've kept it buried for far too long, and you helped me to see what I must now do."

"What do you mean?"

"Nothing that you need worry about. I send my love with you. May you find your gift," Clary said as she hugged Betony. Then, she stepped onto the terrace and floated away toward the Water of the Cloud, and Betony knew she must be thinking of Bindweed again.

"Climb aboard," shouted Crofton as she ran toward the pod. She was surprised when she stepped inside because the pod had no separate rooms. It was one large open circular area similar to the Commons on the long-range exploration vessel, except the pilot seat was in the center of the circle. The viewspace also circled the perimeter, so in any direction she looked, she could see outside the pod. There were several chairs behind the pilot seat and storage compartments above the viewspace, where Pili was loading the provisions that

Clary had given them. She helped herself to a seat to the right of the pilot's seat, making sure to buckle the safety harness.

Crofton climbed into the pilot seat, and Pili sat down beside her. She was glad that she was no longer terrified of exiting and entering atmospheres because it would have made her appear weak, and she wanted nothing to add to Crofton's reservations about taking her along. The take-off was much smoother and quieter than she had anticipated. If not for the viewspace, she wouldn't have known they were in open space. She could tell by the way the stars were whizzing by that this pod was built for speed and stealth.

"How did you manage to get this pod without Tussock knowing Rue and I escaped?" she asked hesitantly. She wasn't sure if Crofton was in the mood for conversation, since he seemed absorbed with the controls. Pili was busy pushing buttons on the arm of his chair, possibly programming the coordinates in as navigator.

"One of my contacts brought it to me. Apparently, the Free Frats have come up with a ploy to explain my prolonged absence, though we didn't have time to exchange much information before he had to leave. Luckily, we got this beauty before Clary called. I'm not sure how we would have managed to transport you with two space gliders," he replied.

"Do you mind if I ask you a few questions? I have only been a part of this planetary system for a short time," she asked.

"Go ahead. You're part of the team now, aren't you?" Crofton answered, and she felt much more at ease. She was part of his team.

"How many Free Frats are there?"

"It's hard to say. We're recruiting more and more every day, but there's not enough. We're still a minority by a large margin."

"How do you keep from getting caught?"

"Three A's," Pili answered her this time. "Alertim. Attentivim. Awarim."

"If one of us is caught, many innocent people will suffer - people who've never even heard of Free Frats - family, friends, the guy who happens to be walking on the street where the arrest is made. For each arrest in Noxia, regardless of the infraction, five additional people are punished - whether they are guilty or not."

"What do you mean by punished?"

"For minor infractions, a person might lose a finger or a toe or he or she might be branded with the seed of shame on his or her forehead. The Punisher who carries out the torture may even go as far as cutting off an arm or a leg, maybe an ear or a tongue - whatever suits his pleasure that day. For serious infractions like treachery, a person's eyes are gouged out, and he or she is sentenced to life in the Pit of Punishment - a place where just enough light filters in each day to keep a person barely alive - tortured for years. The laws are pretty loose, so what constitutes treachery on one day may constitute a minor infraction the next day. Everyone basically lives in terror every second of every day." Betony felt a lump in her throat at his unexpected response. Torture. She wasn't familiar with this kind of cruelty.

"How did you come to organize the Free Frats if you are risking that kind of punishment?"

"Two reasons, really. My father joined the Elite Guard when Tussock took power, and he was close friends with the Chief Guard, who is second in command only to Tussock himself. In my father's day, that man went by the name of Bindweed. I'm sure you're acquainted. Around this time, Tussock procured a pod - inside was an Ancient. Tussock thought she had a gift, and when he couldn't find out what it was, he was enraged. Bindweed took pity on her and rescued her from a terrible fate, fleeing Noxia. As retribution for his treachery, five of his friends were rounded up and punished. My father was among them, although at the time we were told he was killed when his pod malfunctioned upon leaving the atmosphere for Space Patrol. Normally, Tussock would have used their punishment as an example to others, but he didn't want anyone to know his own Chief Guard had betrayed him and escaped, thus the secrecy.

"Having no idea any of this had happened, I naturally joined the Elite Guard when I was no longer considered a seedling. My oldest brother, Pickerel, was also in the Guard. We had served together for a while when he was sent on a special mission. Though he wasn't supposed to tell anyone, he confided in me that he was taking a mechanism to Eudora's surface, but he didn't know what it was. That was the last time I ever saw Pick's eyes. When he was returning home, he received a transmission from Tussock, congratulating him on furthering the Noxian realm. He was horrified to learn that he'd helped annihilate an entire planet, but by that time the plague had been unleashed. The damage was done. It was only a matter of hours before it was all over for the Eudorans.

"Pick received a second transmission before he reached Noxia, ordering him and two Space Patrols to destroy a seed-pod that had been launched from the planet's surface. One of the Space Patrollers got to the seed-pod before he did and blasted it. Pick shot the Space Patroller down and tried to rescue the seed-pod, but the second Space Patroller took him by surprise. In the resulting firefight, the seed-pod was destroyed. My brother was escorted back to Noxia, arrested, and sent to the Pit along with five of his friends. I suppose it was my luck that I wasn't among the five that went to the Pit with him, although knowing he was there was torture enough. Unlike my father, Pick's punishment was a public affair on the steps of Tussock's palace, and I was forced to watch the whole thing.

"Several months later, quite by accident, I discovered a secret passageway to the Pit. I snuck down to see Pick, and he told me the whole story. That is also when I learned of the true fate of my father, for Pick had found him in the Pit barely alive, though I never would have recognized him myself. At that moment, I decided something had to be done by someone, so I appointed myself and have been on my crusade ever since, plotting patiently, gathering allies, although before you, they were all Noxians, except Clary. I've just been biding my time, waiting for Tussock to slip up. But I want to be clear about my motivation. I do not fight for revenge. I would be no better than Tussock if I did. I fight for freedom. I fight to free my father and my brother from the Pit. I fight for all the Noxians who live under Tussock's reign."

"I'm so sorry," Betony whispered. No wonder Crofton was so full of anger and hatred all the time. "I had no idea."

"You're lucky then," he replied simply. "I'm sorry you have to be burdened with it now." And so was she.

"I know you deeply dislike the Brotherhood, and I can't help but wonder if any of that has to do with Bindweed. He is, after all, responsible for your father's incarceration." The question caught Crofton off guard, and he took a few moments to collect his thoughts.

"I did think to find an advocate in him, and I won't say that I'm not more than a little disappointed that he hasn't responded to my constant queries, groveling really. I would have thought he would be the first to support an uprising against Tussock. I mean, sure, he escaped himself, but he left people behind. People like my father, whose condition is rapidly deteriorating. But I also believe that if Bindweed were going to act, he would've acted by now. I think the whole lot of them have left us to our own devices to sort this mess out."

"Except Rue," Betony interjected defensively.

"Yes, except for your precious Rue. Anyway, Bindweed holds no blame for Tussock's rise to power, and that is where my dislike really comes into play. He simply left and never looked back."

"What do you mean?"

"I think it's time for a little Noxian history lesson. You'd be surprised at all the connections in the story. Tussock rose to power under a cloak of lies and deceit and murder – the typical tyrannical story, although some speculate that his thirst for domination initially resulted from Ranunculus's refusal to collaborate with him."

"Ranunculus? I had no idea he was a part of Noxian history."

"Ranunculus has always had a scientific following of the 'elite,' even when he was still on Quamir before the Brotherhood was officially founded. Tussock needed a place to develop his plots and ideas for overtaking the current leader of Noxia, Borreria. He was granted admission into Ranunculus's little group until Ranunculus discovered his true intentions. He was expelled immediately, so he returned to Noxia to form his own group. He had gleaned enough of Ranunculus's information and educational material that he was well on his way. You see, Borreria banned all books and educational institutions because he felt that ignorance was an effective way to maintain control of the Noxian population. It worked until Tussock came along. Tussock had Borreria murdered, but no one blinked an eye because everyone hated Borreria, and they thought there would be improvements under Tussock's reign. Tussock did effect change. He encourages education, research, and intelligence as long as it's closely monitored, and he reaps all the rewards. His tool of choice is fear rather than ignorance; therefore, loyalty to Tussock is only as deep as a person's fear in most cases."

Betony was suddenly grateful that her planet had been destroyed by an act of nature rather than the hand of a heartless dictator. While she still grieved for the loss of her people, she was relieved that they had died knowing only love for one another. She felt that love more strongly now than when she had first been reconnected to her past.

"Rue once mentioned how your ancestors came to inhabit the planet, and I have wondered ever since what is Noxia as a planet like? It's always depicted as a dark circle."

"It is the dark planet, literally – not just because of its history of diabolical rulers. The planet is dark for most of the day. The sun-star shines for one hour and one hour only early in the evening, but its light is so intense that it would burn someone unaccustomed to it. That's why we all have incredibly tanned skin. We practically roast for an entire hour, but because of the intensity of the sun-star for that hour, we are able to harness enough energy to power everything we need until its return the following day. We've also been able to harness the energy from the electrical storm, complete with thunder and lightning, that directly precedes the one hour of light. We use solar heating panels to stave off the cold, so the planet is quite warm even in the absence of the sun-star."

"Couldn't you simply use solar light panels or even sun-star simulators like those on Asa-en-Darah to generate light rather than remain in the dark the majority of the time?"

"Very perceptive. Tussock does use solar light panels, but only for himself. I'll give you a little more backstory into the maniacal man that he is. You see, my father didn't find pleasure in serving as a member of the Elite Guard. He did it more out of necessity, so my brother and I wouldn't grow up in poverty and darkness. Because my father was a member of the Elite Guard, we were able to live within the compound of the castle, and we received the best education possible. That's how Tussock works; he manipulates Noxians into doing his bidding by offering them a better life than they would otherwise have. If they refuse, they face the Punisher. There is no way but his way, and there is no way around him. He must be removed from power, or we will never be free to be what and who we want to be. I just want to be a regular guy, hanging out at the Caverns, pursuing my dreams, settling down to start a family. I didn't ask to lead this rebellion, but if not me, who? I can't live like that anymore, and no other Noxian deserves that life either. Not my brother, not my father, not...well...not anyone." He stopped his reflective speech abruptly, but Betony could tell there was more he wanted to say. He never had an opportunity to express his feelings to anyone but Pick on the rare occasion he was able to visit him in the Pit, and even then, he shielded his brother from the weight he felt upon his own shoulders.

Betony saw Crofton's softer side as he opened up to her, the side that could be a thirty-year-old man rather than a stoic warrior with his eyes fixed on rebellion. She saw his truest, sincerest intentions, as well as the reluctance and self-doubt that he kept so well hidden from the others. She thought of Rue, her reason for being alive – her reason for joining the Free Frat – and the similarities between the two. She wondered if Crofton had an anchor of his own back home – if there was someone, he had stopped himself from naming just a few moments before – someone else he was fighting to free so they could share a brighter future together.

"May I ask you a more personal question?" she asked.

"I'm not sure I have any other personal information to share. You practically know my whole story," he replied.

"Is there anyone in particular waiting for you at home?"

"Nah. A bit too dangerous to fraternize with a member of my gang," he said nonchalantly.

"But there is someone? You're just not willing to pursue her for her own protection?" Betony persisted. Pili cleared his throat and inserted a small devise in each ear as if to give Crofton his privacy.

"I actually broke her heart for her own protection. I doubt she'd have anything to do with me." There was a hint of regret in his voice as he spoke. Betony was fully prepared to change the subject to something more neutral when Crofton unexpectedly continued, "It's not like I meant for it to happen at all. As a member of the Elite Guard, I was assigned to protect Tussock's daughter, Ambulia, for one of my rotations. You'd like her if you met her. She's the only ray of sunshine in her father's dark palace. I gradually fell in love with her over the year I guarded her. I don't know how I could have avoided it. I was practically around her every moment of every day. It was almost as if she became the air I breathed, literally. The feeling was mutual, and she urged me to get her father's blessing, so we could unionize."

"Would Tussock have approved?"

"Surely. I had no fear of being rejected. I'm a decorated member of his own Elite Guard. There could be no better suitor in his eyes."

"Even with your brother in the Pit for treachery?"

"All the better to keep me in line according to Tussock's line of thought. Besides, I still have a mother with whom he can barter for what he wants. On my way to speak to Tussock, I found the secret passageway to the Pit. I wanted to talk to Pick so badly, so I snuck in. You know the rest of the story."

"So, you never spoke to Tussock?"

"I couldn't. The idea of the Free Frats had already hatched, and I couldn't risk her safety."

"But would she have supported you?"

"Of course. She hates her father more than anyone. He had her own mother locked away, but I couldn't risk it. If we were together and I was discovered, she would surely be tortured in front of me. I couldn't bear the thought of it."

"So, what did you do?"

"I requested re-assignment as far away as possible. It was necessary to advance my cause anyway. I had no access to any important information when I was guarding her."

"And you haven't spoken to her since?"

"What could I say to her? I can't tell her the truth or she's as good as dead. I can't lie and tell her I don't love her because I couldn't live with myself if I did that. I jumped on the first Space Patrol off Noxia, and I haven't seen her since. I didn't leave her unprotected though. A trusted associate of mine is watching out for her, and I just try to keep my distance. I don't know what excuse he used for my sudden departure and prolonged absence, and I haven't dared ask him how she is. I don't think I could bear to hear the answer, whether good or bad." In a rare show of tender emotion, Crofton's eyes misted over with tears, but he quickly regained his composure.

"Now, that's enough about me. No more questions," he voiced the conclusion of the conversation. Then, tossing a wad of something slimy he had been eating at Pili, he said, "Get those ridiculous things out of your ears. It's not like you can't hear through them, anyway." Pili's hearty laugh lightened the somber mood in the room, and Betony couldn't help but laugh with him.

"At least you have friends to watch out for you in the Free Frats," she commented.

"Pili's the best friend I could ever ask for. We've been through a lot together," Crofton noted.

"I puttim upim with a lotim crap...fromim you," Pili tossed the food back, hitting Crofton in the side of the face. Crofton glanced at Betony, her mouth posed to ask yet another question regarding their history.

"I see you just can't keep yourself from asking questions, can you? I suppose you want to know about Pili now, right?" She nodded her head with a sheepish smile.

"Oh, all right. I suppose there's no harm in that. Is there, Pilipiliula?" Pili shook his head in disgust at Crofton's use of his full name.

"Pili and I go way back. We were both just young seedlings, although he is a bit older than I am. Pili's reclusive mother lived in a small alcove just around the corner from where I lived. He too lived in the castle compound, and I believe his father was a stone carver for Tussock before he disappeared." Betony saw Pili's eyes darken and his muscles tense at the mention of his father, but he said nothing.

Crofton continued, "I often had the feeling that someone was lurking in the dark corners, watching me, but I could never see anyone. One day, I was outside trying to spark a fire when I noticed a boy standing off in the distance. I motioned for him to come out of his hiding place to join me. He slowly approached, and he has been my silent shadow ever since. In the beginning, Pili never spoke. I only knew his name because I heard his mother call for him once when we were out exploring beyond the border walls. As time wore on, he would try to communicate but the words never came out quite right. He adopted his own language with the strange word combinations and incomplete thoughts that he uses now, but I understand him just the same. Isn't that right, Pili?"

"Crofton gettim meim inim heapim troubles," he announced much to Crofton's delight as he then launched into a string of stories of the mischief they got into as seedlings. It was only an hour later that the third Quamirian moon came into view.

Chapter Thirteen — A Gift

As soon as the hatch was opened, Betony ran toward the small silver building and opened the door. She saw Rue's figure hunched near a desk, and she found her insides fluttering at the thought of seeing him again. Her smile quickly faded, however, when he turned, and she saw his face twisted in pain and surprise.

"Betony?" his voice was choked and raspy, and he spoke as if she were a hallucination. She rushed toward him, flanked on both sides by Crofton and Pili. She put her arm around his waist to support him.

"Rue, what's wrong?" He tried to motion in the direction of his arm. Betony's eyes immediately settled on the Transparency Detector, which was emitting a bright red glow.

"The Transparencies?" she asked. He nodded weakly before collapsing, dragging her to her knees under his weight.

"At least I got to see you again...one more time. I wanted to say goodbye before I left," Rue spoke, each word requiring concentrated effort. His breathing had become laborious.

"Sh," she whispered, pressing her finger to his lips. "I'm here now. You don't have to say goodbye." Rue shook his head.

"It won't be long before..." she couldn't bear to hear him say it. She had seen too much death, too much destruction. It could not claim Rue too. She leaned closer to his face, feeling her life force quicken its transport through her system, her breathing accelerating just as his was slowing. She pressed her lips against his to stop the utterance of that dark word that sucked everything she loved into its vacuum of heartache, the suction of which she could not seem to escape. She suddenly felt a flame ignite inside of her. She opened her eyes to see if she was on fire, but found nothing more than the spontaneous combustion of her heart sensing love for the first time. She saw only Rue's clear blue eyes staring back at her face, a faint smile on his lips. And then he closed his eyes, and his chest was still.

"No!" she cried out, but in the same instant, the internal flame leaped into her arm, pushing it forward. Her outstretched fingers came to rest on his throat. There was that strange sensation again – the same sensation she had felt when she was with Valerian after the solar flare attack. It slowly meandered through her body, filling her with pain, but she did not withdraw her hand. Each new wave of pain that pulsed through her body eventually dissipated into a tingling. The sensations of pain seemed to pass information to her before they dispersed. The pain was generated from a poison.

As she closed her eyes, she could trace the poison through Rue's body to its source. She followed the flow of his life force through his veins and into his heart and back out again until it stopped at the needle that had been implanted in his arm with the Transparency Detector, the source of the deadly poison. She drew the poison into her own body through the touch of her fingertips and released her own healing life force into Rue's body until all the poison was gone. When the pain stopped and the tingling subsided, Betony withdrew her hand. Although his eyes were closed, Rue's chest was rising and falling at regular intervals. She had found her gift at last!

"That must have been some kiss. You were glowing, seriously glowing! Maybe Data Head can give me some pointers on something after all," Crofton exclaimed. Betony was still cradling Rue's head in her lap, having forgotten Pili and Crofton were in the room with her.

"Was he dead?" Crofton asked on a more serious note.

"As close to it as someone can come," she answered.

"And you healed him?"

"That is my gift. I am a healer," she smiled at him.

"Do you mind telling me what a Transparency is and if we should be high-tailing it out of here?"

"Transparencies are invisible pests that attack the life force of their victims. The Brotherhood identified them on Traveriss and has been working tirelessly trying to prevent their spread to other planets. This devise was supposed to detect the Transparencies as they entered the life force and then emit an inoculation that killed them without harming the member of the Brotherhood," Betony explained calmly, but Crofton and Pili were jumping about the room as if trying to avoid the invisible creatures.

"You can calm down. I don't think there are any Transparencies on this moon at all. I think his detector malfunctioned. Rue was being poisoned by the very thing he thought was protecting him," she said as she reached for Rue's arm. She disconnected the detector and withdrew the tubing from the open wound. She then touched the wound, and Crofton and Pili watched in awe as it completely disappeared. Rue started coming around.

"What happened?" he asked feebly.

"Rue, who designed the Transparency Detector?" she asked pointedly.

"Bindweed," he muttered.

"It can't be. Did anyone else have access to the inoculation serum?"

"Why? What's going on?"

"Rue, that inoculation wasn't meant to quickly kill Transparencies. It was poison designed to slowly kill you, and it nearly worked. I suspect all the members of the Brotherhood are being poisoned as we speak."

"It's got to be Bindweed. He came up with the inoculation," Rue said, trying to sit up.

"Did anyone else have access?" she asked again.

"It's the Brotherhood, Betony, founded on the principles of trust and mutual respect for each other. The stuff wasn't exactly under lock and key. Anyone could have had access to it," he quit struggling to get up, finding himself too weak.

"Rue, it's not Bindweed. It's someone else. Anyone but Bindweed," she asserted.

"We'll back her up on that. Bindweed is a Noxian traitor, not a traitor to the Brotherhood. He may not have come forward to help us directly, but I know he would never do anything to give Tussock an edge," Crofton affirmed.

"What are you doing here? What's going on Betony?" Rue was suddenly alarmed. He hadn't noticed the two Noxians in the room with all the commotion.

"Calm down, Rue. Everything is fine. I'll explain it all later, but for now we need to focus on who's behind this," Betony soothed. "If it weren't for them, you'd be dead."

"That's twice I've saved your neck, Beaker Brain," Crofton added.

"Enough with the derogatory comments, Crofton. We're all on the same team now, and I don't see you addressing your Free Frats in those terms," Betony reprimanded.

"You're right, sorry. Old habits die hard," Crofton mumbled.

"Rue, is there anyone else you can think of with a motive?" Betony asked.

"Bindweed hates Ranunculus. Everything points to Bindweed," Rue repeated.

"Bindweed hates Ranunculus, but not for the reasons you suspect," Betony replied. "I'll fill you in on that later too. Trying to figure out who the traitor is ourselves is proving futile, so for right now, we need to warn Ranunculus, if it isn't already too late. Maybe he can pin-point the inside guy on his end," Betony said hopefully.

"The only secure way to communicate with Ranunculus is on Asa-en-Darah," Rue told her. "But I'm on the verge of figuring this devise out," he added, pointing to the table.

Crofton picked it up, "Nifty looking thing, isn't it?"

"I guess you could say that. Another one of Ranunculus's puzzles, but I think it's a communication device with links to Oro, Quamir, Phirun, and Eudora," Rue explained.

"Thus, the key to you being the Great Unifier," Crofton surmised.

"I suppose so," Rue answered.

"Well, what do you propose we do?" Crofton said just as his wrist started flashing red.

"What is that?" Rue asked.

"Communication implant. It's how the Free Frats communicate amongst each other."

"Not very subtle, is it?"

"Only because I have it set to light alert. I can set it to ping only, which gives my wrist a little jolt. Excuse me for a minute," he said, as he inserted into his ears devises similar to those Pili had used earlier. He stepped outside, and Pili went with him, leaving Rue and Betony alone for a few precious moments.

"Betony, what just happened here?" he asked.

"You almost died, but I found my gift, Rue. I'm a healer," she explained.

"You saved me?" he repeated.

"Just like you saved me back on Asa-en-Darah. Rue..."

"Betony," he interrupted. "You don't need to explain anything to me."

"But I do. I didn't mean to hurt you. I watched a sun-star swallow my planet while I was essentially belched out into the unknown."

"Strangely enough, I don't seem to mind intergalactic waste products," he jested. "I'm not trying to minimize what you experienced either. I can't even imagine what you've been through, but it's not all bad, is it? We can be lone wanderers together at least." She bent down and kissed him again.

"What was that for?" he asked with a smile.

"You were looking a little pale," she answered, returning his smile.

"Well, in that case, I'm still feeling a little weak too," he laughed, but her face was suddenly shadowed with concern.

"What? What did I say?" he asked as he finally sat up.

"I could have saved Valerian. I didn't know. I felt the same sensation when I checked to see if he was alive, but I pulled my hand away from his throat, and then the Quamirians came. I could have saved him."

"You did save him."

"What?"

"I didn't tell you this, but the doctor's had no idea how he was even alive,

122

and he was showing marked improvement every hour without them doing anything at all. I had my suspicions about you when I saw that gash on your face heal so quickly without even scabbing over."

"But his face, Rue. You saw his face. If I had known, he could have been whole again, but now..." her voice trailed off as she pictured his disfigured face.

"Oh, Betony," he said as he hugged her close to him. "You don't know Valerian very well at all, do you? It doesn't matter what he looks like. He'll bear it as a sign of valor, as the ultimate Grafting Ceremony that seals his love for Tansy. And he'll be loved all the more for it. It will be a new fashion statement on Phirun. They love and respect him that much." As he finished, Crofton and Pili re-entered the room.

"Sorry to interrupt your little reunion, but we've got to move. Two Noxian Space Patrols are headed in our direction. We'll have to come up with new headquarters since I can't very well take either of you back to Noxia," he said.

"What about Eudora?" Rue suggested. Crofton flinched at the mention of the planet his brother helped destroy.

"Is it safe on Eudora?"

"Ranunculus has been monitoring it for years, and all of the recent reports have come back clean. He was planning to visit there himself until the Transparencies showed up."

"It would make a good hideout since no Noxian Space Patrols go near Eudora. Looks like we'll have to take the risk."

"But we have to get back to Asa-en-Darah to warn Ranunculus about the detectors," Rue said.

"We'll have to split up then. Pili and I will go to Eudora and set up headquarters, while you and Betony go to Asa-en-Darah to send your message.

I've got a team I have to rendezvous with tomorrow morning."

"Sounds good to me," Rue said, as he got to his feet rather shakily, leaning on Betony for support.

"Oh, I almost forgot," Crofton said, turning to Betony. "Clary sent you more suitable clothing. She didn't think you traipsing about the Florenci System in a gown would be very discreet. A dead giveaway that you're an Ancient." He tossed her a bag, and the three men exited so she could change in privacy. Clary had given her native Phirun clothing like Tansy had worn. She pulled on the slightly baggy brown cargo pants and the thin yellow t-shirt. She declined to wear the shoes as she preferred to go barefoot. She assumed her hair was another dead giveaway, so she arranged it in a series of messy knots. It was quite a feat with so much hair, but she managed it in record time. She could hardly wait to actually feel the sun on the back of her neck.

The last tell-tell sign of her true nature was of course the faint green tint of her skin. She looked around the room, which was covered with a thick layer of gray moon dust. She misted her arms with the water from Rue's drinking vessel and then smeared the gray dust on her exposed skin. As her skin drew in the water, it also drew in the moon dust, effectively muting the green shimmer of her Ancient pigmentation. She was beginning to approach a more 'normal' Florenci System appearance, and she could very well have passed for a native Phirun to any untrained eye. With her disguise complete, Betony stepped out of the research station, only to find the three men staring at her with gaping mouths.

"Something the matter?" She looked down to make sure she had put the clothes on correctly. The men seemed to recover, looking awkwardly at each other, and muttering under their breath.

"Beautiful as ever, Betony," Rue stepped forward to escort her to the long-range exploration pod.

"Excuse me," Crofton interjected. "You're not thinking of taking that piece of space junk, are you?"

"Do you have a problem with it?" Rue asked defensively.

"Yeah, by the time you make it to Asa-en-Darah in that meteor bucket, we'll *all* be Ancients. You better take mine. Eudora is closer anyway."

"You're seriously going to let me take your cruiser?" A burst of excitement lit up in Rue's eyes.

"It's either that or space gliders. Either one will get you there faster than that pod."

"I'm opting for the cruiser," Rue accepted with anticipation.

"Be careful with it," cautioned Crofton. "This beauty is a prototype hot off the presses, especially equipped for the Free Frats."

"Where do you get all this stuff?" Rue inquired.

"From Tussock himself. We've infiltrated the technological development branch. Tussock thinks he's manufacturing them for his Elite Guard, and technically, I suppose he is. We give him our specs for approval, and then our inside guys modify them for us. They are specially marked and identity coded so only a Free Frat can unlock their true potential. This particular model is even equipped with a Scrambler, so the Tracers can't find us. The problem is neither can tractor beams, so you'll have to land without Clary's help. This is her first flight off Noxia, so you better bring her back in one piece," Crofton said, while running his hand over the sleek black surface of the cruiser.

Rue was practically gleaming at the thought of occupying the pilot's seat in an actual Noxian cruiser. He had studied them with quiet admiration for years behind Ranunculus's back. He had worked up the courage to approach Ranunculus about building one of his own as a component of his Independent Studies, but his request had been emphatically denied. Ranunculus said the Brotherhood had no use for machines that were only used for joy-riding around the Florenci System at unsafe rates of speed. How Rue wished Ranunculus were here now!

"I owe you one for this," Rue said, pounding Crofton on the back as he walked by.

"I'll add it to your tab," Crofton replied with a smirk.

INTERGALACTIC INTERCEPTION #5

Prey was beside himself. All the signature codes must have been randomized because there were no detectable patterns. He was stuck traveling through space receiving frequent updates about the imminent decimation of the planetary system that had become his home. As he bent down to retrieve the list of the signature codes he had knocked to the floor, he accidently tipped his drinking vessel over, effectively dousing himself with water. He lashed out in anger at the overturned vessel, lacerating it with the sharp spines on his forearm. The pain of the motion in combination with the smearing black ink on the paper, however, jarred his memory into action.

Prey had only been on Traveriss for three days, when he found himself hiding in the lavatory after dodging Stephanotis for the fourth time since his unexpected arrival. Ranunculus had yet to establish the boundaries between Prey and his colleagues, and Stephanotis was in hot pursuit, trying to get his hands on Prey before Ranunculus dropped the ax on his fun. Prey was clinging to the corner of the ceiling, trying to think of a better hiding place, when someone opened the door. It was late at night, and most of the Brotherhood was sound asleep in their quarters.

Prey turned his head to see Bindweed enter. Bindweed stopped in front of the reflector and stared at himself for a while before engaging in the time-consuming task of cropping his hair. He trimmed it down to a half an inch, which took nearly an hour. Poor Prey's legs were trembling from the exertion of holding himself upside down in the corner, and Bindweed didn't appear to be in any hurry since he turned his efforts on his goatee next. Another half an hour passed, and Prey knew he couldn't hold on much longer. Just when he was sure Bindweed was about to leave, Bindweed stripped his long robe off and stepped into the showering facility, which happened to be directly below Prey. Prey lost his grip at the very same moment and lashed out trying to catch himself. Instead, he hit several pipes with the spines on his forelegs, puncturing them as he fell. He landed directly on top of the unsuspecting and naked Bindweed.

Before Bindweed could recover enough to throttle him, Prey limped out of the room at top speed and locked himself in the first room he came across. He found himself in the Paleobotany Room and had to spend the night warding off nightmares of his body displayed in one of the great glass cases as Stephanotis proudly lectured on the evolution of the Mantis insect. Luckily, Ranunculus rescued him the next morning. That very afternoon he had been given his first commission.

But what Prey remembered now was that Bindweed's wet body had been tattooed with black vines, just like the water-smeared ink on his paper. He had completely forgotten about it before, but he knew very well that those marks were the sign of a Noxian. Ranunculus had told him how to recognize a Noxian in case he ever encountered one. He had special orders to report it at once to Ranunculus, which would have been difficult to do since his Communicator was out of order. He now knew that Bindweed must be the Noxian traitor to whom Tussock was referring. He was clearly not in on the conspiracy. Prey's antennae twitched with excitement as he crossed Bindweed's name off the list.

Could he think of any way to rule out anyone else on the list? He thought about the remaining names: Lamium, Lisianthus, Galax, and Rue. Hmmm. Hmmm. He was tapping his foot as he thought. Rue! Rue could be eliminated after all. Rue was too young to be the traitor. The traitor had killed everyone on Eudora, and Rue's pod had not been opened until after Eudora's destruction, much later in fact. Rue had arrived after Prey himself. He smiled at his intelligence as he crossed Rue's name off the list as well. Maybe he should apply to the Brotherhood when this was all said and done. He clearly had the brains for it. Through the process of elimination, he was down to three individuals. But he never had much contact with the remaining three people, so he now stared back at the black letters in their names. He was back to waiting.

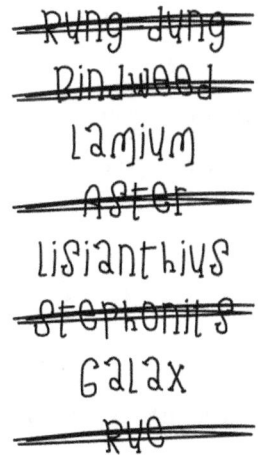

Chapter Fourteen
A Rendezvous

Betony had a difficult time trying to fill Rue in on all the details about Clary, Bindweed, and Crofton that she had gathered in the short time they had been apart. He had the Noxian cruiser racing through space at top speed, and he was clearly more interested in his new 'toy' than he was hearing a tragic love story.

"Rue?" she finally asked in an aggravated tone. "Have you heard anything I've said?"

"Of course, I have. Every word." She had no doubt that he was telling her the truth, but she was still a little perturbed not to be the object of his undivided attention.

"Maybe you could slow down a little before I have no choice but to show you what I ate for lunch today," she demanded.

"No need. We're here," he answered with a grin. Sure enough, he sent out his flash of light, and Asa-en-Darah materialized. Rue had no problem landing the cruiser without a tractor beam, and Betony was glad to be on solid ground again.

"Something's not right," Rue surmised as he walked toward the cottage.

"It's too quiet," Betony agreed. They stepped inside the cottage, but nothing seemed to be out of place. There was no sign of Clary, but she could have been anywhere on the planet's surface, well-hidden in the forests. Rue walked over to the spores and within minutes had composed a message and shot the spore out of the atmosphere on course to Traveriss. They found the locator button with which they could send a signal to Clary, alerting her that they had arrived, but there was no response. They waited several minutes and tried again. Still, there was no response.

"We can't wait much longer," Rue said, pacing around the cottage. "Do you notice anything amiss at all since this morning?" Betony surveyed the area, but nothing caught her eye. The floating terrace was still hovering in place by the cottage.

"I don't see anything, Rue, but this morning Crofton cautioned Clary not to do anything to put herself at risk. It was almost as if he was worried about leaving her here alone," she answered as they walked back to the cruiser. Clary seemed to have vanished. As Rue opened the hatch, Betony noticed that several nearby flowers had been trampled.

"Wait a minute," she said, grabbing Rue's hand and leading him toward the damaged plants several feet away from the landing pad. "These weren't here this morning." They followed the trail of trampled flowers into a small hollow.

"This doesn't look good," Rue commented as he studied their surroundings.

"What?"

"This is about the right size for a space glider. What are the odds that the Free Frats kept one handy on Asa-en-Darah, just in case?"

"You think she left in a space glider on her own?" Betony could hardly believe it.

"That's what it looks like. We'd better get to Eudora," Rue dashed back to the landing spot with Betony in tow. Before leaving, however, he sent another spore to Ranunculus to inform him of Clary's apparent departure from Asa-en-Darah.

Not wanting to damage the cruiser on his first time out, Rue didn't push it to top speed this time, so they didn't arrive on Eudora until the next morning. When they landed, they were unsettled by the sight of a small party of Noxians gathered in a group.

"They must be part of the team Crofton was waiting to rendezvous with this morning. It looks as though they arrived just a few minutes ago," Rue surmised as they opened the hatch to the still swirling dust particles from the landing strip.

"It's still hard to see more than a couple of them gathered in one place since we can't distinguish the good from the bad," Betony told him as they walked toward the group.

"I know what you mean."

As they approached, the men in the group pounded their fists with each other in greeting and then raised their hands in the air, pounding their own fists as a show of their solidarity and commitment to overthrowing Tussock. Crofton nodded his head in their direction as they neared the group.

"This is Rue, our delegate from the Brotherhood, and Betony," he introduced them. Crofton and Pili had been joined by three other men, who were eyeing them suspiciously.

"This is Miramar, Kyasuma, and Boxthorn, otherwise known as Thor," Crofton announced. Kyasuma looked almost identical to Pili, although he wasn't as large, while Miramar was tall and thin with long, stringy, sage colored hair. Thor was bald and wore a spiky collar of thorns around his neck. All were branded with black vine tattoos, but only Kyasuma and Thor bore the mark of the yellow circle. Miramar was marked with a star within a circle, and Betony had no idea what his designation was.

"Let's get down to business, shall we?" Crofton asked, turning his stare back toward the newly arrived Free Frats. Betony was surprised that Rue didn't interrupt with his news of Clary's disappearance, but before she could say anything Thor revealed a jar filled with brightly glowing bugs.

"What have we here?" Crofton asked taking the jar.

"A recent procurement from Tussock's personal safe," Thor answered proudly.

"Do we know what it is?" Crofton never used the terms I or me. He only spoke in terms of we or us as a sign of the collective nature of their fight against evil. If they failed in their mission, they would all suffer the consequences as one.

"Not exactly. At first, we thought it was nothing, but Miramar had the idea to electrically charge the jar, and that's when they started glowing. They must be important though because they were under lock and key. We barely smuggled them out undetected," Thor explained.

"How?" Crofton prodded.

"We found a contact in the Vault. His brother's eyes were gouged out for being late for his guard duty on account that his mother had been seriously injured that morning. The Punisher was in a bad mood that day. He was sent to the Pit. That old Tussock is our greatest recruiter. All we have to do is follow his trail of villainy, and they fall in by the swarms," Thor said.

"What do we know about it? Are they dangerous?" Crofton continued his line of questioning.

"We believe so. Our contact was ordered to secure it in the vacuum seal. We're not sure they're toxic, or if they're the source of the plague that wiped out Eudora, or if they're something entirely new and different. Our contact tells us they are a fairly new acquisition though."

"Good work," Crofton complimented. Essentially, these men were fighting an unknown enemy. They never knew exactly what Tussock was up to, so they merely tried to interfere with anything that seemed important to him, just as they had done when helping Betony and Rue escape. They thwarted Tussock's plans by doing the exact opposite of what they were told, having absolutely no idea what impact their actions might have.

"And there is something else...we've uncovered the nature of the weapon..." Kyasuma said hesitantly.

"Excellent. Excellent. I ought to leave more often. Maybe Tussock has become suspicious of me. By the way, where does he think we are with the Ancient anyway?"

"We told him there was evidence that the solar flares were misfired, destroying both pods. We, Miramar, Thor, and I, are part of the discovery team sent to confirm the findings.," Kyasuma replied.

"Wait, that would mean certain death for whoever fired the weapons, Ky."

"Don't worry. We verified prior to generating the false report that the men who fired them were fully aware they would be killing members of the Elite Guard in the attack."

"But what if they were under threat of their families?"

"They weren't. They volunteered to test the solar flares on their own comrades, and they deserve whatever they get."

"We don't want to be the death of any innocents." Crofton was clearly upset by the news.

"I am well aware of that, Crofton. We all took the same oath. We've all endured the suffering of Tussock's cruelty in one way or another. We would never force that upon someone else."

"I know. I know. I'm sorry. There's just too much death and destruction these days."

"Back to the nature of the new weapon: Tussock has created his own Black Hole," Kyasuma revealed.

"What? That's impossible."

"Well, he's done it."

"What does he plan to do with it?"

"It works like this: He is, as we speak, having sensors put in orbit around each planet. The sensors respond to his controls. Whenever he wishes, he can veil the planet with a dark blanket that keeps the light from the sun-star out as it sucks any light from the planet's surface toward it, so the planet becomes shrouded in darkness."

"Tussock will have complete control of the light. That's how he's planning to conquer the Florenci System?" Crofton was in a state of utter disbelief. He hadn't anticipated such a weapon, and Rue drew in a sharp breath as well.

"It's a brilliant plan, even you have to admit, Crofton. How else would he enslave entire planets? He has to control the one thing they need in order to live."

"May I ask how you came by this information?" Crofton asked pointedly. Ky looked down at the ground, reluctant to answer.

"Ky?" Crofton urged.

"You're not going to like it Crofton," he began.

"Just tell me already," Crofton demanded.

"Clary is on Noxia. She turned herself over to Tussock this morning."

"What?" Crofton yelled, his eyes widening in rage. Betony felt her head start to spin as Rue steadied her. "She did what? How did I know she was going to do something stupid? I told her not to put herself at risk! What was she thinking?" His voice was echoing in the stillness of the morning.

"Crofton, without her we would have never found out about what his real plan was. You know that. We've just been randomly trying to undo whatever it is we think he's trying to do. He's almost ready to test this thing, and we wouldn't have known how to stop it. Tussock doesn't know that Clary has the gift of sight. She knows all his memories, all his plans, and she's been feeding information to us secretly."

"Curses! Curses! Curses!" Crofton was beside himself. "So, Tussock just took her under his wing - not even the least bit suspicious as to why she just happened to show up on Noxia after being in hiding all these years?" Again, Ky looked at his feet.

"What did you do?" Crofton inquired.

"It wasn't my fault entirely. She contacted me last night and told me that she needed an escort to Noxia. I was to send a Free Frat to meet her on the meteor belt. She told me you knew all about it, but you were taking care of the Ancient and couldn't get away."

"And you didn't think to verify?"

"Why would I? What reason did she have to lie to me? She's done nothing but help our cause at her own personal risk. So no, I didn't think to verify. I sent Murain to pick her up and escort her to Noxia because he was already on Space Patrol duty in the vicinity. She told Murain to tell Tussock that he found her stranded in the meteor belt, so Murain took her as a prisoner, just as she asked – and he's been promoted for it, by the way."

"How on earth did she get to the meteor belt by herself?"

"Your space glider," Rue joined the interrogation. "When we arrived on Asa-en-Darah, Clary was already gone as was the space glider you hid in the hollow."

"This is unbelievable," Crofton was running his fingers through the spikes of his hair.

"Crofton. She knowim what she doim. She fightim withim us. She one of usim. Without her helpim, we no winim. We dieim in Pit," Pili, who had been silently listening until now, finally added his voice.

"I know. Without her we'd be no closer to uncovering his plans than we were five years ago. We'll just have to ensure nothing happens to her, all right? Do we know who her guard is?"

"Murain," Ky answered, and Crofton breathed a sigh of relief knowing that he was a Free Frat at least.

"Please tell me you have some good news to offset that debacle. Do we at least have any new means of retaliation?" Crofton queried.

"I was hoping you would ask me that. It won't stop the Black Hole, but it will give us a means to defend ourselves while we attempt to disarm the sensors and overtake Tussock on Noxia," Ky said, visibly relieved as well.

"And? I'm not good with suspense, Ky."

"It's a cryostatic light ray. We figured the best way to fight darkness is with light," Ky proclaimed, handing a small weapon to Crofton.

"What exactly does it do?" he asked as he examined the object, which resembled a long silver tube with a trigger.

"When you pull the trigger, a blast of light shoots out at the target. The light, however, freezes the victim's life force for a full day without killing him – true to our oath. We could immobilize the entire Elite Force with these, as well as Tussock himself, if we had a few more of them."

"And who else knows about them?"

"No one but us. Miramar here developed the prototypes. He's a member of the Lead Research Team that reports directly to Tussock," Ky explained as Miramar stepped forward.

"So why is he on a Discovery Team?" Crofton asked suspiciously.

"I also happen to be a forensic expert. I was sent to gather DNA evidence. And if I may note, I joined the Free Frats because I was conscripted into Tussock's service against my will. He's holding my betrothed hostage," Miramar answered, already anticipating the line of questioning.

"And you're willing to sacrifice her life to help us?"

"As soon as the Black Hole is proven effective, we're all as good as dead anyway. A few of my colleagues will be spared to help should any maintenance issues arise, and the rest of us are sure to be eliminated since we will no longer be useful, especially those of us who were forced to work on the project."

"Welcome aboard, Miramar. We can always use a good mind like yours." Crofton held out his fist to Miramar, who bumped it energetically. Miramar was officially the newest member of the Free Frats. The bond that was forged between these brothers was twisted and contorted into a brand of loyalty Betony could barely comprehend. They were forced together out of cruelty and fear as well as determination and hope that they could somehow make a difference in the lives of the Noxian people by accomplishing the unthinkable - overthrowing Tussock. And now the future of the entire Florenci System hinged upon the courage of this little band of brothers.

Knowing she would be of little assistance in carrying large crates of weapons and supplies, Betony wandered off into a meadow as the group dispersed to unload the pods. She must have dozed off in the bright morning sun because she was awakened by voices within close proximity to her. Startled, she sat up, trying to determine the exact location of the conversation. She did not have to look far, however, as the two men approached her. Not wanting to be seen, she hid behind a conveniently located thicket just before Crofton and Thor came into view.

"I am surprised to see you here, Thor. I hope you're not neglecting your assignment." The two men stopped by a nearby tree as Crofton spoke.

"How dare you insinuate any neglect on my part! I was assigned to accompany Ky and Miramar, and I'm not in a position to excuse myself from Tussock's commands. She's being carefully watched," Thor's words carried an angry edge. Betony surmised they must be speaking of Ambulia. Thor must be Crofton's trusted associate charged with watching over her.

"I trust that she is," Crofton replied, surprised by the defensiveness of Thor's retort.

"I might suggest an extraction in the near future, however," Thor said, his voice steadier and less emotionally charged than a few seconds before.

"Impossible. She's safer where she is," Crofton assured him.

"And how would you know anything about that?" Thor seethed, anger once again lapping at the shore of his serenity.

"Excuse me?" Crofton seemed shocked by Thor's apparent disrespect.

Betony had never heard a Free Frat speak to Crofton in such a manner.

"You've just added her to your list of assets to be protected. She's more than just a pawn in your strategic planning," Thor snapped back. Crofton unexpectedly lunged toward Thor, pinning him against the tree by his neck, just above his spiked collar.

"You don't know what she is to me," he said through gritted teeth.

"I know more than you'd like to think! I am the one who had to listen to her inconsolable sobbing as she cried herself to sleep every night after you left. I am the one who has endured the constant pleading for information about your whereabouts. I am the one who has watched her spirit break off piece by piece with each passing day for the last five years as she pines away in your absence. I am the one who tries to reassure her with lies." Crofton loosened his grip, letting Thor slide down the tree to a sitting position to catch his breath.

"Then, I'd consider you the lucky one," he whispered, looking away.

"Lucky? Lucky? It's torture, you know, watching her eyes light up when she talks about you. It's torture when I return from an assignment only to be barraged with questions about you. I understand why you had to leave, but to break her heart like this...isn't there enough heartache on Noxia as it is? Couldn't you spare her?"

"You've fallen in love with her, haven't you?" Crofton continued to avert his eyes, and his voice had a note of dejection in it.

"I tried not to. I did. But you of all people should know how it is – to be constantly in her presence for such long periods of time – to watch her suffer for so long and then one day to hear her finally laugh at something you say or smile when she sees you – to see her dance in the sunlight –"

"Stop. I don't want to hear anymore," Crofton interrupted, but his voice

140

was no more than a whisper.

"I've become her most trusted confidant, but it's not me she needs. It's not me she wants."

"What would you have me do?"

"It's time she knows the truth."

"That would only compromise her safety."

"She'd be safer here than on Noxia."

"But she can't just suddenly disappear - now, can she? It would only make Tussock suspicious, especially in light of the upcoming weapons test. I have to think about all the other people who have put their lives on the line to dethrone Tussock. To make a wrong move now...would jeopardize everything. All the suffering we've endured would be for nothing." Thor made no immediate reply. As much as he hated to admit it, Crofton was right, and he even admired him for his unselfishness.

"I guess we all have to make sacrifices for the cause."

"I'm not sacrificing her, Thor."

"I didn't mean you were. She's the most protected Noxian out there. We both see to that."

"I'm just sorry I can't be there to protect her for myself."

"I'm not. Whatever comes of it. I'm not sorry."

"I guess I should watch my back, eh?"

"Your back is safe with me. I'd never do anything to hurt her, and I know now that you had no intention of hurting her either."

"You're a good man, Thor."

"That means a lot coming from you." Thor rose to his feet, leaving Crofton alone squatted by the tree. Betony could see the turmoil on his face, and she did not envy his position. He had to set his personal interests aside, possibly at the cost of a life he sought only to save, and he wasn't even assured victory in the end. He very well could have fled Noxia as Bindweed did with Clary, leaving the rest of the Noxians to fend for themselves, yet he could not. His courage, his loyalty, and his love demanded more of him, which led him to more difficult paths, more unsettling potential outcomes. He could not live with himself knowing others still suffered, knowing Tussock's reign of terror continued. There could be no happiness for him until freedom had been secured for all Noxians. If – the stars forbid – Ambulia died, he was reluctant yet willing to pay that price, whatever the personal cost to himself or Thor.

Betony found herself silently crying for these people whom she barely knew. By the time she pulled herself together, Crofton had gone. She meandered back to the landing site, met by a worried Rue.

"Where have you been? I've been looking all over for you," Rue asked, but he recanted as soon as he saw the look in her eyes. "What's wrong?"

"Another dose of reality, that's all. I've just got a glimpse of what this war is really costing – of what's at stake if we lose," she answered. He didn't press her for any more information. Instead, he gathered her into his arms in a tight embrace. The quiet thudding of his heart reminded her of the flipside of their situation. She felt fortunate to know exactly what they were fighting for, and it was a fight for which she too was willing to sacrifice everything: the chance to be with Rue in peace without the threat of death constantly hanging over them.

"I think it's about time we have a little target practice. What do you say, Rue?" Ky called out, holding a cryostatic light ray in each hand. Rue's lips curved into a wry smile as Betony pushed him away playfully.

"Go. Shoot with your friends," she urged as he bounded off with the others.

Chapter Fifteen
An Abduction

While the men were testing the cryostatic light rays like little seedlings with brand new toys, Betony wandered over to look at the strange bugs that were glowing in the jar. She bent closer to inspect them, and her mind was suddenly a swirl of colors blurred together, waiting for the final painting to be unveiled. As she concentrated, a memory emerged unbidden. Her people, the people of Unn, had called them Sparklers. They were invisible unless there was a lightning storm that sent static electricity through the air. Then, they shimmered just like these little glow bugs. They were harmless to her people, and they cohabited Unn in peace. She only recalled one incidence of a recorded attack, but it was a defensive assault provoked by a misunderstanding.

A spore herder had accidentally corralled several Sparklers when he was hunting for weed spores. The weed spores had infested the Red Wood, threatening to cause soil erosion, and thus the destruction of Betony's family. The spore herders were one of the only species on her planet that had mobility, so they offered to help control the weed population. When the Sparklers couldn't get free, they called for reinforcements. Sparklers entered the spore herder's body and drained his life force, which resulted in his death. It was an unfortunate accident, and afterward, Betony's people had learned to communicate with the Sparklers to work out their differences in nonviolent ways. She leaned closer to the jar and began to make a vibrating noise at varying pitches. Pili came up behind her as she was trying to communicate with the Sparklers.

"Great. Clary stickim us with crazy girl," he laughed.

"I think she's trying to communicate with them," Rue observed as he stopped at Pili's side. For several minutes Betony changed the pitch and speed of the vibrations in an effort to establish a communications link as the remaining Free Frats gathered around her, watching curiously. Just as she was about to give up, she hit the right combination, and the Sparklers began emitting the sound back to her.

"Oh my," Betony whispered as she listened to the high-pitched sound. The bugs were still glowing in the jar and were now flying in circles so fast they were nothing more than a blur.

"What's going on here? What does she think she's doing to them?" Crofton approached the jar, reaching out to push Betony out of the way, but Rue thwarted his effort.

"She's communicating with them, I think," he reasoned as he restrained Crofton.

"I don't hear anything," Crofton muttered.

"They must be communicating in such a high pitch we can't hear, but as an Ancient, Betony can," Rue explained as they fell back into silence and watched for several minutes as the bugs began to fly erratically in the small space, hitting the glass several times.

"Oh my," Betony repeated, shaking her head in disbelief. Rue bent down and gently touched her shoulder.

"What is it?" he whispered, breaking her concentration.

"These are your Transparencies, Rue. This is their queen. She was just recently appointed her own kingdom and sent with a convoy to settle a new planet in a nearby planetary system when she was abducted by men who were marked with Noxian tattoos. Only she and her closest advisors were captured. The rest of her convoy was pursuing her captors, but she lost communication with them after entering this inhabited space. She hasn't been able to re-establish communication since," Betony told him.

"So, the Transparencies are somehow part of Tussock's plan? What – to eliminate the Brotherhood?"

"More like distract them for a time. Didn't you say that Ranunculus was planning a visit here but postponed his trip because of the Transparencies?" Crofton asked.

"Or both," Betony clarified. "Not only did the arrival of the Transparencies on Traveriss postpone an investigative trip that might have revealed clues to the destruction of Eudora, but it also provided the means by which to poison every member of the Brotherhood."

"So, the Transparencies near Traveriss must be the queen's convoy," Crofton inferred, and Betony nodded her head in agreement. "And exactly how do you know all this?"

"A similar species inhabited my planet. They speak a different dialect, but I can understand most of what they are saying," she explained.

"Can't you just tell them that we will let the queen go, and they can find their convoy and leave?" Rue asked.

"I'm afraid it's not going to be that easy," Betony replied.

"Of course not," Crofton rolled his eyes. "What's the hang up?"

"They are demanding retribution. They don't understand mercy nor do they forgive mistakes. Even if we weren't directly involved, we will be held accountable because we are of the same species as the abductors. They don't distinguish differences like we do. This is a grievous crime, and they will attack unless they receive retribution. I had hoped to explain to them the circumstances regarding the abduction, but this is a more primitive species than those that existed on my planet."

"What do they want us to do? Pay them? Allow them to kidnap someone from our planetary system? Tell them that they can be my guests. Tussock is all theirs. I'll even lead the way," Crofton offered.

"It's not that simple, Crofton. If you open that jar, they will attack the first life forms they come in contact with. There's no telling how many people will be killed before they feel justice has been served. I'm afraid for now, we can only continue to hold them captive and hope their convoy doesn't find us until we can figure out what else to do."

"This doesn't make sense to me. Why all of a sudden is all of this happening? I can't figure out what provoked it," Rue wondered.

"Tussock is a very patient man, Rue, and so it seems is the traitor on your end. This has been a carefully orchestrated plan that has been in the making for years. It's just now coming together in its entirety. Even Ranunculus has known Tussock is plotting something, thus the embargo. As for the provocation, Tussock is easy. He's motivated by an insatiable desire for power and control. As for his cohort, well, that's the mystery, isn't it?" Crofton offered his insight as he picked up the jar of Transparencies that were now invisible.

"We'd better get these to a safe place. Rue, why don't you try to find a suitable headquarters among the abandoned buildings, if you can find them. I have some things to discuss with Ky." Rue resented taking orders from the likes of Crofton, particularly when he felt as though he were being excluded from an important meeting.

"Fine, but I'd like to be included when you discuss the Black Hole. I'd like to know exactly what we're up against, and you may actually find me to be an asset to your cause if you'd give me the chance. You know nothing about me aside from the fact that I am from Traveriss. I have been personally tutored by Ranunculus himself. Grudges aside, even you have to acknowledge that he is the greatest scientist in this quadrant," Rue replied.

"Unfortunately, I would have to agree with you on that point," Crofton admitted as Rue turned to go.

"And Rue," Crofton added, "you're mistaken if you believe that I think of you as anything but my equal, maybe my superior in some aspects. As much as I hate to admit it, you're a key component to the success of this campaign. Don't think I don't know that."

"I appreciate your confidence in me. And for what it's worth, you're all right yourself, for a Noxian, that is," Rue said as he started down the cobblestone path, not waiting for Crofton's comeback.

"He really is a nice guy if you get passed the rough exterior," Betony commented as she walked by Rue's side.

"His last speech must have pained him as much to say as it surprised me to hear. You're right though. I can't help but respect him, even if he is a little rough around the edges." Rue stopped momentarily in order to determine which direction they should begin their search.

"This is a beautiful planet," Betony noted as she surveyed her surroundings. Eudora occupied a favorable position to the sun-star, so its green vegetation flourished. The path was shaded by a high canopy of trees that obscured the view ahead. "Do you know much about Eudora?"

"Not really. The planet hasn't been inhabited since before my seed-pod was opened. I asked Ranunculus about it once, but he only told me 'Rue, my boy, you focus on life and let me focus on death.' I know the destruction of the Eudoran people has been his top priority ever since I've known him. Last year, he finally let me help him analyze the samples he gathered from the planet's surface. In the past, there were faint traces of a foreign organism that hadn't been present prior to the plague, if that's what it was. In recent months, the samples have all come back clean like I already told Crofton. I am quite surprised that everything looks as it does. Whatever destroyed the people here must have been engineered only to attack their life forces. Everything else seems undisturbed."

"You know nothing of the people?" In answer to her question, Rue shook his head as they continued to walk. The path descended gradually until it abruptly ended at the edge of a river. As they emerged from the canopy of trees, they found themselves standing in a broad valley floor bordered on each side with lush mountainous slopes. Betony's eye caught a flash of orange at the far end of the valley. Rue saw the fiery orange waterfall cascading down the side of a rocky incline at about the same time.

"Wow, look at that! I've never seen anything like it. That waterfall is reflecting the sunset so it looks like it's on fire. Amazing! Let's take a closer look." He grabbed Betony's hand as they maneuvered around the rocky banks of the river. The touch of his skin against hers sent a shiver of pleasure through her arm.

Something had started to grow inside of her that first night when Rue had given her his coat. The growth was slow at first with only little spurts every now and again when she allowed herself to think of him, but the more time she spent with him, the more it grew until she felt her heart might burst. This was surely the feeling of love Tansy had tried to explain to her. It was a different feeling than the familial love she experienced when she reclaimed her memories. This kind of love made her feel as though a summer breeze had been set free inside of her, rustling emotions to life that had settled in a deep layer of dormancy. When they reached the waterfall several minutes later, Rue led her to a rock and sat down beside her, her hand still grasped in his.

"I don't think I ever thanked you for saving my life," he commented as he turned his gaze upon her. His blue eyes were strengthening the windstorm that was already brewing within her.

"You don't need to thank me for anything. You're the one who save me first, remember?"

"But I do. I do need to thank you. Not only for saving my life, but for coming out of your room after we left Valerian on Quamir. Valerian is the only friend I have ever had, and when he almost died, well...I don't want to even think about it. I was at the lowest point I've been in my entire life. You don't know what you've done for me," he tried to explain.

"Would it surprise you so much to discover that you've had the same impact on me? I know my actions on Asa-en-Darah may have given you a different impression, but when I saw your face peering down at me through the water, I thought you were death's last attempt at tormenting me before engulfing me. For some reason, I thought if I let death finally claim me, my pain would cease. It seemed to be hunting me. I thought if I was gone, death would be satisfied, so you, Tansy, and Valerian would be safe. How twisted that

149

seems now that I know more about the situation! Somehow, I knew I hadn't succeeded in pacifying death though. The entire time I was unconscious, I could feel my hand still tingling where you had last touched it," Betony let her voice trail off, not wanting to relive that darkness.

"That's because I was holding your hand the whole time, just as I am now. Isn't it ironic that when I saw you on the Quamirian moon I was sure I had died myself? I wonder why it is that near-death experiences keep bringing us together – although I wouldn't change any of it for the world. Betony, I love you." He lowered his voice as he spoke and moved his head closer to hers until he was kissing her. The black slate she had just uncovered in her heart as she recounted her experience suddenly burst into light. There could be no darkness with Rue by her side. Her grief and despair began to retreat. She felt only the sweet sensation of his lips pressed against hers and her arms wrapped around his neck. She could hear only the thunderous roar of the fiery waterfall, but it was no match for the sound of her own heartbeat thudding inside her chest, surging happiness to every cell of her body.

When Rue pulled away, she leaned close to his ear and whispered, "I love you more."

"Hey!" The moment was interrupted by a shout from Crofton. "Have you two love birds had a chance to pull yourself away from each other long enough to find anything?" Rue rose to his feet as Crofton approached, not embarrassed in the slightest at having been caught kissing Betony.

"We were just about to check behind the waterfall," his face beamed with a smile he could not conceal.

"Yeah right," Crofton's sarcasm made Betony laugh. Crofton led the way through the rocks of the riverbank and up a small incline where they stood behind the waterfall. Oddly enough, where they expected to find solid rock, they found a gaping hole in the cavern with a staircase leading inward and upward. Betony also noted that she did not feel the spray of the waterfall even though she was standing quite near it.

"What have we here?" Crofton mumbled as he ascended the stairs. Several feet into the darkness, a stream of sunlight appeared from an unseen source. As they looked forward, they saw two green marble doors blocking their way. Crofton pulled on the handles, but the doors did not budge. They explored the small entrance way, but there was no other way in, aside from the doors.

"Looks like we'll be making our own headquarters after all," Crofton said. "Unless, of course, you can think of a way in, Rue." Rue examined the doors himself, but could find no way to open them either.

"It looks as if someone has locked this place up tight and thrown away the key. It's odd though because I haven't seen any other dwelling places. I understood that Eudora was inhabited by over a million people at the time of its destruction. Where did they live?" Rue asked.

"Good question," Crofton led the search party back out of the cavern. "It makes you wonder about this place though, doesn't it? A little bit creepy, a little bit magical."

"A fairytale without a happy ending," Betony added, recalling the stories her people had passed down through the generations. Eudora was certainly a mystical place with a tragic end.

INTERGALACTIC INTERCEPTION #6

The pressure had gotten to Prey. Before he had discovered this treachery, he would have claimed no allegiance to Ranunculus at all. Now, however, the old man's life was in danger, and Prey could do nothing but listen.

He couldn't help himself when the stress triggered his incessant cleaning ritual. He began with his front legs, cleaning each thoroughly, right down to the tiniest spine in between the two parts of each leg. Then he moved to his head, running one leg over his head followed by the other, paying special attention to cleaning his eyes. Next, he focused on his antennae, using his front legs to pull them into his mouth one at a time. Onward he continued in his elaborate grooming until his entire body was clean. Then, he began again, unable to control himself as his obsessive-compulsiveness kicked into high gear. By the fifth go around, he was tiring of the procedure and was almost relieved to hear the buzzer signaling another incoming communication.

> Voice 1: You wouldn't be trying to hide something from me now, would you, old friend? A report is well overdue.
>
> Tussock: I ran into a little snafu with my plan, but it doesn't affect the outcome you desired.
>
> Voice 1: Explain yourself.
>
> Tussock: The weapon was misfired and destroyed both vessels: the

one containing your escort, as well as the one containing the Ancient and the Traveling Guardians.

Voice 1: Tut, tut, tut. Too bad for you.

Tussock: Not all is lost.

Voice 1: You mean they're not dead?

Tussock: I'm sure they're dead. I've sent a team to investigate and bring me any remains - not that there would be much left of them.

Voice 1: Then, how can you feel that you have not come up short?

Tussock: Let's just say, I've made a recent acquisition myself that I've long sought after.

Voice 1: The other Ancient?

Tussock: Perhaps.

Voice 1: Then, you've discovered the whereabouts of her hiding place?

Tussock: Maybe, maybe not. That is none of your concern, now is it?

Voice 1: No, I suppose it's not.

Tussock: And how are things with the Brotherhood?

Voice 1: Everything is going according to plan. The Brotherhood should be dissolved, shall we say, in a few days.

Tussock: And there is no antidote that could possibly thwart this plan of yours?

Voice 1: Not unless you have an Adahi spider on hand. Only its venom can cure anyone now, and since they don't exist in the Florenci System, I'd say my plan is pretty much fail-safe. Wouldn't you agree?

Tussock: Adahi spiders, you say? That's the deadliest spider reported within five quadrants, according to my sources. Just the mention of the name makes even me shudder. I'd say it's a two-fold blessing we'll never come across one.

Voice 1: Touché.

The line went dead, but Prey's heart began to race. An Adahi spider? Did he really just say that an Adahi spider could cure the members of the Brotherhood? Prey couldn't believe his luck! It just so happened that Prey had picked up an Adahi spider on a refueling station in the neighboring planetary system on his last mission. Knowing how deadly they were to Florencies, he had locked it away in his pod.

Adahi spiders were a delicacy in his planetary system, and he had praised the stars when he happened across it. He had fed it vigilantly, waiting for his next birthday celebration before savoring each bite of the tasty treat. He had even affectionately given it the name of Smuggler, and he didn't typically name creatures he intended to eat. Now, it seemed he may have to sacrifice his prized possession. If Ranunculus knew Prey had been keeping that spider on his vessel, particularly when it was docked on Traveriss, Prey figured he would hand him over to Stephanotis personally and supply the scalpel himself as well.

Prey tapped the locked cabinet where Smuggler was imprisoned, fat and waiting. He had the cure right here. This latest communication from the wormhole gave him a sliver of hope.

Wait a minute. Wormhole communication? Wormhole communication! Sometimes Prey's stupidity astounded even himself. If he was receiving communications through a wormhole that meant that there was a wormhole nearby. While his eyes were pre-occupied during flight school, his ear occasionally caught a useful tidbit of information; therefore, he knew that a wormhole was the fastest way to travel from point A to point B. The danger in using the wormhole was that a pilot could never be sure exactly where point B was, but Prey knew exactly where point B was. It was in the Florenci System, somewhere near Traveriss.

How much precious time he had wasted when his answer was within earshot the entire time! As he set his radar to scan for the opening of the wormhole, he consoled himself with the thought that had he discovered is idiocy any sooner he wouldn't have known that he was in sole possession of the antidote. He would have made it to Traveriss with nothing more than a report of a conspiracy against the Brotherhood. Now, however, he was actually privy to useful knowledge that just might make him a hero. The radar beeped loudly as it detected the wormhole's opening. Prey set his coordinates and braced himself.

Chapter Sixteen
A Matter of Royalty

Ky, Miramar, and Thor left Eudora just before the sun-star set. After their departure, Crofton, Pili, Rue, and Betony made makeshift headquarters in a grove not far from the landing field. Having no other alternative, they slept on the ground under the stars. After finally adjusting to fluffy bedding, Betony was surprised at how comfortable she was on the hard surface, but she realized that her comfort probably had more to do with the fact that she was snuggled next to Rue.

The following day, Rue resumed his efforts in trying to get Ranunculus's communication device to work. He assumed there was a particular sequence in which each of the planets had to be activated, and he had yet to figure it out. When he placed the seed in the middle of the device where it appeared to go, nothing happened, much to his frustration. The day passed slowly for Betony, who tried to communicate once again with the Transparencies. Even they refused to cooperate, and Betony was forced to give up. She tried to forage for food, but having no knowledge of the plant life on Eudora, she came back with only a few berries, which no one dared to eat. Night fell again, and Betony rested peacefully nestled next to Rue. When morning came, she found Rue gone.

"He's out exploring," Crofton announced when he noticed she was awake.

"I'm headed in the opposite direction to see if I can find anything myself. By the way, we're expecting visitors this morning," he added as he walked through the trees and out of sight. Betony helped herself to a breakfast of two seasoned tubers that Clary had sent with them. No sooner had she finished than she heard a pod land nearby. Crofton must not have gone very far away because she saw him approaching the landing field just seconds after it touched down. She drew closer to get a better view of the unexpected visitors.

"Lia?" Crofton exclaimed.

"It's Ambulia to you," a beautiful woman snapped as she walked out of the pod. Although she bore no tattoos identifying her as Noxian, she had the brown Noxian skin that seemed to shimmer in the early morning sunlight. She was clad in sleek black pants over which she wore a black tunic top. The tunic had yellow thread running through it in circular patterns. Her dark green hair was arranged in rows of micro braids that had been gathered in a knot at the base of her neck. Shadowed with rage, her deep green eyes glared at Crofton. Crofton looked to Ky for an explanation, but Ambulia was accustomed to being her own voice.

"Surprised to learn that I'm your latest recruit? I wouldn't want to impose on all the 'male bonding' you've been up to lately."

"That's not what this is about, and you know it."

"How would I know anything? You didn't bother to tell me before you left, and I'm not a mind reader like your *other* friend."

"What other friend?"

"As if you don't know – the one with whom you've been spending all your time, planning and plotting the overthrow of my father. That *other* friend!"

"Are you kidding me? You think Clary and I are...are what exactly?"

"This is hardly the time or place for that discussion, you worthless piece of mold." Ambulia seemed to morph into a carnivorous plant as she practically ate the fearless leader of the Free Frats alive right in front of them. Crofton stepped forward in protest, and that was all Ambulia needed. She slapped him across the face so hard her handprint remained long after impact. Crofton stood there stunned, as did Ky, Pili, and Thor. Betony waited for Crofton's retaliatory move. If Ambulia was Crofton's ray of light, as he had once told Betony, Noxia must be a very bleak place indeed.

"That's for leaving me behind," Ambulia growled. "And this is for not bothering to give me an explanation." She slapped him again across the other side of the face and then turned and walked away. All eyes were on Crofton, whose face still bore the marks of Ambulia's angry rebuff.

"Excuse me," he muttered to the group as he followed Ambulia into the shrubbery. Betony was trying to decide whether Crofton was incredibly brave or insanely stupid for following her, but she could see now why Crofton thought so highly of Ambulia. They were two peas of the same pod. Ambulia kept up with him stride for stride, which was the precise kind of companion someone like Crofton needed. She was self-assured just as he was, not submissive and weak. She didn't cower to fear and intimidation; she fought it. She didn't sit back silently; she proactively spoke her mind. It was too bad Crofton hadn't used that to his advantage when he founded the Fraternity for Freedom, but then again, he had hoped to protect her, whether she wanted his protection or not. He must have known she would have protested and tried to follow him. Love certainly had a thorny stem. A person was likely to get pricked at least once or twice while trying to hold onto it.

Though Crofton and Ambulia were quite a distance away by now, the onlookers could still hear muffled yelling, although they were pretending not to listen. The shrubs weren't tall enough to obscure the quarreling couple completely from view, and Betony felt herself drawn to their heated conversation.

"Just leave me alone, Crofton!"

"I know there's nothing I can say –"

"Aren't you the least bit curious as to where my father thinks I am?" she interrupted.

"Now that you mention it, how did you get away?"

"He thinks I'm at the Gorge of Grief," she replied curtly.

"What? Why would you be there?"

"Think about it, Crofton. It's certainly not beyond the scope of your intellect," she said sardonically.

"Did someone die?"

"Very good. There may be hope for you yet."

"But who? Are you going to tell me, or are we going to play this little game for the rest of the day?" he asked, annoyed.

"My mother," she stated flatly, although her eyes were misting over with tears.

"I'm so sorry," his voice was much softer and kinder than Betony had ever heard it. He moved toward Ambulia, but she stepped away from him. "Lia, I didn't know."

"I find that hard to believe, Crofton, with all your Free Frats swarming around gathering intelligence for you."

"I've been a little preoccupied lately, if you haven't noticed."

"Oh, that's right. You've been saving people you don't even know while leaving those you supposedly love to rot on Noxia."

"Lia, my father and Pick are being slowly tortured to death in the Pit." It was Ambulia's turn to be shocked; apparently, no one had told her the story in its entirety. Crofton continued, "That's right. The morning I left, I found out my father is alive, being tortured for a crime he didn't commit - guilt by association. How could I start a life with you knowing that - knowing that what I was about to do would put you in the greatest danger if I was ever discovered, yet also knowing I had to do it? Lia, I was trying to protect you," he tried to explain.

"Oh, you left under the guise that I would be safer without you? Is that what you're trying to tell me? Ask me how my mother died." She was met with only strained silence.

"Ask me how my mother died," she demanded again.

"Fine. How did she die?" he relented.

"After a failed attempt at poisoning Tussock. Please note you're not the only adversary he has. She tried to escape, knowing full well her next stop was the Pit. Her own personal guard killed her. You know what the sad thing about it is? He killed her so she wouldn't have to suffer in the Pit. He respected her enough to let her die with her dignity intact. How can such a thing as a mercy killing like that exist? Even sadder still for me is that I knew I was safe when you were my personal guard. That's the only time I've ever felt safe in my life, but when you left...when you left...you left me for dead without so much as a warning. You might as well have killed me yourself. You weren't protecting me. You were protecting your cause. You were afraid that if I knew your plan they could torture me into revealing information and compromising your effort."

"You know that isn't true, Ambulia."

160

"I don't know what I know anymore, Crofton. The only things I'm certain of are uncertainty, fear, and death."

"I'm sorry about your mother –"

"You're sorry?" Ambulia raised her hand as if she might slap Crofton yet again, but he grabbed her arm and pulled her sharply into his embrace.

"I'm sorry for hurting you. I'm sorry for leaving. Lia, I'm sorry." Crofton lifted Ambulia's chin ever so gently and stared into her eyes.

"You left me. You promised you would never leave me, and you left me."

"But I'm here now. You're here now. We'll fight. We'll end this – together. I do love you, Lia. You can't doubt that. Whatever has happened, however flawed my reasoning, I did it because I love you. And do you know how I know that we can win this war? I'm not fighting for revenge. I'm fighting for freedom. I'm fighting for the freedom to love you without fear, without boundaries. I want to be free to love you without your father using that love against me – to control me and keep me in submission to his reign of terror. I'm fighting for you." He then kissed her very passionately, yet more tenderly than Betony would have thought him capable.

"Oh, you don't know how much I've missed you," he whispered in her ear before pressing his lips against hers again. All was well. Betony withdrew her gaze and retreated to headquarters to give them privacy, happy that love had weathered the rocky terrain of the Noxian rebellion, at least for Ambulia and Crofton.

At the same time, Betony couldn't help but feel a pang of pity for Thor, whom she noticed had accompanied Ambulia off the pod. He must have seen his chance to extract Ambulia without drawing attention to her absence. He hadn't lingered near the landing pod to witness the exchange between the two lovers. Instead, he had withdrawn into the meadow that Betony had become so fond of – the same meadow in which she had overheard Thor profess his undying love for Ambulia. Betony knew his heart must be breaking into a thousand pieces at the reunion, and yet when he emerged from the meadow a short time later, his expression was unreadable. He had somehow managed to veil any feelings he was experiencing. The forbidden love he felt for the woman he had so faithfully guarded, protected, and comforted for all these years was locked somewhere securely inside him never to be set free. The fire of his love had to be extinguished, and the smoldering coals were burning holes in his heart. Betony grieved for Thor as much as she rejoiced for Crofton. Why did happiness for one seem only to come at the expense of another?

About an hour later, Betony caught sight of Rue's purple hair making its way through the shrubbery toward her, and her mood lightened instantly. A smile of hope and gratitude settled on her face as she reached for his hand when he emerged from the bushes. He sensed the tension of the gathered group as he scanned their faces. Rue looked at Betony uncertainly.

"Did I miss something?" he asked.

"I'd say," Ky affirmed with a chuckle that he quickly stifled as Crofton and Ambulia came within earshot after their long retreat. Crofton was struggling himself to maintain his stoic demeanor since a smile was teasing the corners of his mouth upward. Ambulia seemed more docile as well.

"What's with the Eudoran?" Ambulia mused aloud as they neared the group.

"What are you talking about now?" Crofton questioned in confusion.

"The Eudoran," she answered, pointing at Rue. "Where'd you find him? I thought they had all been murdered."

"He's not Eudoran," Crofton insisted. "He's the delegate from Traveriss."

"No," she protested smugly. "He's a Eudoran." Rue said nothing, but listened with great interest at the exchange.

"And just how, may I ask, have you come to that conclusion?" Crofton inquired, irritation accentuating each word as though her assertion were a challenge to his intelligence and authority.

"Only Eudorans have blue eyes," she announced. Everyone seemed to be mulling that fact over in his or her mind, trying to decide if she were telling the truth.

"How do you know that?" Crofton demanded.

"Do you know how many hours I've spent in the archives, studying everything there is to study about the Florenci System, trying to find something to use against my father? There are hundreds of books about Eudora in there. Knowledge is my father's real weapon of choice. The more he knows about those he wishes to rule, the easier it becomes to force them into submission. Every Eudoran was born with blue eyes. It's their distinguishing characteristic. The Eudorans were the easiest to identify," she expounded.

"But surely Ranunculus would have known that," Rue interjected.

"Who said he didn't?" she asked.

"But why wouldn't he have told me where I came from? He had no reason to hide it from me," Rue was now pacing circles around Betony, trying to make sense of this new information.

"Unless he thought he was protecting you," Betony added, thinking about the cause of the spat between Crofton and Ambulia just a short while before.

"Protecting me? From what?"

"Not what, but who: Tussock, of course," Ambulia answered.

"Think about it, Rue. Ranunculus never let you leave Traveriss for any reason, until now, and that's because he knew you wouldn't be coming back since he had appointed you to be the Great Unifier," Betony was piecing the puzzle together.

"But how? How did I end up on Traveriss in the first place?"

"My brother," Crofton exclaimed excitedly. "You were in the seed-pod my brother was commanded to destroy after he unknowingly delivered the plague to the planet's surface. One seed-pod was launched before everyone died, and my brother tried to save it, but another Space Patrol damaged it. Pick thought it had been destroyed in the firefight that ultimately landed him in the Pit."

"Ranunculus must have found you floating in deep space years later," Betony deduced.

"This is incredible," Rue stammered, finally sitting down on the ground. "This is my home planet? Tussock destroyed them all."

"Tussock and someone who later became a member of the Brotherhood. Don't forget, Tussock only delivered the poison, he didn't concoct it himself. Besides, he would much rather rule planets than eliminate potential slaves. Whoever did this has a personal vendetta against Eudora and its monarchy," Ky inferred.

"Of course. It all makes sense now. Ranunculus must have hidden all the information about Eudora from me, and I never bothered to ask where any of it was since the planet was uninhabited. The thought never even crossed my mind," Rue breathed.

"Well, I must admit that Tussock's archive was filled by ill-gotten means, but that's beside the point. I'm puzzled about why you in particular are here. Why did they save you?" Ambulia proposed. "Unless..." her eyes widened as she made some internal connection. She walked over to Rue.

"Get up and take your shirt off," she demanded in a tone no one would have dared refuse.

"Excuse me?" Rue squeaked uncomfortably.

"Just do it," she ordered, and this time he took his shirt off. "Now spit in my hand."

"What? I am not spitting in your hand," he objected.

"Do you want to know who you are or not?" she challenged. She needed to say no more. Rue obediently spat in her hand. In a sense, he had waited his entire life for this moment. She gathered a pinch of Eudoran soil from the ground, mixing it with the spit, and then she rubbed it on Rue's back in the space between his shoulder blades.

"Anyone have any Eudoran water?" she asked. Three drinking vessels were tipped in her direction. She took the nearest one from Pili and rinsed the mud mixture off to reveal a gray etching of rays of light breaking through the clouds. Everyone crowded around to see as they uttered a few oohs and ahhs.

"What? What do you see?" Rue asked. Ky produced two small reflectors from the pouch he had slung over his shoulder. Crofton took one, positioning it so Rue could see the intricate, miniature mural that now adorned his back.

"What does it mean?" he asked.

"You are the heir to the throne of Eudora," Ambulia enlightened him. "This is the Crest of Hope – a reminder that the monarchy must always be the ray of light to the Eudoran people, no matter what comes their way. All male heirs bear the marking, but it's not visible to the naked eye unless, of course, a person happens to know how to make it appear with a mixture of the nobility's life force and the Eudoran elements of life: water and soil.

"Typically, the eldest son is born with the mark, but in rare cases it skips several offspring, so a younger son becomes the king. There was a case a few decades back when the elder son did not bear the mark. He attempted to murder his father, but his plot was thwarted. As punishment for the unprecedented act, he was given a pod and banished from Eudora forever, as I recall. The timing seems about right, so you very well could be the heir that was born later. You must have been stuck in that seed-pod as a last resort to save the monarchial order." Everyone was staring at Ambulia in complete surprise.

"Like I said," Ambulia shrugged, "I've spent a lot of time in the archives. Who knew I'd prove to be so valuable as a walking history book?"

Rue had silently put his shirt back and disappeared down the path leading to the river without uttering a single word. Betony turned to follow him, but Ambulia grabbed her arm.

"Just let him go. He probably needs some time alone," she insisted, but Betony shook her arm loose.

"He never just let me go, and I'm not about to turn my back on him now either," she stated as she started down the path. Much to her relief, Ambulia didn't protest, and no one else tried to follow her.

Chapter Seventeen
A Voice from the Past

By the time Betony caught up to Rue, he was standing at the entrance to the marble doors. He must have run the entire way because he was huffing and puffing as he ran his finger over a symbol that had been carved into the marble just above the left door handle. Betony approached quietly, not wanting to disturb him, yet feeling an uneasiness creep over her at the sound of the waterfall behind her. She wasn't sure what to say to him.

"Are you okay?" She wished she could have retracted the words as soon as she spoke them. Of course he wasn't okay. He had just learned that his entire planet had been destroyed by a member of the Brotherhood, someone he had known and trusted his entire life, only to find that he, possibly even a relative, was a murderer.

"Surprisingly, I am. I always knew something bad had happened to my people. I had hoped one day to be reunited with them, but more than that, I kept asking myself the question, why me? Why was I spared? Why was I not destroyed with the others? What is my purpose? And now, at least I know." He turned toward her as he spoke, and she rushed into his arms.

"You're so much better than I could ever be. I tried to kill myself when I learned of my past. I had never even entertained the possibility that I was the only one left, but you...you just take everything in stride as if it were the most natural thing in the world to find out that you are the King of Eudora."

"Betony, there is no Eudora. I am king of nothing - of no one. There are no subjects here. I know nothing of this planet's history or of its people. I am just a man, a member of the Botanical Brotherhood, and nothing more."

"Rue, you know that isn't true. It's clear to me that Ranunculus knew who you were, or at least strongly suspected it. That is why he asked you to be the Great Unifier. You were meant to be a leader from birth."

"But I have no training. I wasn't reared to be a leader."

"Rue, remember when we were prisoners on Quamir? We all looked to you to save us. Tansy and Valerian trusted you to lead them, and if Crofton hadn't come along, I'm sure you would have found a way to save us yourself. I've always felt safe with you. There's just something about you - about your aura that draws people to you. Even people like Crofton." Rue brushed his hand over the symbol again, and Betony realized it was the same symbol that was etched into his back.

"That's the Crest of Hope - the same one you have embedded in your skin," she observed.

"I figured as much, but there's something strange about this one." He grabbed her hand and traced the symbol with her finger. "Do you feel that impression right in the center?" Betony nodded her head.

"That's it!" Rue exclaimed, fumbling in a leather case he had secured to the belt loop of his pants. His hands were shaking as he withdrew the ancient seed Clary had given him with the communication device. He pressed the seed into the barely noticeable impression and waited patiently as the seconds ticked by. At last, the gigantic doors began to slide open.

He entered cautiously, mesmerized by his surroundings. The inner chamber resembled an extravagant castle with unending stone spiral steps leading to upper levels. A small fountain of water was centered in the middle of the foyer, and a giant chandelier of green vines with bright blue flowers that looked like raindrops hovered mid-air above the fountain. The interior was well lit, which Betony hadn't expected since the building was hidden in a mountainside. As she looked at the walls, she was surprised to find herself staring at a city arranged in ten tiers, stretching as far as the eye could see.

The walls were made of glass just as those at the hospital on Quamir. These walls, however, appeared to be made of special one-way glass in which Betony could see out from the inside but not in from the outside. The steep valley walls and the waterfall were nothing more than an optical illusion protecting the capital city of Eudora. Betony pulled herself away from the glass to find Rue staring at an empty pedestal by the far wall, fingering the Crest of Hope that was etched on its dusty surface.

She stepped closer as he turned the tiny seed over and over in his hand before finally placing it at the center of the crest. Something flickered and faded. Rue removed the seed and replaced it again. A holographic image of a man appeared before them. The image was so life-like Betony felt she could reach out and touch him. He was slightly taller than Rue and withered with age, but the resemblance was unmistakable. Rue took a step back, his arms searching for something with which to steady himself. Betony was by his side in an instant providing the support he now needed. The holographic image cleared its throat and began to speak.

"My name..." his voice broke and a few moments passed before he tried to speak again. "My name is Protea, and you must be my son, Rue, for this message was programmed for him and him alone. Rue, I should find great happiness that you are alive and well since I cannot say the same for the rest of our race. If you are safe, at least in that, he who seeks to destroy us has failed.

"Rue, I wish you did not bear this burden alone. I had hoped to train you and teach you and love you as has been the pattern for generations as a king passes the kingdom to his son, but this cannot be the case, and I must put aside my wishes and my grief as I watch all those around me succumb to the silent grasp of death. I once looked out these glass walls to watch with tranquility the daily bustle of this great city. I drew strength and joy from it, but now I must watch with a tear-streaked face as those I have so deeply loved die, one by one for no apparent reason. I can do nothing but watch...and wait.

"However, before I go to the great beyond, Rue, I wish to give you a mission. Consider it my last request. For some time, it has been my greatest desire to unify our planetary system that we all may benefit from each other, drawing on strengths and fortifying weaknesses of each planet that our planetary system can flourish, and of course, squelching the ever-present threat of a Noxian invasion. I have spent years laying the groundwork for this unification process, and I am on the brink of accomplishing the once unthinkable. I have met with the leaders of Phirun, Oro, and Quamir, and we are on the verge of making a pact and beginning the process of establishing interplanetary communications and travel. But now, I fear all is lost. Surely, the others will believe the annihilation of this planet was a repercussion of our talks, but I do not believe it is. I believe it is an act of revenge by one who should by all rights be your closest advisor – your brother. I have felt for some time that he would try again to exact revenge on me and on you for being passed over for the throne, but I never foresaw such a large scale and merciless act as this.

"We are bound by the tradition of our fathers, and the crown can only be

170

passed to one who bears the mark. Sadly now, we see why that is so. Your brother has no heart; thus, he could not bear the mark. Your other brothers are far better men than the eldest, but they too are lacking what you are not. Thus, it is up to you, Rue. It is up to you to claim your title as the new Eudoran King. It is up to you to keep our memory alive. Rebuild Eudora. It is up to you to be the Great Unifier. Son, you are the one.

"I have given you a great task of which you must feel inadequately prepared, but let me assure you, my son, that you are the one. I feel it in my heart. I feel it in my life force. I know your strength. I know your heart. Also know, Rue, that you are not alone. I have friends in the Florenci System. Call upon them. Galax of Phirun. Stephanotis of Phirun. Aster of Quamir. Datura of Oro. Seek them out. They can be trusted. Rue, you must find Ranunculus of Quamir. It is with him I was collaborating to establish a communications link among our planets. It was nearly finished. He had taken it back to Quamir with him for a few more tweaks, and he is not expected to return for another three weeks. By then, it will be too late. I sent the first key with you in your escape pod, which is the key you used to open the castle, and the key you used to retrieve this message. The second key lies in this pedestal itself. The device must first be charged on this pedestal," the man faltered as he spoke the last words as a beautiful golden-haired woman came into view. She grabbed him around the waist to support his weight, though she, too, looked frail and weak. Tears streamed down her cheeks as she stared in Rue's direction and mouthed the words, "I love you." The two images flickered several times before disappearing.

"No!" Rue cried out as he rushed forward to where the images were last seen, but no one was there. He slumped to his knees, his hands covering his face as he silently wept at the first and last memory he would ever have of his parents. He wept for his people. He wept for his wayward brother. He wept for Ranunculus, but most of all he wept for himself. He wept the tears he had held back since he was a seedling, the dam of grief quietly breaking after years of faithful construction.

Betony knelt by his side, wrapping her arm around his back as he rocked back and forth, but she said nothing, for nothing could be said. Instead, she found herself humming a tune unfamiliar even to herself. Rue let his hands drop from his face at the sound of her voice.

"What is that song?" he whispered, staring at her with a bewildered expression on his face.

"I...I don't really know," she answered. "It just came into my head. Why do you ask?"

"I know that song. I've heard it before. I've heard it before here. Here in this castle," he said, rising to his feet and offering her his hand.

"Your memories? Have you regained your memories?"

"Not a memory but a feeling. A strange feeling that I have been here before – that I belong here."

"You're home, Rue. You do belong here," she affirmed.

"But it's more than that. It's the feeling that here I was loved. I've never known that feeling before. Here I was loved, and I can feel it even though they are gone."

"I know the feeling," Betony acknowledged as she smiled up at him. A voice from the past, ghostly images preserved over decades of time, an ancient seed containing a message – each one linked the present to the past and the past to the future.

"I guess there's no need to find Ranunculus. It seems he found me first and led me to the rest of my father's friends as well, except for Datura of Oro. He was never a part of the Brotherhood. They must have all known I was Eudoran. I wonder now though why Ranunculus formed the Brotherhood. Were these men no longer welcome on their home planets as permanent citizens after Eudora was destroyed for fear that their planets too would be annihilated? Did they leave voluntarily when their leaders no longer wished to unify? Was the Brotherhood a guise for something else?" Rue wondered aloud.

"An answer only leads to more questions," Betony commented. "I think the idea of unification just fizzled – perhaps partially from fear but more so due to the lack of leadership. From listening to Clary's interactions with Ranunculus prior to the Brotherhood's inception, I think he left voluntarily to pursue his scientific interests. He was never meant to be the Great Unifier, and he knew that. He had to wait until the right person came along for the job, so why not use the time doing what he loves?"

"You know, I think you just may be right...yet again." Rue pulled her into a tight embrace. In this place she too was loved, even though it was not her home. She was beginning to understand why Rue bore the Crest of Hope. He was the crepuscular ray that streamed through the darkest cloud cover, emitting the much-needed light. He was her ray of hope.

INTERGALACTIC INTERCEPTION #7

Prey was bracing himself for the rough ride through the wormhole. His eyes were having trouble focusing as his pod picked up speed. The walls were shaking. All indicator lights were flickering. Every alarm seemed to be sounding. He only hoped the pod would hold together. He was, therefore, more than surprised when a voice broke through all the chaos. It took a moment before he realized that he was receiving an outgoing communication from Traveriss. Prey barely recognized the hysterical voice on the other end. The breathing was erratic – the voice lacking its usual strength and confidence. Ranunculus sounded scared and weak.

Ranunculus: Bindweed? Bindweed! Come in Bindweed!

No response.

Ranunculus: Bindweed. Answer me you fool! Had I known you would do something so stupid, I never would have told you Clary was gone!

No response.

Ranunculus: Bindweed? I know you can hear me you numb-skull! What do you plan on doing if you find her? Dying at her feet, if Tussock doesn't kill you first? There's too much poison in you now. With no antidote, it's only a matter of time. You may not even make it to Noxia, and you don't know for sure that's where she is.

Bindweed: But I have to try. Even if I die trying, I have to try. I should have gone to her long before now, even if she can care for me only as a friend. She has been alone too long, and now look what's happened. I should have gone back, and now it's too late. Goodbye, Ranunculus.

Static.

Chapter Eighteen
A Call for Help

Rue and Betony lingered in the castle alone together for a while longer. Rue was trying to absorb all that had happened to him in less than a day's time. His entire life, his entire future had been completely altered when he chose to embrace his new identity. Now he had a sense of purpose and a mission to complete.

"We better get back to the others. I think it's time I put that communicator to use as it was intended," he said as he rose to his feet. They walked back to their makeshift headquarters by the landing pad, surprising Crofton and his crew.

"Let's move," Rue stated.

"What?" Crofton wasn't sure how to interpret Rue's new demeanor. He had been expecting Rue to be wallowing in grief or anguish for a while, certainly not for him to come marching back to camp within an hour's time to get back down to business.

"I've unlocked the castle, and I think we should move our headquarters down there. It's much more secure, and the communicator can only be operated from within the castle walls," he explained.

"How did all this come about?" Crofton wondered.

"You could say that knowing my true identity opened the doors for me. I had the power to do it all along, I just didn't realize it. Thank you, Ambulia," he said.

"You're very welcome," she responded, and then turning to Crofton, she added, "You heard the king. Let's move."

"I didn't mean it like that," Rue interjected before Crofton could say anything. "This is your show, Crofton. I'll do everything I can to help, but you're still calling the shots. I may be a Eudoran king, but the scope of this uprising is far broader than Eudora. I simply meant to suggest that relocating would be beneficial for us all. The castle seems to be in good repair, and it is more secure than sleeping out in the open." Rue extended his hand to help Crofton from his sitting position. Crofton accepted the gesture and together, they packed up their meager supplies and hiked down to the castle.

Once inside, the group broke off to explore the surroundings in search of suitable accommodations for sleeping and conducting planning meetings. There were hundreds of rooms from which to choose, but ultimately the group agreed to stay on the second floor, close to the castle entrance. There was also a large conference room on the second floor with murals of the planetary system painted on the walls and ceiling. When Pili leaned on a pedestal, he inadvertently discovered a three-dimensional map of the entire quadrant bearing a striking resemblance to the one Betony had seen on Traveriss. By the time everyone was settled and had eaten dinner, the sky had nestled itself in a blanket of darkness as it bedded down for the night.

"There's not much use in doing anything tonight," Crofton observed with a yawn. "I say we get some sleep and start with a fresh plan first thing in the morning." There was no complaint as each of them retired to their quarters. Betony had chosen a room next to Rue's, though she would have preferred to sleep in the same room. She had been looking forward to falling asleep with the gentle lullaby of his breathing, which chased her nightmares away. She did not want to admit to herself that the darkness still haunted her. She was afraid that it might simply envelope her in its black midst and whisk her away where no one could hear her desperate cries for help. She pushed the thought out of her head, focusing instead on the blue of Rue's eyes. She imagined his breathing in tandem with her own and finally drifted off to sleep.

She awoke in the morning while the sky was still a drowsy gray, the sun-star not fully emerged from its nightly hibernation. There was no point trying to go back to sleep, so she decided to roam the castle instead. As she stepped out of her room, she was startled by a dark figure scurrying down the hall toward her. She recognized Ambulia at once, though she had stopped abruptly when she noticed Betony. There was a moment of awkward silence as Betony realized that Ambulia was sneaking out of Crofton's room.

"It's not what you think," Ambulia blurted out.

"It's none of my business," Betony said, having been introduced to the high moral standards of the Florenci System by Tansy, the same moral codes upon which each planet vowed to keep after the Thrip invasion.

"But it's not what you think," Ambulia tried again.

"You really don't need to explain anything to me," Betony reassured her.

"But I want too. I don't want you to think...to think...well, whatever it is you may be thinking. I have violated no moral code."

"Really Ambulia..."

"It's just that I haven't been able to sleep since my mother's death. I feel as though I should have...I could have saved her, or at least helped her in some way. I knew...I always knew Tussock would kill her because she could not give him a male heir. So much time went by, I guess I became complacent, less vigilant on her behalf."

"You can't blame yourself for what happened."

"I know, but I do anyway. It's worse at night when the darkness comes. Her face haunts me. I hear her dying screams. When Thor told me about the Free Frats and told me he could take me to Crofton..." Ambulia couldn't find the right words to express how she felt in Crofton's presence. At that moment, Betony also realized Thor's true motivation for bringing Ambulia to Eudora, and it had nothing to do with timing. He could endure Ambulia's suffering no longer, and he knew that only one person could console her shattered heart. He had performed the most selfless act Betony had witnessed thus far, and no one would ever know of his heroic deed. Betony knew Ambulia suspected nothing of Thor's true feelings for her since Ambulia looked at Thor as though he were a dear friend, and nothing more.

"With Crofton, you feel safe. The night doesn't seem so black. When he's near you, the sound of his breathing, the smell of his skin, the rhythmic pumping of his life force next to you pushes the nightmares away – dissolves the ghostly faces – silences the screams. Yes, I understand more than you could know the soothing power of a simple touch by someone you love – a single word, however casual..." Betony allowed her voice to trail off, not realizing Rue had been awakened by the noise outside his room and was listening.

Ambulia moved toward Betony and embraced her as she would a sister. She had so little female companionship in her young life on Noxia, and she found Betony to be a star breaking through her long night. Someone finally understood exactly how she felt. Ambulia had been independent all her life, out of necessity more than desire. Now that she felt so dependent on Crofton just to endure such a simple thing as sleeping through the night, she felt weak and helpless. She felt like the seedling she had never been allowed to be. As she embraced Betony, her unspoken fears of incompetence were appeased. She wasn't sure if it was the mystical castle or Betony herself, but she relished the feeling nonetheless.

When Ambulia finally turned to go back to her room, Betony was left alone again in the hallway, still slightly perplexed at the exchange. She jumped when she felt a tap on her shoulder. She found herself face to face with Rue when she turned around. He gently pulled her into his room, his eyes sparkling in the faint morning light. She was surprised when he bent toward her to give her a kiss.

"Why didn't you tell me?" he asked, sincerely concerned.

"Tell you what?"

"I heard what you said to Ambulia," he admitted as Betony blushed, deeply embarrassed.

"No. No. Don't be embarrassed. I didn't mean to eavesdrop on you. I heard voices and peeked out my door to see what was going on. I'm sorry. I really didn't mean to embarrass you, but you should have told me how you felt. Why didn't you tell me?" He was hurt that she had not trusted him enough to share her feelings with him after all they had been through together.

"What was I supposed to say? I'm afraid of the dark? And I know very well it's not appropriate for a couple who is not unionized to share the same bed. Tansy told me as much," her eyes had filled with tears. He hugged her tightly to him.

"It's not the dark that frightens you, Betony. It's the images of all the horrible things that have happened to you - to us. The dark can't hurt you and neither can your memories. You're safe here. You're safe with me."

"I'm not afraid of the darkness that surrounds me. It's the darkness that tries to creep inside me that frightens me most, but you are what keeps the darkness at bay, Rue," she whispered. He smiled as he cupped her face in his hands and kissed her again as if anchoring her to the light.

"I'm not worried about what other people think, Betony. If being near me helps you to sleep, you will be sleeping in here from now on, and I might as well admit that I sleep better when I can feel you by my side as well. So, for the sake of sleep, we'll adjust our sleeping accommodations," he said as she returned his smile. The door was slightly ajar, so Crofton let himself in without knocking. When he saw Rue and Betony, he quickly back-stepped into the hallway.

"So sorry about that," he said as he cleared his throat. "I guess I should have knocked."

"It's fine," Rue assured him, rolling his eyes at the insinuation behind Crofton's apology, especially after Ambulia had just snuck out of his room. "Is there something you needed?"

"I just received a message from Noxia. Tussock is readying himself to test the Black Hole in one week's time. We'd better get a move on that communicator."

"It won't take me long to set up. We can transmit a message within a few minutes. What exactly do you want me to say?"

"That's up to you now, isn't it? You are the Great Unifier, right?"

"Let me ask this," Rue shrugged Crofton's comment aside, "what do you hope to accomplish by contacting them?"

"Right now, I think we ought to inform them about the imminent danger they are in. At the very least, we need to speak to representatives of each planet to secure their support in our fight against Tussock. Even if we can disable the Black Hole, Tussock won't give up. He'll find the leaks. He'll eliminate me and my Free Frats, and he'll start anew. Knowledge is power. That's Tussock's motto, and right now he has all the power because no one else knows what he's up to. If we can publicize this, we can empower the people."

"Well, let's give this thing a test run." Rue grabbed the communicator from a bedside table and headed down the stairs.

A communal breath was held in anticipation as Rue put the devise on the pedestal and inserted the seed. They knew the activation was complete when all the buttons on the face of it lit up. Rue pushed three of the buttons, squared his shoulders, and began to speak into the device.

"My fellow Florencies. A vow that has been in place for at least a century has been broken. I'm sure you are all familiar with the pact that was made with the Pursuers who now inhabit Noxia. We have recently received intelligence that Tussock of Noxia is about to launch an offensive to overtake each of our planets. We have no choice but to unite to enforce the century old pact that has allowed us to live in peace. There was a time when you joined together with Protea, King of Eudora, to begin the unification process, and I now ask you to reconvene that assembly. Time is of the utmost importance in this matter, and I ask for your immediate response on this channel."

Not a second after Rue finished, a face appeared above the pedestal.

"Who is this?" a voice said. "What kind of hoax are you playing calling in on the Eudoran line?"

"I am Rue, formerly of Traveriss, a protégé of Ranunculus of the Botanical Brotherhood. And this is not a hoax. I call from the Eudoran line because I am the sole survivor of the Eudoran people. I am Rue, the son of Protea, rightful heir of the Eudoran throne."

"This is preposterous!" Another head appeared next to the first. "Ranunculus shows up months ago to tell me to be on the alert for a communication from the old line, and suddenly the King of Eudora announces himself and declares a state of emergency."

"May I ask your names?" Rue queried patiently.

"I am Spurge of Oro," came the first man's reply.

"And I am Bluet of Quamir," the second answered.

"Aconite of Phirun," a third head appeared next to the others.

"Yes, I thought I recognized you, Bluet. You must remember me from the incident that occurred recently on your planet when two pods were shot out of the sky by a Noxian weapon orbiting your planet."

"Rue?" Bluet said as if questioning himself. "Yes, I do remember the name and the incident to which you refer, but I don't recall that your destination was Eudora."

"Certain items of information have only come to light very recently - my identity being one of them, but I assure you that the Noxian threat is real. If we do not act now, we will be at Tussock's mercy."

"Exactly what is the nature of this threat?" Aconite asked.

"I dare not discuss it over this line. We must meet. I hope you will agree to send a delegation to Eudora's surface to discuss the matter further."

"On what grounds?" Spurge objected.

"On the grounds that your life is in danger - your entire planet is in danger."

"How can we be sure this isn't some kind of a trap?" Bluet asked.

"You have to trust me as the son of Protea - as an understudy of Ranunculus."

"Surely, you can tell he is Eudoran," Aconite spoke to the others. "He's got the signature blue eyes, and he does bear a striking resemblance to his father."

"But who is that in the background there? It looks as though you're surrounded by Noxians - members of the Elite Guard if my eyesight isn't failing me," Spurge observed.

"You are correct. Bluet will recall that these are the same Noxians I was with on Quamir's surface. They saved me from an assassination attempt - the same attempt that injured Valerian and Tansy, the two Phirunite Traveling Guardians who accompanied me. If not for these brave men, we would all be dead, and we would know nothing of Tussock's plans. They are Noxian rebels, fighting to free themselves from Tussock's reign."

"I can verify that information, although only two Noxians were there at the time," Bluet confirmed.

"These are reinforcements," Rue explained. "They brought us the intelligence we wish to relay to you."

"I have received word from Valerian about that incident on Quamir," Aconite offered his affirmation to Rue's words as well. Betony's eyes widened at the mention of Valerian. They had received no word on his condition, and the fact that he was able to send a message to Phirun was encouraging.

"Gentlemen, I trust these Noxians with my life. It was Ranunculus who gave me this communicator so I could contact you. I know you must trust him, or else you wouldn't have responded so quickly to this call for help," Rue added.

"And Ranunculus is where exactly?"

"He's been detained on Traveriss and has asked me to stand in his place."

"Under the circumstances, I see my choices are limited. I will agree to meet with you with a few of my trusted councilors, but be advised that my planet will be on red alert and ready to defend itself," Aconite warned. Spurge and Bluet hesitantly agreed as well.

"Now, there is the matter of travel. Do you have means by which you can reach Eudora within a day?"

"Certainly. Ranunculus made sure we have high-speed pods on hand and in working order at all times in case such an incident were to occur," Spurge revealed, the revelation echoed by both Bluet and Aconite. Rue tried to suppress his surprise.

"Very well then. I will be expecting you tomorrow morning, and thank you for your cooperation," Rue said. The three heads disappeared as suddenly as they had materialized.

"I think that went better than could be expected," Rue surmised, turning to the others.

"I still have my reservations, Rue. They don't trust us, and we cannot move forward without trust," Crofton voiced his concerns.

"We cannot move forward without their assistance either. They will come to trust you as I have after they've met you. Believe me," Rue put forward his fist. Crofton smiled and punched it with his own fist, which was the signature greeting of the Free Frats.

The rest of the day was consumed in a flurry of activity. Rue and the Free Frats were busy working on star charts and importing three dimensional replicas of the Black Hole into the castle's computer systems. Betony stayed out of the way since she understood very little of the technical aspects of what they were up against. She left that in more experienced hands. She decided to retreat to the meadow to get some fresh air and was surprised to find Pili there, plucking the petals from a white flower.

"Pili? Are you all right?" Pili looked up with surprise when she spoke. He nodded his head as Betony sat beside him.

"I thought you'd be with the others, preparing for tomorrow."

"Not smartim," he answered, tapping his finger to his forehead.

"Oh, don't say that, Pili. Surely, you're just as smart as everyone else in there."

"Otherssi not thinkim so. Me musclim and brawnim." The look of dejection on his face revealed his feelings more clearly than he could articulate with words.

"They are a little full of themselves these days, aren't they?" A slow smile spread across his face, but the longing was still in his eyes.

"Quite frankly, I'm just in the way myself. I don't understand a thing they're talking about now. My people were far from technologically advanced. They spent their time relishing nature and soaking up the light from the sun-stars. I feel myself drawn to these beautiful surroundings even now, and I was about to do a little exploring. I could use some company, if you're up for a hike." Pili rose to his feet and offered his arm to her as her escort. She tucked her arm through the boulders of his muscles, and they spent the rest of the afternoon exploring their surroundings.

All around them, they discovered traces of the abandoned lives that had been so unexpectedly snuffed out. They found several caves that appeared to at one time have been popular hangouts for Eudoran seedlings on the cuff of maturity. They happened across a surprisingly well-preserved book of sketches sitting on a rocky cliff, the coloring stick still intact by its side as if its owner had been absorbed by a passing breeze. The book contained sketches of beautiful people – men, women, and children going about their ordinary lives with their names scrawled underneath each picture: Arnica, Knautia, Mugwort, Squill. It was heartbreaking. Pili put the sketchbook in his bag, so they could add it to the castle's archives. To take her mind off the tragic events that had happened, Betony told Pili stories from her people – stories of happiness and hope, and even a fairytale or two. Before they knew it, the sun was setting behind the mountain tops. As they entered the castle steps, Pili gathered Betony up in a hug that nearly suffocated her.

"Thankim," he said softly.

"It was my pleasure," she replied as they slipped inside, their absence having gone unnoticed by the others.

She was cradled in Rue's arms that night but unable to sleep because of his restlessness. He twitched, fidgeted, and tossed his head, no doubt tormented by thoughts of the events that laid wait for him in the days ahead. Maybe he too was haunted by the ghosts of his past as she had been by hers. Did they call to him in his sleep? Did they beckon for him to join them in death's dark parade as they marched through his mind? She began to hum the song that seemed to emanate from the castle itself. As she hummed the mystical melody, she felt Rue's tense body relax next to her. His eyelids stopped fluttering, and his breathing slowed into synchronization with the song. She traced the features of his handsome face with her fingers, memorizing every detail as she continued to hum. When she was sure he was in a deep and peaceful sleep, she cuddled up next to him and succumbed to a dreamless sleep herself.

Chapter Nineteen
A Lost Tale

Though the sun-star still lingered in its slumber, the sound of an arriving pod awakened Betony the next morning. Rue was on his feet and out the door before she could utter a word. She heard voices in the hallway and realized the Free Frats were also forming a welcoming party to escort their guests to the castle, though they had not been expecting anyone to arrive this early. Betony stepped into the foyer near the front door and sat down on the fountain bench to wait. While Betony felt as though an entire day passed before they finally returned, it had been less than an hour when the door opened at last.

A decrepit man, bent with age and leaning heavily on a wooden cane entered slowly. He was followed by three strange men whose eyes were wide as they studied their new surroundings. Betony recognized the man in the middle as Spurge, who answered Rue's initial call. Rue stepped forward to guide the old man to a bench near the door so he could rest from his arduous trek to the castle. The three men who accompanied him remained standing as the Free Frats filed into the foyer. Betony noted the absence of Ambulia, but before she had a chance to consider possible reasons, the old man spoke.

"I am Datura of Oro," his voice crackled like the dying embers of a fire.

"It is my pleasure to meet you. My father spoke of you as a trusted friend." Datura eyed Rue suspiciously, prompting Rue to add, "Of course, I never knew my father. He left a message for me before he died, which I recently discovered."

"Before he was murdered," Datura corrected. "I know more of this tale than you may think...bear more of the responsibility for what happened than I wish to admit."

"Please follow me, and we'll go somewhere we can talk," Rue's intrigue danced in his voice. As he motioned for Betony to follow, he walked by Datura's side, steadying him as they went. The Free Frats were curious as well, but allowed Rue his privacy as he closed the door and sat down next to Datura.

"So, you have a story to tell?" he inquired. Datura tapped his cane on the floor - once, twice, three times before he finally spoke.

"I don't know how I ever became entangled in it in the first place. I wish it were not mine to tell..." The old man was reluctant to relinquish his hold on the knowledge that haunted his days. Rue placed his hand on Datura's shoulder.

"Datura, whatever information you can give me so we can piece this puzzle together once and for all will be kept in the strictest confidence - whatever implications it may have for you." Datura shook his head emphatically.

"Boy," he said, his voice no more than a whisper, "I am not concerned about my welfare. It is for your sake I hesitate."

"I am not a boy, Datura. I am a man - a man whose past is a mystery that can only be unraveled one story at a time. It is my past you are unraveling, Datura, not me. I seek only for the truth. It is only with the truth that my memories can be set free."

"A true Eudoran king, I see."

"That I cannot say. Maybe you can shed some light on what exactly a true

Eudoran king is."

"Ah," Datura shook his head back and forth slowly as he spoke. "My tale is more of what a Eudoran king is not, but you can infer as you wish. My association with Eudora began when your father called for representatives of each planet to come to an interplanetary summit meeting many years ago. I suppose it was similar to the call you made yesterday, although the invitations were delivered personally by your father's ambassadors. There was no other way to communicate planet to planet back then.

"Your father was a great man with a great vision – a charismatic leader who magnetized others toward him by his very nature of goodness. The summit meeting went well, and plans were made to begin a unification process among Phirun, Quamir, Oro, and Eudora. The groundwork was laid when all the representatives unanimously agreed to go forward. The summit was adjourned, so we could return to our planets and gather support from our own citizenry. It was during this break that the eldest of Protea's sons came of age to be tested for the mark of the heir. His name was Liatrus, and he was a very ambitious young man. He was among those attending the summit and was most outspoken about including all planets in the unification. The rest of us were opposed to admitting Noxia.

"You see, Noxia was in a barbaric state of affairs. Some, a very few I might add, were fortunate enough to escape Borreria's brutality, and your father offered them asylum on Eudora when no other planet would admit them. I'm not sure how much you know of Noxian history, but Borreria was the ruler before Tussock came to power. Interesting how word spreads among planets, even without convenient means of communication, eh? It was from these refugees that we learned about the situation on Noxia. We decided it would be best to unify our planets first, and deal with Noxia later. Protea had hoped to liberate the Noxians from their oppression, but he felt he could not do it alone. Liatrus thought his father was being unreasonable in refusing to invite Noxian representatives. I don't think he trusted the refugees, and he was upset that his father so readily believed their unsubstantiated stories. At any rate, when we left, we could all tell the relationship between Protea and Liatrus was strained.

"It was during this heightened tension that Liatrus found out he was not the heir to the throne. He was enraged. For the previous five generations, you see, the firstborn had borne the mark. There were recorded incidents in the Eudoran archives of the mark being borne by a younger son, but this was a rarity. Liatrus blamed his father. He felt his father had removed the mark from him by some sort of trickery to punish him for openly disagreeing with his decisions during the summit meetings. He tried to incite a riot, but he had no support. Protea's subjects were loyal. They all knew the true character of Liatrus. Honestly, the rest of us merely tolerated him at the summit meetings out of respect for Protea. He was everything Protea was not – rude, demeaning, arrogant.

"When his attempts failed, Liatrus resorted to plotting Protea's murder. He planned to kill your father in his sleep with a dagger. On the appointed night, he crept into your parents' sleeping chamber, unaware that your mother had been unable to sleep since she was with seedling. She saw the glint of the dagger in the moonlight and instinctively flung her body over Protea's. The dagger delivered a near-fatal blow. Ixora, your dear mother, survived, but the seedling she carried did not. It was the first murder in recorded Eudoran history. Protea had no choice but to act decisively. Liatrus was banished from Eudora, given a pod, and sent away.

"To this day, I do not know why your father allowed him to leave. The crime required his life, but your father could not bear to carry out the punishment. Protea feared Liatrus would go to Noxia to request assistance from Borreria to start a war to overthrow his father, but Liatrus did not go to Noxia. Instead, he went to Ranunculus of Quamir. He respected Ranunculus and hoped to become one of his young apprentices. He had heard that Ranunculus had allowed a young, zealous Noxian named Tussock to work with him. He hoped Ranunculus would grant his petition as well, but Ranunculus quickly rejected him when he learned of his treachery. Angry, Liatrus left Quamir. I don't think even he knew at the time exactly where he would go when his first plan failed. While he spoke of allowing Noxia to send representatives to the summit, I think he was personally too fearful go to Noxia. Talk was one thing, but taking action was quite another, considering that the young Tussock had confirmed the stories of brutality that the refugees told.

"As it turns out, his pod crash landed on Oro, which is how I come into the story. Orons are nomadic, reclusive people in general. While there are groups or families that congregate together, for the most part, we keep to ourselves. There are no organized cities as there are on other planets because Oro is nothing but a vast desert. Liatrus wandered in the desert for days. He did not know how to find water or food. He was on the brink of starvation, which would have been just recompense for his crime. If only Phacelia had not found him! Oh, if I could turn back time...but she did find him. She found him and took pity on him. She was mesmerized by his handsome face, flattered by his deceptive words, and lured under his spell. She nursed him back to health against her father's wishes.

"You see, her father knew Liatrus quite well for he had sat with him during the summit meetings. Word had even reached him by means of Ranunculus of the murder Liatrus had committed. Phacelia's father warned her of the newcomer's cunning ways, but she refused to listen. She gave into the young man's persistent seduction. When her father tried to intervene, the foolish girl ran away with him. Her father searched Oro's endless golden desert year after year, hoping to recover his only offspring – ready to forgive and accept her back into his arms though that is not the custom of the Oron people. When his efforts proved fruitless, he returned to his home and entered into seclusion, overcome by grief. He was a broken man, and he may have died that way too if not for Phacelia's return. Yes, she came back for a short time with her son.

"Liatrus had become careless the more comfortable he became in the desert, and he was bitten by a poisonous serpent. Phacelia tried to draw the poison out by sucking the wound. The venom was strong, too strong. Liatrus died within an hour. Phacelia was weakened, but her son heeded her urgent pleadings and carried her back to her father as she told him the way. It was too late to help her, however. She died within days, but not before her father noticed that her son had been poisoned too. He surely had been poisoned but by a different means. He had been poisoned by his father's words, and there was no deadlier poison for that boy than his own father. Liatrus's endless discourses about how he had been wronged and his right to the Eudoran throne stolen seeped deep into the very soul of his son. The hatred and anger his father sparked inside him had burst into all-consuming flames of rage right before his grandfather's eyes. He was determined to avenge the death of his parents.

"His grandfather was a stranger to him, and the boy would not allow him to speak to him or touch him or come within close proximity of him. If he tried, the boy became violent, and so he withdrew, hoping that in time he could connect with his grandson once his grief had abated some. But that was not to be. The boy was gone as soon as his mother drew in her last breath.

"Her father heard rumor that the boy had finished rebuilding the wrecked pod that he had once worked on with Liatrus. He heard rumor that his grandson had left Oro, and then he heard nothing. For two long years, he heard nothing until Ranunculus paid him a visit. You see, Phacelia's father had withdrawn from the unification process for all those years. He resented Protea for not dealing with Liatrus on Eudora. He blamed Protea for the loss of his daughter, and he let the hatred fester inside him. He understood from his successor that the process had stalled several times. There were squabbles over the terms of the pact and concerns about interplanetary travel and communication. The process moved at a snail's pace, much to Protea's frustration. By this time, Borreria had also been overthrown by Tussock, who proved to be even more ruthless, which only further complicated matters.

"Ranunculus had gone to great trouble to track down this former Oron delegate, so he listened as Ranunculus told him that every living soul on Eudora had been killed. There was no explanation. Ranunculus told him that the unification summits were suspended indefinitely as no one could agree on who should lead the effort. There were fears about what happened on Eudora. People felt more secure withdrawing to their own planets, where they were oblivious to the happenings of their neighbors. Protea's dream seemed to die with him. Ranunculus told him that he had formed a Botanical Brotherhood and even created his own planet. He asked him to join him, but the bereaved father's interest in science had dried up with the departure of his daughter. He wanted only to be left alone to sing his death chants as the sun-star continued to rise and fall each day. He called to the sand to return his body to her realm. He wanted only to die," Datura ended his story with a dry click of his tongue. He leaned back and closed his eyes.

"But what does this have to do with you?" Rue finally asked. Datura's gray eyes slowly opened, and he stared at Rue for quite some time, his hand wringing a strand of hair, brown and brittle with age.

"I am Phacelia's father. This is my story. My grandson is the only person capable of killing the population of an entire planet. The instant Ranunculus told me of the mysterious death of every living soul on Eudora, only Eudora, I knew he was the mastermind behind it. I saw the hatred in his eyes. I heard his vile ranting when he thought he was alone at his mother's bedside. I heard him swear an oath of revenge, and yet in my despondency, I let him go. I did not try to stop him. I simply let him go and never looked back. 'How much harm could one boy do, particularly when he is on his own?' I reasoned. I was a grief-stricken old man. What could I do? That's how I tried to justify my inaction, but I knew better. He was my seed, my responsibility; therefore, I must also bear partial blame for his actions." Datura's fail frame gave way to violent shaking as he sobbed. Rue put his arm around him to comfort him.

"Datura," the old man looked up at Rue. "You are not to blame for another man's actions, no matter who he is. You can get lost in the maze of what-ifs, struggling your whole life to find a way out, or you can let them go and watch the maze crumble to the ground, allowing yourself to be a free man. You've done your time in the maze. It's time to let it go. Reconcile yourself to the fact that what's done is done. We must move forward now, not backward."

"You are a true Eudoran king – so like your father."

"Datura, there is one thing I must ask of you. Whoever is behind this heinous crime has worked his way into Ranunculus's affections and has become a member of the Botanical Brotherhood. I was raised by those seven men, and I'm baffled by the man's identity. He must be an incredibly good actor to fool Ranunculus – to betray the entire Brotherhood while working side by side with us for all these years. He is a master of disguise to conceal his true hatred to such a degree that he is considered a trusted colleague, even a friend. He has eradicated my people and attempted to poison me, which would have been my end if not for Betony. It is time for this charade to end. Datura, what is your grandson's name?"

"Rue, I'm afraid it wouldn't make a difference even if I knew."

"What do you mean?

"His name was never spoken within the walls of my tent. His mother only called him 'son.' I daresay if I had known who he was, I would not be talking to you now."

"I see."

"Now I have told you what I came to say. I wish to return to Oro to die – for my time has come. The sand can claim my bones now that my conscience has been appeased."

"Will you be taking the others back with you too, then?" Rue asked anxiously.

"No. They stay behind to help sort this mess out. I trust you will return them safely to Oro when their work is done."

"If it is ever done," Rue muttered. Datura placed a frail hand on Rue's shoulder.

"You are Protea's son, King of Eudora. You will finish what your father could not." Datura turned his back toward them and hobbled out the door.

Chapter Twenty
A Plan

No sooner had Datura's pod disappeared in the sky then another pod landed. Betony recognized the face of the first man who stepped out as Bluet, the Quamirian Ambassador. Behind him, a short man with blue hair followed, shadowed by a tall man. When the fourth man emerged, Betony's gaze stopped at his eyes. She knew those eyes. She watched curiously as he descended the ramp, limping awkwardly.

Before the door of recognition had fully creaked open for Betony, Rue was at the man's side, gathering him into a friendly embrace. Valerian? Betony blinked her eyes in surprise. It was impossible, and yet the man standing before her now was undoubtedly Valerian. She would never forget his eyes, his image. They were forever etched in her memory. So much had happened since she had last seen him and his reappearance was so unexpected, she had to dig a little to uncover the memory. She stared at him now, unable to help herself.

His head had been shaved, which drastically altered his appearance in and of itself. She moved to his face, hardly able to believe the transformation. The right side of his face was completely unscathed, but the left side was riddled with scars and disfigurement. The skin was too taut by his left eye, causing the eyelid to droop. The left side of his mouth was drawn into a permanent frown and remained paralyzed as he spoke. In fact, the whole left side of his body was impaired and scarred, while his right side was perfectly intact. As Betony continued to assess his appearance, Valerian's eyes met hers. She quickly looked away, embarrassed to have been caught gawking at his shocking yet remarkable image.

Crofton also recognized him as the man who had risked his life trying to rescue Salsola and Tornillo, his Noxian comrades who lost their lives the day of the deadly blast. He greeted Valerian warmly by putting his arm around his shoulder. It was only at that moment that Betony registered the conversation around her.

"Well, well. What do we have here?" Crofton was saying.

"A walking miracle, I'd say," Rue answered, patting Valerian on the back. "By the stars, it's good to see you again."

"Do I understand correctly that I am now to address you as King Rue?" The right side of Valerian's mouth curved into a smile.

"We do have a lot of catching up to do, my friend," Rue said as they approached Betony.

"And how exactly did you happen to come by this lovely Phirunite maiden?" Valerian asked as he winked at Betony with his right eye. She instinctively hugged him, though the comment drew the attention of Bluet, who had been watching the exchange with increasing curiosity.

"You look...good..." Betony stammered.

"Considering I woke up on the wrong side of the bed this morning, you mean," he jested, pointing to the left side his face with his mangled left hand. "Yes, even I have to admit, my looks are awe-inspiring, to say the least," he laughed. Rue had been right about Valerian. His magnetic personality thrived despite his tribulation.

"And Tansy?"

"Ah, Tansy. She has quite the following on Quamir. I'll be hard pressed to get her back to Phirun when all this is over. I daresay she wouldn't even consider returning unless I promise a spaceway between the two planets, which may be a possibility in the near future if all goes well. By the way, did I happen to mention that we unionized?" Valerian never had been at a loss for words.

"Oh, congratulations," Betony wasn't the only one who was taken by surprise at the announcement.

"When did this happen?" Rue asked.

"Just before one of my grafting procedures. We asked ourselves, 'What's the point of waiting?' Your priorities change a little after a near death experience," Rue and Betony exchanged glances, but said nothing of their own brief acquaintances with death.

"Anyway," Valerian continued, "I figured since I was going under the knife anyway, we might as well make it the Grafting Ceremony." He pulled down his shirt just enough to show the star-shaped graft over his heart. Their reunion, however, was cut short by the arrival of the last pod from Phirun. When Aconite and his party had disembarked, everyone walked to the castle to begin the meeting.

They assembled in the conference room that had been prepared the day before. Betony was surprised to see Ambulia lurking in the corner with Thor since she had not seen her the entire morning. Perhaps Crofton was keeping her away for some reason.

Rue stood and began to explain the seriousness of their situation, beginning with the weapons test on Quamir. He did not tell the entire story. He didn't mention Betony, the existence of Asa-en-Darah, or the disappearance of Clary.

He also chose not to mention the Transparencies since as far as they knew there had been no evidence that the queen's convoy had left the vicinity of Traveriss, although he did mention the poisoning of the Brotherhood. He focused on the atrocities of Tussock and his colleague who had infiltrated the Brotherhood.

"So, we can expect no help from the Brotherhood, then?" Aconite queried.

"At this point, we don't even know if they are alive. I sent them a warning about the poisoning, but I have not been in contact with them since my departure from Traveriss," Rue explained. "I don't think we should depend on anyone but those of us in this room right now and the citizens we represent. Now that you understand a little bit of the background, I've asked Crofton to elaborate more on the present threat that has recently come to light." Crofton stood and told them about the Black Hole and Tussock's plan to enslave all the planets in the Florenci System.

"I daresay you wouldn't have called us here if you didn't have some sort of a plan," Spurge prodded.

"Do you know how to destroy this thing?" one of the Phirunite ambassadors asked.

"I don't think destroying it is the answer at this point," Miramar stepped forward.

"What do you mean, 'Not destroy it?'" Bluet queried.

"If we destroy the Black Hole, it's only a matter of time before Tussock tries again with something else. We must stop him once and for all...now," Crofton explained.

"But you're proposing intragalactic warfare. There isn't time to make the necessary preparations. Didn't you say we had less than a week before he tests this thing?" Aconite voiced his concerns.

"We must act now while we have the element of surprise. Tussock won't be expecting it, and we have to destroy him before he has time to launch another offensive. Right now, I can guarantee the accuracy of my information, but after we attempt to thwart the Black Hole test, Tussock will surely know his security has been breached. This is our only chance to take him out," Crofton clarified.

"We don't even have an army nor do we have a wealth of trained soldiers to call upon from our own planets. Quamir has only a small-scale peace keeping force at best," Bluet argued.

"Same with Oro," reiterated Spurge.

"Phirun as well," came Aconite's echo.

"You've got to listen to Crofton. Tussock will be able to organize another offensive strike far faster than we can organize ourselves defensively. We must take him out on Noxia before he can plan anything else – like the genetically-engineered virus that wiped out the entire population of my planet." After hearing Datura's tale, Betony couldn't help but wonder what had happened to the Noxian rebels who had taken refuge on the planet if the virus was genetically-engineered to eradicate only Eudorans. They must have died as well, even though they had a different genetic makeup.

"I wasn't anticipating warfare when I came here," Spurge finally broke the silence.

"What exactly were you expecting? Do you not understand that Tussock is planning to take over your planets? You do not know what it's like to live under his reign. If you did, you would volunteer every man, woman, and child to fight against him rather than allow your planet to fall into his hands. I understand your hesitancy. I understand your reluctance to engage him, but we have no other choice. You've turned your back on us Noxians for years, believing that as long as his terror didn't affect you, all was well. By turning a blind eye to his atrocity, you merely bought him enough time to devise a means by which to conquer you. And he will, unless you do something about it before it's too late. I, for one, will be drawing on numbers from my own rebel forces," Crofton chastised.

"But they will be no match for Tussock's army," countered Aconite.

"There are two types of men in Tussock's army: those who serve him out of loyalty and those who serve out of fear. There are more of the latter, and if you will stand with us, they will see that we don't stand alone. They may be swayed to turn on him," Crofton speculated.

"May? They may be swayed?" Bluet wasn't convinced. "You're gambling lives, and the cards aren't stacked in your favor."

"This wasn't my gamble. You look to Tussock to see who dealt the cards and forced us all into this game in the first place. I'm only trying to make do with what I have. The chance is slim to none; I know that. I've known that ever since I founded the Free Frats, but it is a chance I must take. Death is inevitable, my friends, but I would rather die fighting the tyranny, defending those I love, than cowering under a rock in fear. I will fight." There was no noise to be heard at the conclusion of Crofton's speech as each man at the table contemplated the predicament. Rue rose to his feet, crossing the room until he stood shoulder to shoulder with Crofton.

"Stand with him with whatever meager forces you can muster," he urged.

"Easy for you to say since you're a one-man Eudoran show," one of the

Orons commented rather spitefully.

"Aren't you perceptive? I stand alone as the sole survivor of the worst crime that evil has ever masterminded, but I do not fight alone. I fight with generations of Eudoran strength within me. I fight for their memory. I fight for their honor. I fight for those whose voices Tussock has silenced. We fight as one," Rue exclaimed with a fierce look on his face that made Betony believe that he could very well win this war single-handedly. Valerian rose and took his place beside Rue.

"I will join Eudora and the Free Frats, and I hope my fellow Phirunites will join me," he looked at Aconite and the three Phirunites who accompanied him. One by one each delegate stood, pledging his commitment to the cause.

"Now that we're agreed, we need to come up with a game plan," Crofton pressed forward while the momentum was in his favor. "We need to make it look as though the Black Hole is working. Once the test is successfully complete, Tussock plans to send three prisoner pods to the surface of each planet. The orders are for one thousand high-ranking and influential prisoners to be taken from each planet. If we can commandeer the vessels, we can transport our troops to Noxia.

"I have instructed my Free Frats to volunteer for any assignments relating to transporting prisoners or testing the Black Hole. With any luck, we won't have to commandeer the vessels at all - my Free Frats will be aboard to help. Tussock will be none the wiser, believing that frightened prisoners will be aboard. Now, for those of you unfamiliar with Noxia, the planet is dark most of the time. You won't be able to see without special lenses, but I can provide those to you. You must simply instruct each soldier to insert the lenses into his eyes. There is one hour of light each day, but it's a more intense light than you could possibly bear. The prisoners are to be dressed in special solar suits that absorb the light, thus protecting the wearer. The suits are transparent and fit underneath your regular clothing. Those will be aboard each pod, so we can take no more than one thousand per pod. Any non-natives who are not in their suits will be burned alive. Any questions so far?"

"The blaring question in my mind is how we plan to get around the Black Hole," Valerian responded.

"You may understand this better than anyone, Valerian, since you're a light marshal. We'll have to make it look as though the Black Hole is sucking away light. The only way to do this is if someone manually overrides the Black Hole, forcing it to capture and redirect the light to the planet's surface. To Tussock and his team of scientists it will appear as though the Black Hole is actually working. Miramar has figured out how to bypass the sensors orbiting each planet, so instead of shielding the planet from the sun-star, they will draw light from the sun-star and re-route it to the Black Hole, which in and of itself is nothing more than a sensor orbiting Noxia. The person acting as the light marshal will bear the most danger in this part of the mission as he will be exposed to the heat from the light being routed to the Black Hole if he doesn't get everything set up before Tussock activates the sensors," Rue detailed the plan.

"Hey, I'm practically fireproof by now anyway. I think I'm your guy," Valerian volunteered to be the light marshal as Rue breathed a sigh of relief. Valerian's surprising arrival at the meeting couldn't have worked out more in their favor. Rue knew Valerian's expertise as a light marshal would ensure the success of the first phase of their mission. Had he not shown up, their chances of launching a surprise attack on Tussock would have been slim to none.

"What about weapons?" Aconite asked.

"We have a limited supply of cryostatic light rays, which maim rather than destroy the enemy. Aside from that, we don't have much. There is a large store of old decommissioned weapons in the Pit, where Tussock keeps his prisoners, but getting to them may be difficult since the Pit is located within the border walls that separate the castle from everything else," Ky answered the question.

"We'll have to do it the old-fashioned way, then," Spurge suggested, "with hunting weapons and the like."

"What weaponry will Tussock be armed with?" a Phirunite asked.

"They have ray guns, but only the Elite Guard will have those. The rest will use spears, dart guns, and bows. Essentially, we'll be equally matched as far as weaponry in those regards," Crofton said.

"It's the numbers where we'll fall short," Bluet surmised. "By the way, how many troops does Tussock have at his disposal?"

"There are only one hundred members of the Elite Guard, but the regular Guard is nearly to fifty thousand as Tussock has been increasing recruiting efforts in light of his pending attack." Bluet's mouth dropped open.

"Fifty thousand to three thousand? Those are the odds?"

"Not exactly. I have at least a thousand Free Frats if not more, and don't forget we'll have the element of surprise. The Guard won't be able to mobilize all fifty thousand immediately. There will be a lot of confusion and chaos when we arrive. All we need to do is capture Tussock, and the game is over. Like I said before, his true loyalists are few and far between," Crofton explained.

"And if we fail?" Aconite's eyes were downcast as he asked the question that was on everyone's mind.

"Prepare your planet to defend itself," came Rue's reply. The gravity of the situation that had slowly been seeping toward them finally descended upon the room, nearly extinguishing the small flicker of hope Crofton had tried to ignite.

"For now, you should return to your planets and get everything in order, except for Valerian. We'll need to formulate a strategy for you. As for the rest of you, we'll be in touch," Rue directed.

The meeting had lasted most of the morning. After the delegates were offered a mid-day meal, they somberly boarded their pods to return to their planets and relay the dire circumstances of the entire Florenci System.

CHAPTER TWENTY-ONE: A HOMECOMING

When Prey finally emerged from the wormhole, he was disoriented. He had no idea how much time had lapsed, and he only hoped that he wasn't too late. He took a moment to ensure his pod was still in working order. The peristaltic movement of the wormhole sucking him through its darkened chamber had taken its toll on the small pod, and there were times when Prey thought for sure the vessel would be squeezed to bits as it was swallowed through the vortex of time and space. The control panel, however, seemed to be in working order, for the most part.

Breathing a sigh of relief, Prey turned his attention to his coordinates. He was hovering in space not far from Traveriss, but far enough away that he hadn't tripped any security alarms that he well knew had been placed strategically along the outer shield. Old Run-Dung appeared to be more than a little paranoid about unwanted guests dropping in on him. After one too many late-night arrivals that had triggered alerts, awakening the Brotherhood, Run-Dung had finally agreed to give Prey the access codes to disable the alarms. As Prey recalled, permission was granted after a conversation that went something like this:

"Him again!" (Lisianthus with a bad case of bed head)

"Welcome home, Prey! So nice to see you again!" (Stephanotis with a creepy smile)

"If you insist on allowing this creature to stay here, at least have the decency to give him the codes so he isn't a constant nuisance!" (the ever-pleasant Bindweed)

"I do say that is an excellent idea." (Ranunculus, clapping his hands together)

And so, Prey punched in the codes to disable the security system and enter Traveriss's atmosphere undetected. He was trembling with fear as he pressed the buttons – fear for what was awaiting him on the planet's surface. Traveriss was a place he customarily associated with utter and complete boredom with only the twisted excitement of his ongoing hide-and-seek game with Stephanotis breaking the monotony between commissions. Now, however, he didn't know what to expect, and he had never been much for suspense, unless of course it involved a romantic tryst. This certainly was not that.

He steered the pod toward his docking station, unnerved by the unsteadiness with which he maneuvered it. He had to get in control of himself. As the pod docked and powered down, he took several deep breaths before unlatching the windowless kennel in which he kept his prized Adahi spider, Smuggler. He debated with himself. Should he take the cage with him or leave it aboard until he could scope out the situation? Ultimately, he decided to stash it in a nearby compartment that he often used to hide contraband from Ranunculus. He knew it would be safe there. He crept out of the pod, the box under his foreleg.

Though the lighting was dim at best, it nearly blinded Prey, whose eyes had been accustomed to the blackness of deep space. He waited a moment for his eyes to adjust. He then inched toward the compartment, which he had made sure was easily accessible when he first found it, just in case he needed to make an emergency exit or entrance. The only sound was the clicking of his own feet across the hard floor, which seemed to resonate more loudly than he would have liked. He might as well have grabbed a megaphone, announcing his arrival, with as much noise as he was making. His body was definitely not designed for stealth.

Finally, he reached the cubby hole and slid the cage safely inside. His heart was pounding and his breathing erratic as he contemplated his next move. The pressure was causing him to hear things as well. He was picking up an incessant buzzing noise, but he could not seem to locate its origin. What a time to go crazy! He tried to shake it off, chalking it up to nerves as he plotted his next move. Where would he be most likely to find Run-Dung and least likely to run into the traitor? Think. Think. Think. Well, Ranunculus and the others were sick, weren't they? His best bet would be to check the medical facility, hoping that the traitor had left them for dead and hoping beyond hope that the poison had not yet claimed its victory. With his next course of action mapped out, he set off down the corridor at a snail's pace – that's why he hated snails, by the way - they were too slow and took the fun out of his hunting experience. He kept turning his head 300° to keep a lookout for anything suspicious.

Chapter Twenty-Two
A Silent Exit

The days that followed were filled with technical discussions, strategy planning, formulating, and preparing. Crofton and Rue were frequently communicating with Aconite, Bluet, and Spurge, relaying plans, organizing commanders over the gathering troops, answering questions, assuaging growing fears and concerns, and offering optimistic encouragement. Noxians were coming and going as Free Frat Space Patrollers frequently landed on the planet's surface to aid in the battle plans. Betony seemed to be in the way more often than not. She had found several plant books while scouring the vast library one morning and had since gone on daily expeditions to find edible plants and berries. On occasion, Pili would unexpectedly join her. Those were the expeditions she liked best. One afternoon, just two days before the scheduled test day, they were walking along the river's edge when Betony noticed footprints in the mud.

"Where do you suppose those came from?" she asked.

"Feetim," Pili replied with a grin.

"Very funny," she said, playfully pushing him. "I didn't see anyone leave the castle this morning, did you?"

"People comim goim always," he answered.

"But surely not this far when there's so much to be done, and look at how small this print is." Pili shrugged his shoulders, unconcerned, and started moving along the river's edge again. Betony attempted to follow the footprints, but they disappeared when the wet mud met the grass and shrubbery. It was to remain an unsolved mystery after all. She ran back toward Pili.

"So have you been given your assignment yet?" she asked as she stopped to inspect the purple bud of a flowering bush.

"Not yetim, go where needim." Pili probably hadn't even asked Crofton about his assignment. He simply did as Crofton told him to, no questions asked. Betony hadn't dared ask Rue where she fit into all the plans either. He was so distracted lately that she had hardly spoken to him. Rue spent most of his time in deep conversations with Valerian, and she didn't want to intrude, especially since she felt she had so little to contribute now. She had kept her distance from Valerian since their ill-fated conversation the morning after he arrived. Ambulia had asked Valerian if he was in constant pain since he should have still been in a Quamirian medical facility recovering. He had unconvincingly told her that the pain was sporadic at best. Betony pulled him aside later and offered her services as a healer, but he quickly declined.

"Thanks, but no thanks. You've already done enough," he had said. Betony had taken him to mean that she shouldn't have interfered in the first place, although Rue later assured her that she had misinterpreted Valerian's meaning. Valerian felt that his healing was a rite of passage he must go through on his own from that point on to make him a better person and build his character. He didn't want to take the easy way out, thus missing out on all the experience that had already helped him redefine who he was as an individual. Maybe that was so, but Betony still kept her distance.

More than anything, Betony was worried. She worried about Rue. She worried about her role in the events to come, and she worried about the outcome. She knew the odds of success were not in their favor. She and Rue had already evaded death more than once, and she taunted it even now with her every breath. Surely, it would come for her or Rue or both of them this time, and if it did, she wouldn't be afforded the opportunity to relish her last days of life with the one she loved.

"Bee!" Pili was calling her. He had taken to calling her Bee since it was easier to pronounce. She looked in his direction, unaware of how long she had been lost in her own thoughts.

"You comim?"

"Sorry. I'll be right there," she called back as she darted toward him.

They were all sitting at the Great Table for dinner that night before the big day. Still Rue had said nothing to Betony, and she was more than a little angry with him. She had stood by him and supported him, and he chose to tell her nothing. She tried to rationalize his silence in the beginning, but the last two days every time she tried to broach the subject, he took evasive measures – a sudden call he had to make or a tired yawn followed by a sudden deep sleep from which he could not be stirred. Her irritation was apparent to everyone, but only Pili had offered any consolation: "He tellim when timem." She had her suspicions that she hadn't been factored into the plan at all. Surely, he wouldn't leave her by herself on Eudora. Then again, Ranunculus had done just that to Clary. Betony stewed all through dinner, not talking to anyone, although she doubted anyone noticed. When everyone had dispersed to other parts of the castle, Betony remained sitting at the table with her arms crossed as did Rue. Rue leaned toward her, turning her face toward him with his hand.

"Why the long face?" he asked, peering at her intently. She rolled her eyes and turned her head away, saying nothing.

"Come on. Now is not the time for hard feelings," he whispered, leaning close to her ear.

"What about me, Rue? What do you plan to do with me or have I surpassed my usefulness to you? Is this a rite of passage Eudoran boys must go through alone to prove to themselves that they can be kings?" she asked bitterly as she rose to her feet and walked across the room, turning her back toward him. He did not follow her.

"That's not fair, and you know it," he retorted.

"Not fair? Is it fair that you have chosen to exclude me from your crusade without so much as consulting me on the matter? Did you think me too frail and delicate to help? Would I only be in the way?"

"Betony –"

"I'm going, Rue. I am going, and you can't stop me. I am only subject to your will if I so choose. Rue, you didn't like it when the Brotherhood chose your fate without consulting you, and I don't like it when you do that to me. It's my life; it's my choice. If you didn't want me by your side always, then you should have let death claim its victory over me at the waterfall. You can't save me only to abandon me later, whatever your reasoning. Rue, I am because you are. I go where you go. Betrothed or not. Unionized or not. You can't sever that bond without severing me in the process. You might as well cut my heart out and feed it to one of the carnivorous plants on the South Side," she interrupted.

"Betony, if you were captured, you would be Tussock's ultimate victory. You have to understand that, but I know better than to argue with you," he was behind her now, so close she could feel his breath on her neck, slowly melting her glacier of anger as he exhaled.

"Have I told you recently how much I love you? What began as a youthful infatuation with your beauty has grown into such a deeply-rooted love in such a short amount of time that sometimes I'm afraid I'm still on Traveriss only dreaming. You never belonged to Unn. You've always belonged with me – the ancient guardian to my heart, which never truly beat until I met you," he turned her toward him as he spoke. She looked up into his eyes, staring as the ocean of blue carried away her melting glacier. He hugged her close to him. Minutes passed, but he did not move nor did she wish him to. She knew he was saying goodbye in the only way she would have permitted him to – without actually saying the words.

"Don't be angry with me, not tonight. We can sort this out in the morning." He kissed her once, twice.

"Come, have one last drink with me. Crofton found the castle's store of exotic fruit juices. I thought we could drink some... for luck," he coaxed when he finally pulled away. He strode to a table with two small vessels already filled with an amber liquid.

"For love," she said as she took the vessel from him.

"For victory," he offered. She drank the small amount of liquid in one swallow, surprised at its bitter taste. When she looked at Rue, a fog of sadness had settled over his features. He was placing his still full vessel on the table as he took hers from her hand. She meant to ask him what was going on, but found herself falling, first into his outstretched arms and then into a deep and dreamless sleep.

Betony awoke with a start. Realizing where she was, she calmed down, but only for a moment. The castle was too quiet, and the eerie silence had awakened her. Rue was nowhere in sight. She jumped to her feet and rushed to Crofton's room. Empty. She checked for Valerian, Ky, and Thor. Every room was empty. She raced down the stairs, panic gripping at each breath as she went, but the only sound was her bare feet tapping the stone steps as she descended the spirals until she reached the foyer. By the doors stood Pili with his arms folded, a sentinel of dashed hopes, securing her loneliness.

"You nottim go. Orders."

"Whose orders?"

"Crofton. Rue. Both agreeim."

"Why? Because I'm not a warrior princess like Ambulia?" Pili only laughed, a sad laugh that echoed in the silence.

"You safim here."

"I don't want to be safe here," she shouted, moving a step closer to him. "I can help there. What if someone gets hurt? I can help. You've seen me heal." Pili shook his head no.

"Please," she pleaded. He did not move.

"Please," she begged, tears coming to her eyes. Pili seemed unaffected by her groveling, which enraged her. He was supposed to be her friend! She rushed forward, fists flailing at him, pounding his chest. He didn't budge. She slumped down in a heap, sobbing. After a few minutes, she felt Pili's strong arms pick her up. He carried her to the circular bench that surrounded the fountain. As he gently sat her down, he sat beside her, patting her shoulder as she cried.

"I wantim to goim too. Mustim obeyim orders. I protectim you," Pili said in a forlorn tone.

"From what Pili? There's nothing here, and when this is all said and done, we may be the only two left. I joined Crofton to help, not to hold him or his men back." Instead of responding, Pili pulled an envelope from the pack he kept slung around his shoulder.

"Fromim Rue," he said, handing her the envelope before resuming his post by the door. Betony retired to her room before opening the envelope. She would have known it was from Rue even if Pili hadn't told her. The envelope carried his all too familiar scent – a smell that made Betony's heart ache for him all the more. As she unfolded the paper, something fell out. She bent down, frantically searching for whatever had fallen when her hand brushed across a seed. It was not any seed, but **the** seed Rue had used to open the castle door and to operate the communicator.

She recognized his handwriting from the star charts upon which he had jotted notes when they were traveling to Asa-en-Darah – his small neat script, each letter perfectly formed in perfectly straight rows. How life had changed since then! She had barely known Rue and never would have imagined how much her life would be intertwined with his. Her eyes drifted to the page, and she heard Rue's deep voice speaking the words in her head.

My Beloved Betony,

> *I am entrusting this to you for safekeeping. It is not only the key to this castle, the key to the communicator, and the key to my past, but it is also the key to my heart. You are the only one I could ever trust to guard it for me. I know you're angry with me for leaving you behind and tricking you into drinking the sleeping juice. I am sorry. I can imagine the look on your beautiful face as you read this, but I felt it necessary. You are my personal secret weapon – the sunlight that keeps me going – I can't bear to take you into the black of the endless Noxian night for fear it may extinguish your light. Crofton agrees that someone should stay at headquarters. Is it selfish to recommend you? Absolutely. Is it painful to leave you behind when my greatest desire is to have you by my side always? Excruciatingly. Am I afraid to leave you alone, possibly forever? Petrified. Why did I do it, then? Because I love you more than life itself – because you are life itself – because without you there is no life itself. Remember, I am always with you. I'm the blue sky watching over you by day. And when you feel the blackness edging toward you, don't be afraid. It is only me wrapping you in my embrace to shield you from the night.*

> *Until we meet again,*

> *Rue*

Betony closed her fingers tightly around the small seed in her hand. She easily recognized the subtle knocking on the door of her heart. The darkness of death and despair was announcing its arrival yet again. She was tempted to open the door, just a crack, but she knew that once opened, it could not be shut again. Focus. She needed to focus her mind on something else.

How had the Florenci System gone from a peaceful tolerance to the brink of warfare in such a short time? What was to be a relatively short journey to Asa-en-Darah to retrieve her memories now found her wrapped up in a dangerous conspiracy that threatened not only her life, but also the life of her newfound friends and the man she loved. Even amidst the hatred, distrust, and violence, love had still, little by little, nudged itself into her heart, opening a new world of emotion and awakening her gift. Clary had been right.

Love was the true source of real power. The love for family and friends motivated Crofton and the Free Frats. The love of their planets prompted the Orons, Quamirians, and Phirunites to join the fight from which they otherwise would have shirked. She thought of Tansy's love for Valerian and her love for Rue. The planets revolved around love; it was essential, maybe even more so than a sun-star. A sun-star allowed them to exist, but love allowed them to live, and so she focused on all the love she had felt during the short time since her seed-pod had been opened.

CHAPTER TWENTY-THREE: A HEAD WILL ROLL

Prey inched along the wall as he neared the medical facility, trying to stay out of sight. Too bad his eyes weren't removable so he could peek into the glass window. He stood on the tips of his hindlegs, straining his neck so he could see inside. He had predicted correctly. He saw their bodies, lying nearly lifeless on the makeshift tables. The room had only been equipped with one table before, but now there were five. He could barely make out the slow, staggered rise and fall of the five chests as he watched. He scanned the rest of the room, but there was no sign of anyone else. He paused to look down the corridor before opening the door, and again, he saw no one. He turned the door handle, somewhat awkwardly, as his forelegs were not exactly designed for such a maneuver. He crept inside and scanned the faces for Run-Dung. His was the body lying closest to the door.

"Ranunculus?" he whispered, his voice raspy from lack of use.

"Who's there?" came the response, though Prey did not recognize his voice. It was feeble and barely audible.

"It's me. Prey. I've just returned," he explained.

"You must go. Go now," Run-dung commanded.

"I'm here to help you. I can help."

"It isn't safe. Leave. Just leave. Will you listen to me for once?" Run-dung

219

was pleading with him, the very tone of his voice evoking so much pity that Prey almost obeyed its insistent command, but it was not to be. Prey heard the swishing of a robe behind him. He turned to see who had entered. The silver sheen of the sword glinted in his line of sight a split second before it sliced through the air, severing his head from his body. The robed-figure of Lamium had struck with such force that Prey's head thudded to the ground next to Lamium's foot with a loud splat.

"And just what did you think you were going to do, you wretched insect?" His cackle clawed through the mournful silence, ripping to tiny shreds the glimmer of hope that had manifest itself at Prey's unexpected arrival. Lamium glanced in the direction of Ranunculus and the others.

"Don't you want to know why?" Lamium sneered, but no one had strength enough to respond. "You, my friend, are a prideful prude, denying my father entrance into your beloved circle when he was banished from his own planet and failing to give him refuge even in light of the injustice he was dealt. You give this creature a safe haven," he said walking to Prey's head and kicking it so it crashed again into his lifeless body, "but you refuse to help one of your own kind. And then you dare expel one of the greatest minds in the Florenci System because he doesn't have the same objectives as you. Tut-tut, Ranunculus. Poor judgments indeed. And now look at you. You are nothing. A few breaths from your own demise by the hands of those upon whom you turned your back. For Eudora!" Lamium's voice echoed as he ended his soliloquy with a triumphant shout.

"The... people... of... Eudora... are... better... off... dead... than... to... have... you... for... a... leader... and... I... only... wish... the... same... fate... on... the... Noxians... if... you... and...Tussock... plan... to... rule... over... them,"

Ranunculus struggled to reply. Lamium rushed toward him angrily, grabbing the front of his robe and shaking him.

"How dare you speak to me like that, old man," Lamium spat in his face, letting Ranunculus's body slump back to the table as he released his grip. "You never did know what was best for anyone. Just look at what happened to your young protégé –the poor orphaned seedling to whom you were a great savior. While it was to exact revenge upon you personally that I came here initially, I was most fortunate when you discovered that damaged pod floating aimlessly. It should have been destroyed, but you had to go poking about. Didn't you? Oh well, it made for a livelier game for me. He's gone now anyway, despite your heroic efforts - blown to bits."

"Or... so you... were told," Ranunculus managed to utter through shallow breaths.

"You know nothing!" Lamium struck Ranunculus in the face, but the seed of doubt had been planted nonetheless.

"Evil... will... never triumph... over... good - and you - you... Lamium... of... Oro - you will be justly... compensated... for... your.... murderous... treachery. I will... personally... assure... you... of... that... even... in... my... death." Ranunculus's words dealt the last blow to Lamium. Even at death's door, Ranunculus refused to acknowledge Lamium's power. Lamium struck him again and rushed from the room. A few moments later, a pod was heard leaving the launch with Lamium on board.

Chapter Twenty-Four
An Unexpected Visitor

Betony huddled next to Pili just as the sun was setting on Eudora. The Free Frats were scheduled to arrive at the Black Hole at this time, and Pili was waiting for a transmission from Crofton, who had promised to keep them apprised of their progress. Pili had given one of his ear buds to Betony, so she could listen as well. The silence was aggravating. She wished they could hear every communication that was made among the Free Frats, but Crofton had reserved a special frequency for updating them so they didn't get alarmed if something didn't go as planned. Finally, Pili's wrist flashed bright red.

"Phase one successful. Valerian disarmed Black Hole. Sensors have been disarmed. Light re-routed to planets. Prisoner pods launched." They both breathed a sigh of relief, although phase one of their assault had never worried Betony much. Phase two held the most danger, and it wasn't scheduled to begin until the following evening just after the Noxian sunrise. They had to allow for travel time, and Crofton estimated that it would take no more than a day to get the prisoners back to Noxia since those pods had been loaded with speed enhancers. Tussock wanted his prisoners on Noxia as soon as possible.

"Now, we wait some more, I guess," Betony said. Pili nodded in agreement. "And Pili, I'm sorry about this morning, and I'm sorry that you are stuck here seed-watching me." Pili looked away without responding, so Betony retreated to her room. She knew he was upset at having been left behind, probably more so than she was. He had shadowed Crofton his entire life, and now Crofton had left him behind. Betony felt the tears slipping down her cheeks. She sat in her room, misery tapping at her heart like rain on a window. As she watched darkness descend upon the world outside, she heard a tap at her door.

"Come in, Pili," she called.

"Bringim foodim," he said as he pushed open the door, carrying a tray.

"Pili, you didn't have to do that. Besides, I'm not really hungry."

"Eatim. Drinkim. Keep strongim."

"Really. I'm not hungry."

"Eatim. Drinkim."

"If you insist, I suppose I have no choice in the matter," she picked up a bowl of berries and plopped one into her mouth. After she had eaten a little of what he had brought, he urged her to drink some water. Though she wasn't really thirsty, she complied. She recognized the bitter taste as it raced down her throat, and she shot a disapproving look at Pili.

"Did he put you up to this? I'll be just –" she hadn't finished her sentence before sleep had seized control of her consciousness.

Betony awoke the next morning, but her mind was still in a haze. She was upset that Rue would ask Pili to drug her. She knew Rue was just trying to protect her, but she was getting tired of everyone feeling as though she had to be protected. She could protect herself. She marched downstairs to give Pili a piece of her mind. She found him staring blankly into the fountain. Her angry approach startled him.

"Let's get one thing clear here. You are not Rue's puppet. You are not Crofton's puppet. You don't have to do their bidding. I can sleep on my own, okay? Don't ever do that again!" she reprimanded him, wagging her finger in his face. Again, he looked away, saying nothing.

"Pili, what's wrong?" she was suddenly concerned. He was acting very strangely.

"Wantim be normalim. Tiredim of stupidim. Not needim," his voice was sharp and angry. He wanted so badly to communicate his feelings, and he couldn't. Betony immediately regretted her tirade. She had treated him like a seedling. Everyone treated him like a seedling. He felt betrayed by Crofton, and he couldn't even vent his feelings. She had never seen him so angry before. He burst out the front door of the castle, ran down to the river, and started hefting boulders into it. She did not try to stop him. Instead, she watched and waited for more than an hour. He finally collapsed on the bank of the river and broke down. She doubted he had ever cried before. He kept his feelings locked inside of his mountain of muscle, tough and strong, but the avalanche had finally come. The face of his mountain was crumbling. Betony walked to where he was laying and bent over him. His eyes were closed, but he felt her shadow the sun-star. He opened his eyes, surprised to find her so close to him, and quickly wiped away his tears. She offered her hand to help him up. He took it.

"Do you feel better now?" she asked tentatively. He nodded his head. "Listen, I'm really sorry about what I said back there. It wasn't meant for you.

I was just venting my frustration, and you happen to be the only one here. Friends?" A smile broke through his somber countenance as he pulled her into a hug.

"Friendim," he agreed as he released her.

"How about a walk?" Betony had grown fond of their walks together over the past few days.

"Walkim clearim mind," he agreed as he offered her his arm.

They had walked for a while when Betony stopped to inspect a flower she hadn't noticed before. As she bent down, she noticed the familiar ballet of swirling leaves that accompanied a landing pod. She looked up to see a familiar-looking pod sinking slowly out of the sky toward the ground. Pili looked alarmed. He had not received a communication that someone would be landing.

"That looks just like the pod Rue and I flew to Asa-en-Darah," she observed. Pili tensed. He knew as well as she did that if it was a member of the Brotherhood, they wouldn't have received word of their coming.

"Go insidim," Pili commanded, a hint of fear and uncertainty in his eyes.

"Don't go, Pili. Come with me. Whoever it is can't get inside the castle once we lock the door," she protested.

"No. You goim," he demanded. She turned toward the castle, which was nothing more than a speck in the distance. She turned back to Pili, but he had already started up the incline toward the landing strip. She headed forward along the rocky path to the castle, resisting the urge to run. She walked as fast as she dared, but it wasn't fast enough for her. She was nearing the river when she heard the bushes rustling behind her. She knew it wasn't Pili because he hardly ever made a noise. She whirled around.

Her pursuer stopped instantaneously, temporarily stunned by the person he saw standing before him, someone who was supposed to be dead. Betony's eyes settled on Lamium, as she contemplated why he was on Eudora. He took a step toward her.

"Ranunculus sent me... to bring you back," he cooed. Her eyes shifted to the Transparency detector still attached to his arm, the blue glow indicating its functionality, and no doubt filled with the real inoculation. The traitor had come home to claim his throne, no doubt. She quickly surveyed her surroundings. The terrain was now flat, and she could probably make it back to the castle ahead of him. She didn't know what secrets his father had revealed to him or if he even knew of the castle's existence or location. She decided to take the chance since it appeared he had either killed Pili or knocked him unconscious. She hoped for the latter, but given Lamium's murderous history, she held little confidence in a good outcome.

"Save your lies, Lamium." His eyes narrowed.

"Choose your words carefully, young lady. You have no one to protect you now."

"Who said I needed protecting?" He cocked his head back and let out a shrill laugh.

"Apparently, you don't know who you're up against."

"Oh, but I do - a coward who fights his battles in the shadows with mechanized viruses and hidden poisons." His nostrils flared, but she didn't back down. "Aren't you even a little bit surprised to see me here?"

"A mere bump in the road. That's what I get for leaving my affairs in incapable hands, but enough of this idle chit chat. More important is the fact that I have found you now," he hissed the words.

"You may have found me, but you won't catch me," she turned her back to him and ran as fast as her legs would carry her. He was in pursuit, though his legs kept getting caught up in his flowing robes. She was nearing the waterfall, when she slipped on a wet rock. She rolled toward the river, sensing her body flushing out the pain of a broken ankle. She felt the bone mending as she came to a stop at the water's edge, facedown. Her clumsiness gave Lamium enough time to catch up to her, and he was upon her before she could move. He grabbed her hair, jerking her head upward as she whimpered in pain.

"Where's your sarcasm now, my sweet? You will respect-" Betony's head fell forward, and she heard Lamium's body fall with a thump to her side. She looked up in surprise to see a small child staring at her with a rock in one of her hands. Betony backed away from Lamium cautiously as she saw two more individuals, who appeared to be Noxians, dragging Pili toward them with great effort. When they neared Betony's location, they dropped his body in the mud, panting at their exertion.

"Wh-who are you?" she asked trying to calm her voice, but her eyes were wide with fear.

"Live," it was the child who answered her, pointing into the bushes.

"You live here? On Eudora?" The child nodded in response. "But how?"

"Live," the child repeated. The female Noxian who had been dragging Pili dumped a wooden bowl of water over Pili's face. He woke up sputtering and choking. His eyes widened as he recognized a fellow Noxian hovering above him. As he struggled to get to his feet, the male Noxian rushed forward to help.

"Pili, they saved me. The child says they live here," and then she remembered. "They were leaving the footprints in the mud. They are the Noxian rebels Protea allowed to live here when they escaped from Noxia all those years ago. They weren't killed by the virus because it was genetically-altered to kill only Eudorans." The Noxian couple smiled at her.

"Can you not speak?" she asked. Pili walked toward the man and woman whose skin was withered with age. They opened their mouths, and Pili looked away in repulsion. Their tongues had been cut out.

"A Noxian Punisher did this?" Betony asked. They nodded in response. Betony walked toward the woman. "I am an Ancient," she said. The woman nodded as if she already knew that, which meant she must have been on Noxia when Clary was found.

"I can heal you if you would like." The woman didn't move, so Betony placed her finger on her throat. She instantly felt the pain, but she didn't cower this time. She felt her life force rush into the woman's body drawing in the dead and scarred cells from the woman's tongue. Her life force rushed to through the woman's body instructing it to grow new cells. The woman's body at first tried to reject the instructions, pushing the life force away. Betony persisted. The woman's resistance buckled under the pressure, and the cells answered the call to grow. Within minutes the woman's tongue had been healed. She turned next to the man and followed the same routine until, his tongue had regenerated itself.

"Thank you!" the woman exclaimed. "Thank you!" The tears were streaming down her cheeks. Although Betony felt slightly fatigued, she helped Pili tie Lamium up with a rope from his satchel. After securing him to a tree near the river, the group made their way back to the castle. As they walked, the Noxians recounted their story. The man's name was Calden and his wife was Yerba. Calden worked in Tussock's research labs, and Yerba was a cook in Tussock's house, which she considered a great honor. They had both grown up in a poor village known as the Grub, but Calden had worked hard to get into school, where he was recognized for his academic prowess. He was recruited by Tussock and gladly accepted the offer to escape the poverty and squalor in which he had been forced to live. He took Yerba with him as his wife before entering Tussock's academy, where he excelled.

He was assigned to a research team and lived a life of relative leisure. He tried to ignore the brutality around him, until Yerba found a starving orphan named Bracken outside her kitchens begging for food. Knowing it was against the law to feed vagabonds, she gave the seedling some tubers and sent him on his way. The only problem was he kept coming back. One month passed by, and Yerba got careless. One day, she was caught sneaking him food. Tussock's guardsmen rounded up Calden, Yerba, Bracken, and two other servants in the kitchen who had been with Yerba outside. Calden's and Yerba's tongues were cut out. The two servant girls each had a finger cut off, and poor Bracken was sentenced to life in the Pit.

Yerba couldn't bear to live on Noxia any longer. She begged Calden to plan an escape, so Calden did. They were too young to have their lives snuffed out from under them. Calden had been developing an atmospheric solar propulsion suit to enable a person to fly into space without a pod. When two suits were ready for testing, and Calden was confident they were fully functional, he stole them. When they arrived on Eudora, they were welcomed by Protea and accepted by the Eudoran people. They lived happily in a cave dwelling outside the protections of the castle, until everyone began mysteriously dying – everyone except Calden and Yerba. They waited for someone to come to save them, but no one did. They had no choice but to adapt, living off the land, alone. In their old age, they unexpectedly bore a seedling whom they named

Starthistle. Because her parents could not speak, she spoke very little. With Calden nearing the death age, they tried to teach the young child as much as they could to ensure her survival when they were both gone.

When the pods came bearing Noxians, members of the Elite Guard no less, they feared that Tussock had finally come for them. But as they watched and listened, they knew they were different than the guardsmen they had known on Noxia. Then, the ships bearing the others came, just as they had done in Protea's day. Calden and Yerba knew that a king had returned, but still they feared. They often followed Pili and Betony on their walks, and Starthistle began to pick up a few words. They came to like Betony, and they knew they could trust her. Then, they saw everyone leave, and they assumed they were alone again, until today. They were about to approach Pili and Betony when the pod landed. Betony knew the rest of the story. She was amazed that they had survived for so long, and she noticed the Pili openly wept as they told them their story and repeatedly thanked her for healing them.

"What do we do now?" Calden asked.

"I don't know about you, but I'm not just going to sit around here and wait," Betony said. "We now have a pod." Pili's eyes lit up.

"Goim to Noxia," he said.

"We're doing no good just sitting around here, now are we?"

"May we come too?" Calden inquired. "I would like nothing more than to ensure my daughter's future is secure. Given our age, we may not be of much help, but we would like to accompany you anyway. We owe at least that much to Bracken." They decided to leave Lamium on Eudora and let Rue deal with him upon his return. They gathered a few meager supplies and locked the castle.

"Wait!" Betony exclaimed. She ran back to the castle and reappeared carrying what appeared to be an empty bottle. "You never know if these might come in handy." Calden and Yerba exchanged confused glances, but Betony didn't bother to elaborate. They set off for Noxia in Lamium's pod.

CHAPTER TWENTY-FIVE: A TRUCE OF SORTS

"Prey?" Stephanotis choked out the words. "Prey! Answer me! I know you aren't dead, tricky little rascal. Unlike Lamium, I've done my research on you. I certainly never found your species beneath me. Now get up, quick!" Stephanotis had found a little burst of energy, possibly the adrenaline rush from the events he had just witnessed. Prey had never experienced such pain before. He'd come close a time or two, but he had always managed a narrow escape, until now. He knew he could live for several days without his head attached, but it was a gory thought. He could clearly make out Stephanotis's voice, so there was no sense pretending he couldn't. More than his life was at stake, and now he had effectively been given a death sentence so he figured he might as well do something admirable in his last days.

He could see his body lying beside him, if only he could make his forelegs move. The first two attempts failed. He wasn't even sure it was possible with a complete severing, but he tried again. There, at last! A small movement. The forelegs seemed to be flailing about without regard to the instructions he was trying to send. He could not control their movements. The sharp spines on his left foreleg cut his head as it swung a little too close. Finally, they grasped his head and set it back on his neck. He rose to his feet and staggered out of the room, ignoring the desperate shouts from Stephanotis and the others. He knew what he had to do.

He was too wobbly on his legs, so he lifted his wings to fly. He usually reserved his wings only to catch the eye of a passing female, but he'd have to make an exception. He wished he were trying to find a mate rather than inching closer to his own death with every passing second. He rushed to the cubby hole to extract Smuggler. With his forelegs busy holding his head, he used his middle legs to carry the kennel, which meant he would have to use his hindlegs to cover the distance back to the medical facility. The kennel added too much weight for him to fly back. The trip took twice as long since his body was acting of its own accord, not to mention the fact that his head was being balanced on his neck like a rock on a skewer. He finally rounded the last corner, the Adahi spider less than happy about all the jostling.

Prey entered the room quietly, hoping that no one would notice him as they struggled to continue breathing. Luck was not on his side, as usual. Stephanotis had actually managed to raise himself up, and he was watching Prey with curiosity. Prey set the kennel on the floor, knowing full well that as soon as he opened the door Smuggler would seek its first target, then a second, followed by a third and fourth and on and on until all threats had been eliminated, even if those threats were barely clinging to life. It would bite anything and everything in sight as long as its senses detected foreign life forms in the air, which was one reason this species was so deadly, aside from its venom, of course. The spider would also try to attack him, so he would have to be on his feet when that moment came. He hoped his forelegs would react instinctively since his true hunting skills had been severely impaired. Oh, how he hated to waste such a treat – he wouldn't be able to eat it once he had killed it. Darn that Lamium, anyway. He had so looked forward to it, but alas, what choice did he really have?

He slowly lifted the kennel lid, making sure it was pointed in the direction of the Brotherhood's tables. He did not have to worry about the spider reaching them from the floor. Its amazing jumping abilities were a contributing factor in Prey's great admiration for this delectable snack. He rarely liked to work for what he got, but the thrill of hunting an Adahi spider was an exception to his work philosophy. It was more sport and pleasure than work anyway.

As soon as Stephanotis caught sight of the creature Prey had unloosed upon them, his eyes registered fear. Prey liked that look on him, and he had waited far too long to see it. He was glad he would get a little pleasure for his pain at any rate. He would have tried to reassure Stephanotis, but his vocal cords had been severed in the decapitation. Okay, if he were being truly honest as he probably ought to, given that his days were limited, he wouldn't have offered reassurance to Stephanotis even if he could talk. Payback was far too sweet for that. He would relish the memory of the look on Stephanotis's face until his dying day, which he hated to remind himself was sooner than he would like.

Smuggler went right to work. Thankfully, the members of the Brotherhood were so near death's door, they did not resist, and Prey highly doubted they felt any pain, or any more pain than they were already experiencing. He watched as Smuggler jumped with flying grace to the table on which Run-Dung laid. It sunk its fangs deep into the throat of its victim. Ranunculus let out only a raspy sigh as Smuggler moved to Stephanotis, who had laid down and closed his eyes in disgust. He made no sound as the venom entered his life force, attacking the poison that was killing him. On to Galax, Aster, and Lisianthus, and now for the tricky part. Smuggler turned, assessing the air. His legs twitched. Prey knew he had been detected. The only way for Prey to kill Smuggler was to put his head in a safe place to free up his forelegs for the fight. His forelegs, after all, were armed with the sharp spines. His head rolled as it was dropped by his own legs, but he kept his eyes fixed on Smuggler.

He was moving slowly, stealthily, for he had sensed that this victim was more advanced in the defensive arts than his former targets. Prey watched his own body adjust its weight, first by leaning on two legs, and then on the other two. He was a natural-born predator, a ferocious hunter, and he would enjoy watching himself in action, assuming he came out the winner. As Smuggler approached, Prey's forelegs raised instinctively. His thorax and abdomen were completely still, and he had noted his coloring had changed as well, adjusting to the dim light in the room. He was fascinated with himself.

Smuggler crept closer and closer, but Prey's body made no movement in response. When Smuggler was within striking distance, he watched his forelegs sweep down in a motion so fast that he was barely able to track it with his excellent vision. And there, his forelegs held the struggling spider, waiting for Prey to indulge himself in the delicacy. While Prey often resorted to eating his meals dead these days, he preferred to eat them alive. He began salivating as he watched Smuggler continue to struggle. Oh, what he wouldn't give for just a taste, but it would do him no good. He couldn't move his head, and even if he did get a bite, he wouldn't feel the satisfaction as it filled his empty stomach. He resigned himself to watching as the time ticked by, drool pooling beneath his head. Smuggler finally stopped resisting. His big, furry body hung limp in Prey's forelegs. The fight was over.

Only then did Prey think to check on the members of the Brotherhood.

He had been so caught up in his own selfish desires that he had forgotten the purpose for his self-denial. His mind was suddenly flooded with waves of doubt. What if it hadn't worked? What if his actions had merely sealed their fates? He ventured a look-see at the tables. Prey was pleasantly surprised to find Run-Dung's chest rising and falling at regular intervals, his eyes twitching beneath his closed eyelids. This was a good sign, but suddenly Prey felt faint. True, he knew he could live for days without his head attached to his body, but he hadn't considered, until now, whether he would be conscious or not. He was fortunate that he had done as much as he had in his condition. He would expect Run-Dung to at least construct a shrine, maybe a monument in his honor. That's the least he could do, given the sacrifice Prey had made. Then his vision blurred, and his mind was quiet for the first time since he had been a nymph.

"This is quite the development, I should say," Stephanotis announced. "I never would have expected this in a million years, and I should know. I've studied the Mantid for a while now, always happily surprised by the species."

"I can't say I share your admiration. I always quite detested the revolting creature," Aster countered flatly.

"He saved your life, good man! Have an ounce of gratitude, would you?" Stephanotis chided.

"Gratitude? He sicked an Adahi spider on us!" Aster shouted, rubbing the puncture wounds on his throat, which were still black and sore.

"Should have left you for dead," Stephanotis retorted.

"Enough," Ranunculus joined the conversation. "We owe our lives to Prey, and we're lucky Stephanotis was skilled enough to save him. He very nearly gave his life for us, and I'll not tolerate any more criticism of him. You should be ashamed of yourself, Aster. If there's anyone you should detest right now, it's Lamium."

"Where do you suppose he's gone anyway? Surely, you're not going to let him get away with this?" Galax asked.

"I have no idea what his plans are, but I assume they include both Eudora and Tussock. I propose we head to Noxia. We must see if we can help Bindweed, if he isn't dead already. I suspect that he hadn't been poisoned as long as us since he developed the inoculation and often refilled his transmitter after making a fresh batch before Lamium contaminated it. Rue's warning bought him even more time. Besides, I have some unfinished business to take care of there, but maybe I'm getting ahead of myself now. You are under no obligation to follow me," Ranunculus said.

"Of course, we'll follow you," Lisianthus spoke up. Ranunculus looked to each of his brothers, and each tipped his head forward in approval.

"I appreciate your support," Ranunculus's words surprised them since he rarely articulated gratitude to them.

"What shall we do about the sun-star, Ranunculus? If we arrive during a Noxian sunrise, we'll be incinerated," Galax observed.

"I have been preparing to go to Noxia for quite some time, ever since I first started receiving petitions from that Crofton fellow. I knew the time would come when we would have to intervene. I have developed a solution that we can spray on our bodies that will protect us from the heat of the sun-star, and I also have a store of weapons that we might find useful," Ranunculus told them.

"Weapons?" Stephanotis was surprised. "Certainly, you don't plan to –"

"Stephanotis, my brother, this is a time of war, and I, for one, am tired of standing by, letting innocent people die. We must take decisive action, and end this threat. Unfortunately, we have no idea what we're even walking into," Ranunculus stated firmly.

"I see," Stephanotis let the subject drop, though he had reservations.

Prey had heard the entire conference between the members of the Brotherhood, and he did not like Ranunculus's tone. More shocking, however, was the revelation that Stephanotis had reattached his head, and as far as he could tell, he hadn't given way to his temptation to dissect him. He supposed he should be grateful, but given the exchange he had just heard, he wasn't so sure he was glad to be alive. Noxia? Was Run-Dung insane? Had the venom tainted his mind? Prey was not going. He was going to put all six feet down on this matter.

"The anesthesia is wearing off," Stephanotis announced cheerily to the others. Prey raised himself slowly off the dissection table to which he partially owed his life. The smell of the room made him queasy. His head was pounding with pain as Stephanotis wrapped his gangly arms around him. A hug? Nobody had ever hugged Prey before. He was so stunned that he even resisted the urge to use his spiky spines to snip Stephanotis's ridiculous hair. Instead, he sat motionless and expressionless.

"We're headed to Noxia, Prey," Ranunculus declared as if Noxia were some sort of resort whose exclusive members had recently overcome life-threatening experiences. Prey glowered at Run-Dung, though he doubted Run-

Dung knew that's what he was doing. It was hard to distinguish facial expressions on the Mantid species in general. Nonetheless, he let his antennae flit with dismay.

"Don't you even want to know how I got here?" Prey asked. He did not like the sound of his voice. It was much too high, much too feminine. Apparently, Stephanotis had found tinkering with Prey's body a little too enticing after all. Prey shot Stephanotis an angry look, and Stephanotis shrugged with a smile. Prey didn't need an interpreter to know what that smile meant. Stephanotis was exacting his revenge on Prey for taunting him with Smuggler. He supposed they were even now – a truce of sorts.

"Certainly! Do tell," Stephanotis encouraged him. They listened with fascination as Prey told his story. Of course, he left out a few parts, like the fact that he hadn't bothered to fix the broken communicator before he left Traveriss, and he embellished other parts, like his experience in the wormhole, which became death defying in and of itself. But all in all, they got the general gist of the story, which of course, painted Prey as nothing short of heroic.

"Well, well. We are truly fortunate that you ended up here instead of racing around the galaxies on the back of a comet. I do, however, have something to say to you about smuggling certain delicacies onto the planet when it is strictly forbidden...but maybe...just this time...I'll let it slide," Ranunculus said with a twinkle in his eye.

"Now, on to our next adventure. Prey, you come with me. The rest of you take a separate pod. To Noxia," he instructed as he turned to leave. Prey reluctantly followed. So much for putting his feet down. He hadn't even managed a mild protest.

Chapter Twenty-Six
A Broken Heart

Bindweed had kept himself hidden when he landed on Noxia. He was surprised at how well he remembered the planet's surface. He was also surprised that Tussock had failed to secure his airspace. No alarm had sounded as he entered the Noxian atmosphere, and he was able to land in a small clearing. Although he had been significantly weakened by the poison, he was not as bad off as the rest of the Brotherhood, who, he hated to admit, were probably all dead by now. He snuck into an underground tunnel that led inside the border walls. He had commissioned the tunnel's construction himself as an emergency evacuation. He followed the dark tunnel to its entrance and positioned himself just inside the castle gates, hidden amidst the stone sentinels.

He had only one objective: to save Clary. Nothing else mattered to him at this point. In fact, nothing else had ever mattered to him since he had first met her. He hadn't caught a glimpse of her yet, but he was saving every last ounce of his strength, for the moment would surely come.

As he waited, he allowed his mind to wander back to the days when he had walked the long, dark corridors of the hallway as Tussock's Chief Guard. The memories had been locked away for so long, he had some difficulty removing the rusted padlock that guarded against their escape. Yet, one by one, they came, hesitantly at first for fear that they would be locked away once again, and then more readily as they grew confident in the reality of their freedom. They produced such realistic images of their liberator that he was lost for many hours reacquainting himself with them. He marveled at the vivid picture of Clary emerging from her seed-pod for the first time. He still found himself holding his breath as he gazed upon her beauty.

Their sweet conversations echoed in his ear, filling the empty walls of his heart with happiness once again. He watched too, as a man removed, the images of Tussock and Ranunculus as they snatched his love away. Then, the cloud of Clary's own rejection darkened his mind, forcing a rainstorm from his eyes that he had not expected. Yet he let each drop fall, at last escaping the tortured existence he had contrived for himself. He wept there, in Tussock's statue garden for the first time since he had been a seedling. He wept for his loss, his bitterness, his stubbornness, and his pride.

Clary had never been his lover, though he had certainly desired to advance their relationship to that level. She, however, had been his best friend, his only true friend. He loved her more than anyone or anything he had ever known. She showed him the truth of Tussock's cruelty even when the darkness permeated to his very core. When she rejected his profession of love, he had abandoned her, retreating to seal the cracks in his broken heart with bitterness toward anyone or anything that crossed his way. Now, at death's door and fearing the permanent loss of his beloved Clary, he re-opened the cracks, chipping away at the bitterness until only the raw emotion of sadness remained.

Then, he slowly cemented the cracks closed again with love as he retraced the long journey of his life, memory by memory. He even managed to add a dab of cement out of love for Ranunculus, who had accepted Bindweed despite his bitterness. He had given him a home when he had nowhere to go. He had not judged him because of his past, but he had treated him as an equal. Oh, that things could have been different. He may have counted Ranunculus as a friend, but now he had only to wait – to wait for the chance to right a wrong he should have corrected long ago – to restore a friendship that should have weathered the storm of rejection. He listened. He relished his memories. And he waited, alone.

Chapter Twenty-Seven
A Call to Arms

The first phase of their plan had gone better than they had hoped. Valerian masterfully redirected the Black Hole, while other Free Frats disengaged the sensors around the planets. From the surfaces of the planets, the only sign that anything had taken place was ten seconds of darkness, ten seconds onlookers may have missed if they happened to close their eyes for a moment at just the right time. That was not the case, however. The inhabitants of each planet had been warned, and they had been waiting, eyes fixed toward the sky. An instant of darkness confirmed their deepest fears, fears they hoped had been unwarranted, fears they hoped to evaporate in the continuous stream of sunshine. Instead, ten seconds, ten long seconds of complete darkness, released a downpour of trepidation upon their serenity. They were at war.

Within the hour, the large prisoner vessels arrived, the great bulk of which amazed them. No one had seen anything bigger than a four-man pod, and some had never even seen that. Now, a vessel large enough to transport one thousand men was landing on each of the three planets. Crofton had thanked the stars when he learned that each vessel was also manned by Free Frats. They had a contingency plan in place, but he was grateful that had worked out in their favor. He trusted his Free Frats with his life, and now he was entrusting them with the lives of millions of people.

The Free Frats noted the disdain and hesitation with which they were regarded. The people of these planets, so foreign to them, had been taught to hate and fear Noxians, though Noxians had never committed a crime against them. In fact, their ancestors had once saved the entire planetary system from the Thrip invasion. The Free Frats, however, had no time to assuage any tentativeness. Time was of the essence, so they simply deferred to the leaders of each planet to board the vessels with the men who had volunteered to risk their lives to save those they loved most. The Free Frats, though insulted by their cool reception, respected the courage of the volunteers and were happy to be acquainted with them.

All pods left at varying times so they would reach Noxia simultaneously. When they landed, Crofton wasn't exactly sure what to expect as far as a welcoming party. They had ceased communication with the Noxian planet surface as a precaution, just in case the Black Hole were to pick up their frequency. Only in an emergency was anyone to use his communicator, and they had not received a transmission from the ground team. He had given Rue and the captains of the other forces external communicators as well, so they could lead their forces more effectively, if it came to that. He anticipated that all the Elite Guards had been summoned, and a small portion of the regular Guard - just enough to strike fear into the heart of the prisoners. Tussock surely wouldn't be expecting a fight from the prisoners since they should still be in shock from the unfolding events.

Crofton hoped that Tussock himself would greet them. There would be fewer lives lost if that were the case since they could simply capture him, eliminate his loyalists, and free the people. He knew deep within, however, that Tussock wasn't going to be overtaken that easily. Since Crofton was supposed to be dead, Ky, who had been assigned to escort the prisoner vessels to the planet's surface, emerged from the Noxian pod first. Surveying the situation, he gave Crofton a shake of the head, indicating that Tussock was not present. Since Crofton's first plan of overtaking Tussock had not played out in his favor, he was going to have to try to recruit the members of the Guard who were there in Tussock's absence. If they would join with the Free Frats, they would be better able to capture Tussock. By tapping his finger to his arm, Ky indicated to Crofton that four thousand had gathered to retrieve the prisoners. Most likely they were to form a barrier around the prisoners as they took them within the border walls.

Crofton stepped out of the pod behind Ky. He heard a few gasps from those in the Noxian Guard who recognized him and had probably heard that he had been killed. He signaled to the other Free Frats to open the prisoner vessels by extending his arm into the air with a closed fist, which he then quickly opened. The doors opened, and three thousand men piled out, their weapons hidden from view. The Noxian Guard tensed as they emerged, unsure what to expect. Those who had recognized Crofton were confused by his presence as the commander, and they sensed that something wasn't right. The pods were to have landed one at a time, not all at once.

"What's going on? What are you doing here?" The voice of Charlock, the Chief Guard, broke the strained silence. He was loyal to Tussock in every way.

"There's been a change of plans, Charlock. I've come back from the dead, and I've decided there will be no prisoners. We're here to set them free," Crofton stated calmly. Charlock laughed.

"Very funny, Crofton. Tussock will be glad you've returned, although I was told your DNA remains were found in the wreckage on Quamir."

"There was a slight miscalculation on Tussock's part, and I'm not joking Charlock."

"But you've brought the prisoners, and the Black Hole is already doing its damage as I'm sure you know."

"It appears then, that I know more than you do this time, Charlock. And these are not the prisoners to whom I am referring," Crofton replied stoically as he raised his hand again. The prisoners brandished their weapons, and a rumble was heard throughout the Noxian Guard as they tightened their grips on their own weapons.

"You stupid fool," Charlock sneered as he raised his ray gun toward Crofton. Rue had been listening inside the vessel and finally emerged when he saw Crofton's sign. He came out just as Charlock aimed and instinctively fired his cryostatic light ray. Charlock fell with a thud to the ground as several members of the Elite Guard rushed toward his frozen body. Charlock had not given the command to raise their arms, so the Guard stood, stunned.

"He is not dead, I assure you," Crofton confirmed. "I do not employ the same methods as Tussock, but I do have a proposition for you. Join with me to fight Tussock. Your hearts are not in this war. You fight to protect your families from Tussock not from the rest of the Florenci System. Would you have these men endure the same fate that you have? Would you have them watch their families be cruelly punished for nonsensical crimes they did not commit? Would you really wish that upon another? They have freedom on their planets. They are here to share that freedom with you because in reality, you are the prisoners. They have left their homes to free you from Tussock – to free your families. Join us!" Crofton looked into the eyes of the members of Tussock's army who stood on the front lines, daring another loyalist to fire on him with his glare.

"You serve out of fear," he shouted. "I refuse to let fear determine my future. Join me, and we will be free!" There wasn't a blink. The troops stood still. Tussock's chill laugh shattered the reflective silence from a distance. *Too soon*, Crofton thought to himself. *I only needed a few more minutes alone with them.* No one dared to break rank. Their fear ran deep within their life forces, deeper than Crofton had expected. The odds were not in Crofton's favor anymore. That much was clear.

To join him and lose would mean either certain death or a lifetime of torture for each soldier and his family as well. It was a risk none was willing to take. The sound of Tussock's cruel laugh was enough to make their courage falter, and they stood their ground, muscles tensed, eyes averted from Crofton's defiant stare. He couldn't quite understand their reluctance. He was willing to give his life rather than live under tyranny, but they were satisfied with the status quo, willing to live their lives in fear and desperation.

"They are not willing to pay freedom's price, rat," Tussock's thickly accented voice bellowed with a hint of delight at the unfolding events.

"Then, they will die cowards at their own hands. They will secure a bleak future for those they think they are protecting. Someone will suffer for the treachery that has been committed here today. You'll make sure of that Tussock! At least five hundred will suffer by my estimation. Maybe it will be you," Crofton said, pointing at a soldier in the front, "or you." He pointed to a soldier two rows back who shifted uncomfortably. "And if not today, then maybe tomorrow or next week. Be assured, your time will come. You are only a pawn in this demented game he plays. He doesn't care about you or your families, but I do. I'm willing to die for you, right here and right now. I've put my life on the line for you. We've done the impossible for you by uniting the entire Florenci System. Don't you see what's at stake here?"

"Groveling doesn't suit you, Crofton. I bestowed my highest honors on you only to have you stab me in the back. And I had such hopes for you too. At one time, I even thought you worthy to be my son, fatherless rogue that you are." Tussock had sauntered through the ranks as he spoke, coming almost face to face with Crofton except for a member of the Elite Guard he was using as a shield. He, therefore, saw the flicker of fear that crossed Crofton's face as he mentioned his connection to Ambulia, who was safe inside the second pod that had served as an escort. The emotion only surfaced for a second, but a fatal second it was. A horn blew in the distance, calling to all guardsmen to assemble themselves.

"Ah, interesting," Tussock scratched his chin as he spoke. "And I thought she was mourning the unfortunate death of her mother all this time, but instead she's been consorting with the enemy. Well, well, well. These are difficult times, are they not? But... you've caught me in a generous mood today. You've shown great ingenuity in all that you've accomplished – a trait I greatly admire. With a little humility, you can still be a great leader among the Noxian realm. Yes, be assured this little stunt will not thwart my plans to assert my influence beyond the confines of this small planet. I am willing, however, to negotiate with a great mind like yours. It would be a terrible thing to lose. Surrender without a fight right now, and you will be my new Chief Guard. Of course, I will expect you to marry my daughter as I see that she is the key to controlling that rebellious side of yours. I'll grant you another favor as well. I'll allow you to be the Punisher of those that must suffer the consequences for your brash little outburst. It seems only fair that you dole out the punishment for your faithful followers, doesn't it? I am a man of equity after all." Tussock paused for a moment as if to give Crofton time to contemplate the offer. "What say you, Crofton?"

"I have a better idea, Tussock. Why don't you and I settle our differences man to man – me against you? Winner takes all," Crofton offered with a smile that gave even Tussock an unsettled feeling.

"That would never do. I don't care much for hand-to-hand combat myself. I believe in an even playing field, well, maybe slightly in my favor," he scanned the gathering troops that were responding to his call. "I see I must withdraw my proposition as it is a war you want. If you would rather spill the life force of your own brothers on both sides to prove your point, you can have it your way. But be assured this was your call, not mine. These men are my witnesses. I tried to negotiate peace, but you would rather kill."

"Your kind of war is far more gruesome than mine, Tussock. You separate people from their hope, and you sever them from their souls. You enslave them with your fear and hold their happiness hostage. You take away from them what they value most for your own gratification. You started this war with your cruelty and insatiable desire for power, but I'm going to finish it. Prepare for battle," he shouted, and then he turned toward his meager forces and called out, "To arms!"

"As you wish," Tussock whispered before returning to his place behind the ranks. Crofton returned to the group, who did not need to hear his exchange with Tussock to know that Crofton's recruitment effort had not gone as planned. Most of them had already mentally prepared themselves for the possibility of failure since it seemed an alliance was beyond hope.

"I'm sorry. I underestimated them. Just a few more minutes, and I think I could have swayed them," Crofton confessed to the captains that had gathered around him.

"There were no guarantees, Crofton. We all knew that," Rue reassured him. "Now, to the battle at hand."

Crofton's troops had received a crash course in Noxian battle tactics, as well as the Noxian terrain upon which they would be fighting. Their positions had already been predetermined since they knew exactly where the prisoner vessels had been instructed to land. The Rocky Ridge, which formed a wall from their left to their rear, was filled with caves and rocks, perfect for hiding and shielding themselves from those they were to fight. The downfall was that there was nowhere to retreat as they could not climb over the Rocky Ridge without special equipment.

To their right was the Gorge of Grief. No Noxian would enter the gorge as it was forbidden unless one was in mourning. In front of them lay a flat terrain, from which the Noxians would be fighting. This area extended toward Tussock's border walls. Tussock would be seated on the throne made from carefully positioned rocks that sat along the border wall. Crofton's men would have to push the Noxian troops backward, so the Free Frats could sneak on the periphery of the fighting to get to Tussock. The Free Frats who had been among the Elite Guard and guardsmen had already withdrawn themselves to Crofton's side, except for Murain, who was assigned to protect Clary at all costs.

The battle would not commence until Tussock blew the horn, and in that at least, Crofton would comply since it gave his troops a chance to group. The Free Frats were organized into groups of one hundred, each having its own captain. The captains had taken their hundred to their specified places and still the horn had not sounded.

"Crofton," Thor pulled him aside. "If Tussock knows that Ambulia is among us, he will surely send a group of Elite Guardsman to hunt her down."

"Yes, I know. Thor, I need you to take her to the Gorge of Grief. It's the only place she'll be safe until this is over. You go with her and protect her. If this goes badly...well...take her to Asa-en-Darah in the pod. She'll be safe there at least. I know it's not fair of me to ask that of you, but please...take care of her," Crofton petitioned.

"You know I will. I'll take the route by the Caverns. There should be enough fighting in front of us that we won't be noticed. She's safe with me," Thor assured him, gripping Crofton's forearm before he turned toward Ambulia.

"No!" Ambulia shouted. "I won't go. I won't leave you. You can't tell me what to do. You can't make me leave you!"

"I'm not telling you what to do, I'm asking you to go...for me. I must know you're safe," he bent down to kiss her as Thor looked away from the one thing he would never have. The horn blew. Thor quickly grabbed Ambulia's arm, but she did not resist.

Rue hunched behind a rock formation, his hundred occupying the section of the Rocky Ridge directly in firing range of the Noxians. He gripped his cryostatic light ray with a sweaty palm as he watched the Noxian ranks move forward. He was not too proud to admit that he was more scared than he had ever been in his life. As he waited, he found courage intermingling with the fear until it had overtaken it. He felt his life force, his Eudoran life force, course through his body, and he knew that he had been born for this. He squared his shoulders and fired.

Chapter Twenty-Eight
A Descent into Darkness

Pili flew the pod in silence. In fact, nobody spoke. They were each pondering exactly what they would do when they landed. Betony needed a plan - something she could do - something she alone could do. She knew so little of Crofton's plans, but she recalled hearing more than once that their forces were too few unless they could recruit some of Tussock's men. Had they been successful? What had happened? What would they find when they landed? Pili's communicator had ceased working after they received word that the Black Hole had been shut down. Pili tried to find the new frequency they were using on the planet's surface, but to no avail.

"Approachim Noxia," Pili reported. "Where goim?" She felt a great pressure resting on her heart. *Something she alone could do.* She was a healer. That was her gift. Rue needed an army. That was what he lacked. The answer came like a bolt of lightning streaking across a dark sky.

"To the Pit," Betony answered. A look of horror crossed Pili's face.

"But why would you want to go there?" Yerba spoke the words the others were thinking.

"That is where I must go. It's the only place I can be of any use. Pili, you must take me to the Pit. You know the way, don't you?"

"Not takim youim there," Pili protested adamantly.

"Yerba, Calden. Do you know the way?" she persisted. They reluctantly nodded their heads.

"Good. You can lead me there. Pili, you can stay with StarThistle then." Pili looked at her angrily, but steered the pod onward.

A short time later, the pod sputtered to a stop on the planet's surface, unnoticed by anyone on the ground given the commotion that was already under way and the fact that Noxians were accustomed to Space Patrols launching and landing continuously throughout the course of a day. StarThistle had fallen asleep on Yerba's lap, and Betony could tell by the longing in her eyes that she would not be persuaded to leave her daughter in search of the Pit. Betony looked once again at Pili, but he stared back at her with his arms crossed, shaking his head. Calden was her only hope.

"Calden, are you ready?" He looked to Pili and then to Yerba. Yerba urged him on with a nod.

"I promised to help, and if you're sure this is the only way to help, then I'll lead you to the Pit," he finally relented.

"I've never been more positive about anything in my life," she assured him. Pili turned his back to them in disgust. Betony felt a pang of regret that she had overridden Pili's judgment, but she could see no other way. She turned to follow Calden, her heart pounding in fear that they would be discovered before they reached the Pit. She still wasn't exactly sure what she would do once they arrived, but she knew that Pit was where she needed to be. It was almost as if it was calling to her.

They had to sneak through the border walls, avoiding all paths commonly used, although the streets were mostly empty because many had gathered to watch the battle at the north border wall. Betony was surprised by the amount of light within the border walls. There were lamps every few feet, powered by stored solar energy. An hour later, they approached the Pit's entrance, a small dark opening in the ground.

"Here it is. At least this is the only opening I know of that can be accessed without being seen," he whispered.

"Thank you, Calden. No one will be looking for me in here, so you can go back to Yerba and StarThistle. Keep them safe, and feel free to return to Eudora in the pod. No one will think any less of you," she instructed.

"Good luck to you. May the stars smile brightly on whatever it is you are about to do," he offered as he turned to go.

Betony peered into the hole. She was on her own, battling the darkness once and for all. After a deep breath, she began to lower herself into the opening when she felt rough hands pull her back. Her heart became a sinking rock in a pond of disappointment as she realized she had just been caught.

"No goim withoutim meim," whispered the voice belonging to the arms. She turned around and punched Pili in the arm, although he didn't flinch.

"You scared me half to death! I thought I'd been captured," she exclaimed in hushed tones. Pili smiled at her, and she couldn't resist the urge to hug him for a brief moment as her fear subsided in his presence.

"Thank you for coming," she whispered up at him.

"I goim firstim. Helpim you," he instructed quietly as he dropped his bulky body into the small hole. A few seconds passed, and Betony was worried he had gotten stuck.

"Comim," his voice echoed up to her. She slowly let herself down into the tunnel that would lead to the Pit of Punishment, Tussock's personal lair of evil.

Chapter Twenty-Nine
A Rocky Ridge Indeed

Thor walked as fast as he could with Ambulia over the Rocky Ridge, his cryostatic light ray armed and ready to fire at anyone he happened across. Their progress was slow and frustrating as they swerved around boulders and cracks. He held tightly to her hand, using his body to shield her from any potential attackers. He knew Tussock too well to let his guard down. He would want his daughter back at any cost, not because he loved her, but because he wanted to make an example of her treachery.

"We've got to stop so I can catch my breath," Ambulia pleaded.

"We can't stop until we get to the Gorge," Thor said.

"Thor, please," she begged.

"Fine, but just for a second," he ducked into a dark cavern. Ambulia sat down, panting. Her pants had been torn on the jagged edges of the rocks, and her palms were scraped from breaking her falls when she stumbled. Her face was dusted with dirt, and the knot of braids at the nape of her neck had come loose, so several braids danced around her face. Thor still saw her as a picture of beauty. He stood guard while she caught her breath.

"Here, drink some water," he advised, offering her the leather water jug he had slung around his neck. She did as he directed.

"Thor," she started to say, but Thor heard noise nearby and held up his hand to silence her. He peeked his head out to make sure the way was clear.

"Hurry, we've got to go," he grabbed her hand again, wishing their circumstances were different. Young Noxians often hung out at the Caverns with their friends, and Thor had known more than one Betrothal to take place along this very path. He glanced over his shoulder at the flat terrain that was now swarming with the dark figures of Tussock's army. He looked to the Rocky Ridge at their small band, and he knew that the situation was hopeless. There was no way anyone would be able to break through to the side to capture Tussock. His forces were too strong. He cursed under his breath. How could he possibly keep Ambulia safe from all this? Once the Noxians were swarming the Rocky Ridge, there would be no escape from the Gorge. He paused.

"What's wrong?" Ambulia asked.

"We can't go to the Gorge," he observed.

"But why?"

"We'll be trapped there once Tussock takes the Ridge. We won't be able to get out, and I can't protect you in there."

"Where do we go?"

"We have to get to a pod."

"What? I'm not leaving Noxia, not without Crofton."

"Ambulia, look out there. We aren't going to win this. Crofton will be killed or punished, and you'll be right alongside him. I can't let that happen. He told me to take you to Asa-en-Darah, and that's exactly what I'm going to do."

"Thor, that's ridiculous. We'll never make it to the pod."

"We can. We just have to look like we're fighting on Tussock's side, that's all. Tuck your hair inside your tunic, and keep your head down. Once we're on the periphery, we'll fall in with the troops. They haven't seen me yet, so they won't know I'm with Crofton." Ambulia looked toward the spot she had last seen Crofton, but he was gone from view. She knew Thor had made his mind up, and he would force her to go along with him, so she decided not to protest. She would follow him, waiting for the opportune moment to steal his cryostatic light ray. Thor had been her rock through all of this, but she was not leaving Noxia without Crofton.

"Fine," she relented. She gave in too easily, however, and Thor knew she was scheming again. She couldn't overpower him though, and he wouldn't let her run away, so he started toward the edge of the Gorge. His plan seemed sound, and there was so much confusion around them that it appeared it just might work. He had not, however, anticipated running into his brother, BuckThorn. Thor and his brother could not have been more dissimilar, as BuckThorn was as loyal to Tussock as a moon was to its orbit. It was BuckThorn who had been charged with finding Ambulia, and it was BuckThorn who found her. She was crouched behind a bit of shrubbery, while Thor was plotting their course to the pod when she heard someone approaching.

"Brother," BuckThorn called out in greeting as he spotted Thor. He was accompanied by two men from the Elite Guard. "What are you doing over here? I thought you were on Space Patrol duty."

"Buck," Thor acknowledged him nervously. He scooted the cryostatic light ray toward Ambulia before standing up from his squatting position. "I came in just last night. I was so tired, I didn't even check in, and with all the chaos this morning..."

"Why aren't you in the ranks, then?"

257

"Oh, I thought I'd sneak up this way to see if I could take a few rebels out from behind. Maybe even Crofton himself, if I can get my hands on him," Thor said, but he had chosen his words poorly for Buck looked to his hands and saw no weapon.

"Where is your weapon, brother?" he asked suspiciously.

"I left it in the brush over there. I had to relieve myself, you know, and you can't really do that with a weapon in your hand, now can you?" Thor laughed unpersuasively.

"You're one of them, aren't you?" BuckThorn stepped toward his brother. Ambulia didn't know what to do. There were three of them, all armed with ray guns, and only one cryostatic light ray, which took several seconds to recharge after firing. BuckThorn grabbed Thor by the neck, not even flinching as Thor's thorny collar dug into his hands.

"There will be no traitor from my house, BoxThorn!" he shouted, but Thor took the opportunity to kick the ray gun out of his brother's hand since he was now within close proximity. His brother was caught off guard, and Ambulia poked the cryostatic light ray through the bush, firing on the man next to BuckThorn who had raised his gun toward Thor. He fell instantly to the ground. Thor was still caught in his brother's stranglehold, struggling to free himself. The cryostatic light ray recharged, and Ambulia took aim again. She couldn't get a clear shot at BuckThorn, so she fired on the second man with a direct hit. He slumped to the ground. Thor momentarily broke free from BuckThorn and went for his brother's ray gun. BuckThorn, however, had already grabbed one of his comrade's ray guns and was aiming it at Thor. Ambulia's weapon was still recharging, and she knew she could not wait to make her move.

"Wait!" she called out, creeping out from behind the bush. "It's me you want, not him. I'll come with you, if you let him go." She held the cryostatic light ray to her side, hidden by her tunic.

"Oh, isn't that sweet?" BuckThorn mocked. "She's offering herself as ransom for you, brother! She is a tasty little morsel. No wonder you switched sides, and I daresay Tussock won't mind if I have a little taste before I escort her home." Thor was enraged at the threat, and he lunged toward his brother. Ambulia took aim, but she was too late. BuckThorn got his shot off a split second before she did. Thor fell to the ground followed by BuckThorn. Ambulia rushed to Thor's side.

"Thor," she felt tears stinging her eyes.

"Thor!" she screamed. He opened his eyes, barely able to cling to consciousness.

"I'm so sorry," he whispered through clenched teeth. "Go back. Find the Free Frats. I'm so sorry; I've failed you."

"Thor, don't leave me. Please, don't leave me. Please, hold on for me. You've been my rock all these years," she cried.

"You don't need me, Ambulia. You don't need me anymore." He raised his hand to brush the tears from her face, but found that he was too weak.

"No! Don't...don't say that."

"I would rather die for you than live without you," he managed to say.

"But I'm here, Thor. I'm right here," she reached for his hand as tears spilled down her face.

"I love you, Ambulia," he whispered.

"I love you, too," she echoed, her hands now holding his head.

"No. I *love* you. I will always love you. It's better this way. I couldn't have lived in Crofton's shadow any longer. He has the only thing I ever wanted...you."

"But –" she stammered as she stroked his bald head.

"Sh. You don't have to say anything. Just go. Please go. Don't let my death be in vain." She didn't move at his request. His eyes widened.

"Go!" he shouted with the last of his strength. "Just leave me. Now! If I had to die a thousand of these deaths, I would do it if it meant spending five years with you. I made my choice. Now go," he demanded as his eyes closed. A single tear slipped down his cheek. Ambulia gently rested his head on the ground, retrieved the three ray guns and ran toward the gorge, tears blurring her every step as her best friend lay dead.

The battle was not going well for the Free Frats. They were outnumbered and tiring quickly. Many of the men under Rue's command were badly injured, and the Noxians had managed to close ranks, forcing the Free Frats into a confined area. Rue saw Crofton fighting to his right. He was firing his cryostatic light ray as quickly as it was able to recharge. Hidden by a rock, he scanned the vicinity to calculate his best strategy for attacking the advancing forces. He saw a Noxian, blocked from Crofton's view, carefully taking aim with a spear. Rue had noticed many of those they fought were only maiming their targets when they could have easily killed them. Crofton had been right, this was a battle they did not want to fight, but with courage and conviction failing, they fought for their ruthless leader, hoping to protect those they loved from torture when Crofton's small band of rebels had been beaten. They hoped to be rewarded for their apparent allegiance. Although, there were also those who relished bloodshed. They were loyal supporters of Tussock through and through.

Rue could tell by the smile on his face and the glimmer in his eye, that this Noxian, posed to strike Crofton, belonged to the latter group. Having frozen the last soldier to climb the rocky outcropping that hid him, Rue sprinted full-speed to Crofton's aid, shouting a warning as he ran. Crofton turned to look in his direction just as the spear was thrown. Rue jumped in an effort to deflect the spear, which was on course to strike Crofton in the heart. The spear penetrated Rue's left arm, sinking deep into his flesh. His body fell, full force on top of Crofton, who managed to freeze the Noxian loyalist before he could escape and re-arm.

Rue groaned in pain as Crofton hoisted him over his shoulder to carry him to safer ground. The spear was still protruding from his arm, being jostled with every quick step and hop Crofton took. He set Rue down in the first cave opening he found.

"That wasn't very smart," he muttered as he surveyed the wound.

"Saved your life though, didn't it?" Rue said.

"I'll give you that. Consider your tab settled with me," Crofton conceded.

"Not quite. You helped save me twice."

"But I didn't sustain any bodily harm in the process, Book Worm."

"And I thought we were passed all the conjecture. I thought our relationship had moved to the next level," Rue laughed, grateful to distract himself from the pain searing through his arm. "Besides, I think your girlfriend has proven herself much more worthy of the title of Book Worm." Crofton managed to laugh himself as he grabbed onto the spear.

"Brace yourself," he instructed as he pulled. Rue stifled his urge to cry out as the spear was retracted.

"Just a flesh wound," Rue noted through jagged breaths.

"Where's Betony when you need her?" Crofton mumbled.

"Safe on Eudora where she should be," Rue retorted as he tore his shirt off. "Here use this as a tourniquet." Crofton knotted the cloth tightly around Rue's arm, noting that Rue's solar suit had only been sliced where the spear had struck. The cloth would be enough to protect Rue from the sun-star. Rue rose shakily to his feet.

"Where do you think you're going?" Crofton demanded. "You'll get yourself killed if you go back out there in your condition."

"I'll get myself killed if I stay here too. One way or another I think it's time we came to terms with the fact that none of us will make it out of this life alive," he said with a twinkle in his eye.

"This is no joking matter, Rue. What's wrong with you?"

"It's my coping mechanism."

"Yeah right. As if the members of the Brotherhood have a sense of humor."

"You might be surprised."

"You probably wish you were still back on Traveriss after all this."

"Not really. I had no sense of purpose there aside from writhing in boredom. If I'm going to die, I want to die fighting for a cause I believe in – fighting for the cause I was born to fight. As for now, I can't just sit here watching my friends give their lives. We haven't lost this yet. I think it's time we call in the troops. Let's regroup."

"Now you're speaking my language," Crofton said, offering himself as a crutch under Rue's good arm. They stumbled to the top of the rock outcropping, and Crofton sounded the signal for his men to fall back. He sent a yellow flare into the darkened sky, a sign to Tussock that there was to be a temporary cease-fire.

"To the Gorge," he said into his wrist implant. Tussock himself shot an orange flare into the sky, signaling his men to fall back, as he watched what remained of Crofton's rebels withdraw.

"I expect a full surrender within the hour," Tussock laughed triumphantly.

As the men gathered in the Gorge, Rue tried to maintain his optimism at the sight of their diminished numbers. Many were badly injured like himself. What could Crofton possibly say to rally his troops? He kept a watchful eye for Valerian, whom he had lost sight of within the first few minutes of fighting. The minutes passed slowly as he scanned the horizon. Then he saw it - a movement from the corner of his eye. He squinted. Valerian's proud figure and slight limp were unmistakable. He had managed to maintain his position while everyone else was forced deeper into the Rocky Ridge. Valerian's scarred face came into view, and then the weary faces of his hundred materialized. Not one man had been lost in his battalion. Rue wished he could say the same for his own hundred, of which only fifty remained. He hugged his friend as he stopped beside him.

"So, is it true? We're surrendering?" Valerian asked sharply, pushing Rue away. "I didn't come here just to give up!"

"Of course we're not surrendering," Crofton countered. "Tussock only wants to believe that. He'll have to kill every last one of us." Valerian relaxed at the assurance.

"Doesn't seem as though his men are much for killing. Otherwise, we'd have been wiped out in the first few minutes. They could have easily defeated us by now," a Quamirian soldier observed.

"I tried to tell you. They want to believe in our cause, but they're too afraid to fight with us. Apparently, we didn't look formidable enough to win. They think they're protecting their families by appearing to remain loyal to Tussock. Tussock knows as well as we do that their hearts aren't in it. He only allows this battle to draw on because it amuses him."

"So, do we have a plan?" Valerian asked, but before Crofton could answer, a pod entered the atmosphere. Crofton's troops gathered at the mouth of the Gorge. A mere quarter of a mile separated them from the first line of Tussock's forces. The pod landed directly in between the two groups, coming to rest amid the shrubbery and rocks. The hatch opened slowly.

Chapter Thirty
A Matter of Reunions

Four men stepped out of the pod: Stephanotis, Lisianthus, Galax, and Aster. They were not adorned in the robes they typically wore on Traveriss; instead, they were donning their native clothing, armed with queer weapons. Rue noted the absence of Ranunculus, Bindweed, and Lamium. The four surveyed the scene before them, surprised to find bodies strewn across the battlefield, some of which were merely frozen. Stephanotis found Rue and directed the others toward him.

"I see we've come just in time," Stephanotis observed as he approached.

"Too late for too many," Crofton muttered, tallying their losses as he looked around them in disgust.

"Well, we were detained, you might say. Lucky we've come at all," Aster said bitterly, thrusting his hand to the scabs on his throat. Their conversation was interrupted by the sound of a space glider entering the atmosphere. It touched down near the pod Stephanotis had flown, and Lamium, his robes flowing in the slight breeze, emerged. Rue knew the instant he saw his arrogant swagger that he was staring at the traitor of the Brotherhood, the murderer of his people. A cold chill chased the information down his spine, and his finger twitched on the trigger of his cryostatic light ray. He had been waiting for this particular confrontation.

"Surprised to see me?" Rue asked as Lamium approached him.

"Not you, no! I assumed you were alive when I found the Ancient on Eudora," he smugly replied.

"You were on Eudora?" Panic broke through Rue's once calm and confident demeanor, and Lamium knew he had the upper hand for now.

"Certainly. You didn't think you were the only one with a claim to the throne, did you, Uncle?" His voice was filled with scorn and mockery.

"You have no claim to anything," Rue said.

"Oh, don't I? We shall see about that, won't we? By the way, your little Ancient – she is a fireball, isn't she?"

"What have you done?" Rue asked through gritted teeth.

"The better question would be what haven't I done?" Lamium sneered, distorting his face into a grimace of evil. He turned his back to Rue before he could demand any further information. Turning to Stephanotis, he said, "I am, however, surprised to find you here." Stephanotis smiled, unaffected by Lamium's sudden air of superiority.

"You did feel entomology beneath you. 'A lesser species hardly worth my time,' I believe you once said to me. How wrong you were, as usual, for one lowly insect may very well be your own demise," Stephanotis taunted. For a moment, Lamium lost his composure.

"But I killed that creature with my own hands – one swipe of a sword and his head went rolling. He's surely dead!"

"Maybe. Maybe not," Stephanotis replied with a smile.

"I've had enough of this. I'll deal with you later," Lamium twirled in the direction of the north border wall.

"You can count on it," Stephanotis responded under his breath. Rue raised his cryostatic light ray, but Lamium had disappeared from view before he could pull the trigger. He had failed in stopping his foe from joining with Tussock. Rue buried his face in hands. Stephanotis walked to him, placing a hand on his shoulder.

"I thought she would be safe on Eudora," Rue could barely speak. All of his plans seemed to be crumbling before him.

"Rue, don't take to heart everything Lamium says. He's a man whose tongue is defiled by deceit. Did you leave her locked in the castle?" Rue had forgotten Stephanotis had been part of the planetary summits held on Eudora during his father's reign. Of course, he would know about the castle.

"Yes," Rue affirmed.

"Then, she's safe. Even if Lamium was able to find the castle, without a key, he could not get in," Stephanotis reassured him. "You need to keep your head in the here and now. By my estimation, we're in a tight spot - sorely outnumbered by what 100 to 1?"

"Something like that."

"If I may," Galax interrupted. "I did notice Lamium landed in a space glider. I wonder what happened to the pod he took from Traveriss." Stephanotis glared at him.

"Probably rendezvoused with his cohorts. It is a Noxian space glider, is it not?"

"There were Noxian space gliders on Eudora," Rue said, worry shadowing his blue eyes once again.

"Rue," Stephanotis mused, "whatever has happened is done. It cannot be changed now. We can only look forward from here, and from what I see we have our hands full enough."

"She was right. Death seems to be hunting us," Rue acknowledged to himself. "We'll just have to see if we can evade it one more time."

"May I make an observation?" Galax asked, but before Stephanotis could stop him, he blurted out, "Lamium did use the present tense when referring to the Ancient. He said 'she is' not 'she was.' Details, details. It's all in the details." Galax was pleased with himself.

"Too true, brother," Stephanotis breathed a sigh of relief.

"Thank you, Galax," Rue said, happy to have the support of those who were closest to him – the remaining members of the Brotherhood. They were certainly not groomed soldiers ready to wage war, but Rue couldn't have picked a more loyal band.

"By the way, where's Bindweed?" Rue asked.

"Probably dead somewhere, the old dolt. When Ranunculus received word that Clary had gone missing, Bindweed flew off in a pod before the antidote arrived, not that any of us knew there was an antidote. Now, there's a story for you, another time, of course. Anyway, Bindweed was headed here, but we don't know if he made it. If he did, the poison has surely gotten him by now."

"So, you know about Clary?" Rue asked in disbelief.

"We do now. Too many secrets aren't good for one planetary system to bear," Stephanotis was alluding to Rue's true origins, but Rue merely shrugged his shoulders.

"And where is Ranunculus exactly?"

"He's just behind us with Prey. He insisted on coming alone for some reason." As if on cue, another pod entered the atmosphere. It circled the vicinity twice, before landing near the border wall where Tussock was conferring with his newly appointed Chief Guard.

"That has to be Ranunculus. He clearly miscalculated the landing though," Aster observed, but Rue had a sneaking suspicion Ranunculus had landed exactly where he intended to land.

"I'm going in for a closer look," Rue said. "Cover me." All four members of the Brotherhood flanked him, as well as Crofton and Valerian, as they crept toward the border wall.

"Prey, you stay here," Ranunculus commanded, although he might as well have issued an open invitation for Prey to follow him. Prey waited until Run-dung was barely visible before he crept out of the pod. Disguising himself was no problem in the grayness of the Noxian day, and besides he had built-in camouflage that automatically changed with his surroundings. He followed Run-Dung at a distance, though he wasn't sure exactly why he was putting himself in danger.

He also couldn't shake the feeling that he was being followed and watched. He'd first felt the strange sensation when he landed on Traveriss, but it had steadily strengthened since then. Even with his amplified visual abilities, he could detect nothing, but the feeling persisted, as did his uneasiness. He watched as Ranunculus walked confidently toward Tussock. Run-Dung stopped with a mere ten feet separating him from his archenemy.

"I hope I'm not too late for the festivities," he said to a very surprised Tussock, who thought Lamium had taken care of Ranunculus and the Brotherhood.

"I'm just now assembling the guests of honor, though I didn't think I'd have the pleasure of your company," Tussock replied coolly. He nodded his head, and Murain came forward with Clary. "I believe you two are acquainted."

"Let her go, Tussock," Ranunculus demanded.

"Your commands mean nothing here, old friend. Clary has merely been returned to her rightful home. This little battle is nothing more than a welcome home party." Tussock reached for Clary's arm so he could drag her closer to him, but Murain stepped in the way. One look at Murain's expression of defiance, and Tussock knew where his allegiance lay.

"You will not touch her," Murain said.

"Another traitor, I see," Tussock replied and at the same instant with lightning quick speed, he grabbed Murain's weapon, twisting it toward its owner while Murain's finger was still on the trigger. Murain's eyes were wide with surprise.

"You can die for your cause right now, and I'll deal with your family later," Tussock shouted for all to hear as he pushed Murain's finger, depressing the trigger. As he released the pressure, a burst of light was seen. Murain let out a groan of pain and fell, twitching, onto the ground. Ranunculus raised his own gun, the orange glow indicated that it was set to kill, but before he could pull the trigger, Tussock grabbed Clary. She now stood between Tussock and Run-Dung's glowing laser – a human shield.

"Do it now, mighty Ranunculus! Pull the trigger," prodded Tussock.

"He'll never do it, but I certainly will," Lamium said from behind Tussock. Tussock's face suddenly paled at the sound of the familiar voice. He had not seen the occupant of the space glider, assuming the pilot to be another Free Frat who had unknowingly secured his own death.

"You incompetent idiot. Someone like you can never be trusted to rule this planetary system with all your recent blunders," Lamium reprimanded Tussock in front of the onlookers as if he were a seedling.

"My blunders? It seems to me Ranunculus should already be dead, unless he tapped into the powers of resurrection recently." Lamium dismissed the comment, though rage flared in his eyes.

"I warned you, Tussock. I gave you a second chance," Lamium said.

"Who gave you the right to determine who's worthy to live and die Lamium?" Ranunculus queried. "That is no one's right to bestow. You entered my circle under false pretenses. I was blinded by the great fossil plants you brought to me from the outer reaches of galaxies unknown to me. I was deceived, so preoccupied by the great scientific discoveries you offered, that I could not see you for what you were. You played to my greatest weakness – the great prospect of science and the unknown, and I succumbed to your charms. Blinded by science as so often I am." Run-Dung glanced sorrowfully at Clary, but she wasn't listening. Instead, her wide eyes were scanning the area. She had perceived Ranunculus's memories and knew now that Bindweed might be close at hand. She was frantically searching for him as Ranunculus continued.

"Is there nothing genuine about you aside from your hatred?" The events that took place next happened so quickly Prey had a difficult time piecing everything together. First, there was a noise unlike anything Prey had heard before – a groan of pain or a beastly roar. Prey couldn't tell which.

All eyes turned in the direction of the noise, save two. With Ranunculus distracted, Lamium fired his weapon with a direct hit. As Ranunculus's finger was still on the trigger of his weapon, the sudden jolt caused him to inadvertently squeeze it. Prey followed the burst of light as if in slow motion. It was headed straight for Clary, but just before impact, a staggering figure leaped into view, pushing Clary out of the way. The burst of light grazed the figure hurtling through the air. A startled Tussock had been knocked off balance as Clary was pushed out of his grasp and lay on the ground. The burst of light was still seeking a target; a feature Ranunculus had designed himself. Lamium, who had maintained his position during the commotion, saw only a flash of light before his lights went out forever. All of this happened in the blink of an eye. Thankfully, Prey did not have to blink his many eyes, so he was the silent witness to it all.

Tussock rose to his feet to investigate the aftermath, but more particularly to learn the identity of the man who had risked his life to save Clary. He didn't have to search far. Clary was stooping beside the body of a dying Bindweed. Tussock glanced behind him to see Lamium's lifeless body slumped on the ground. He was relieved that the only man he feared lay dead. This knowledge bolstered his confidence as did the fact that the only man who could possibly secure victory for the opposition lay struggling to breathe in front of him. Tussock decided to let him suffer the last few moments before his death. He hoped he might even catch the demise of the Ancient he so treasured.

"Bindweed, you came for me," Clary whispered while stroking his head. "My Weedeater came for me." Bindweed struggled to open his eyes at the sound of Clary's pet name for him.

"Oh, Bindweed. I'm so sorry. I was so foolish, and then too scared to come to you. I couldn't face your rejection if you had closed the door on me forever. I do love you, my dear Weedeater, more than you will ever know." The look in his eyes told her that his love had grown over the time and distance they had been apart. Never had his bitterness been directed at her. He was too weak to respond, but he didn't have to. Now that he was in her presence, she knew his every memory. She bent down to kiss him as he struggled to cling to life for a precious few more seconds with her.

"Now, isn't this sweet?" Tussock interrupted their reunion. "I've been looking forward to seeing you again too, Bindweed. I have something to give you that's far overdue," he raised his gun to finish his nemesis off before Lamium's poison could claim its victory. Clary, however, had anticipated his move, and she bent forward again to kiss Bindweed. The moment her lips touched his, there was an explosion of light that could be seen even from the Gorge of Grief, where the Free Frats waited nervously. Tussock stumbled backward. When the light dissipated, Clary and Bindweed were gone. Prey watched the entire exchange with interest.

Chapter Thirty-One
A Farewell

Rue rushed to Ranunculus's side, protected by his armed escort.

"Rue, my boy! I knew you'd come through this okay," Ranunculus whispered.

"Ranunculus, what were you thinking?"

"I was trying to right a wrong – finish what I should have finished long ago when Tussock was less powerful, but I've failed miserably, haven't I? I usually do at things of most importance, like you, my boy."

"Why didn't you tell me?"

"I didn't want the past to define you – to define who you became. I didn't want anger to fester in your heart, destroying all that is good in there. Even the strongest man can crumble under such a load. Look what it did to Lamium – poisoned him, it did – ruined him. I didn't want your life to be tainted by want of revenge, but I'm afraid I failed to fill the void I left by not telling you. I thought I might bear the burden of being the Great Unifier, but it was not meant for me. I failed you, my boy, failed you. This is all my fault."

"No, it is my destiny. You simply prepared me to face it. It's always been my fight. You did what you thought was best."

"At least I didn't stifle your nobility," Ranunculus tried to laugh. "Your father was a good and trusted friend. I was lucky I happened across you, but I never counted myself worthy to raise you. The science of the heart is most complicated. One such as I could never master it, although, I admit, my attempts were feeble at best. I fear I shall only be remembered as the man whose quick dismissal of two young minds seeking help created two of the worst monsters this planetary system has ever known. Had I not been so brash...had I taken them under my wing...I may have averted this whole crisis...At least I could have kept an eye on them. But that is that. Rue, I'm not half the man your father was, but please know that I loved you like my own – in my own way. Remember me for that, my boy." His voice was nothing more than a whisper.

Rue was too choked up to reply to his mentor. He simply nodded his head and gathered Ranunculus's frail body up into his arms in the tender embrace of a son to his father. It was the first, last, and only embrace they ever shared as Ranunculus mustered enough of his remaining strength to squeeze back before his arms fell limp to the ground. Rue took one last look at Ranunculus's face, a look of peace lingering on his familiar features. Rue closed the old man's eyelids for the last time and tried to hoist the lifeless body over his shoulder, so he could carry him to safer ground until he could return him to Traveriss.

So much worse was the pain of his grief-stricken heart, he had almost forgotten about the pain radiating from his wounded arm. He buckled under the extra weight, weakened by the loss of his life force. Valerian rushed forward and carefully lifted Ranunculus's lifeless body, cradling him in his arms, a lone tear escaping his rapid blinks. Crofton helped Rue to his feet, allowing him to lean on him as they turned to go.

"We will finish this, Crofton!" Tussock shouted. It was too bad they couldn't have taken him out and spared a few lives, but he had been surrounded by his own personal guard just after the flash of light in which Clary and Bindweed vanished.

"Yes, we will. My army will be prepared to engage you at the Rocky Ridge in half an hour," Crofton stated.

"Your army? How you deceive yourself, Crofton! Had you accepted my offer, you could have commanded an army. You have nothing more than a fledging band of weaklings you are leading to their deaths, and if by chance, some survive, they will make a perfect addition to the Pit. I'll even do you a favor, even though you are a sniveling traitor. I'll arrange for a little family reunion: you and Pickerel and even dear old dad, if he's still around." Tussock laughed maniacally as Crofton left with the others.

Crofton's hope had begun to flicker as night descended upon them, the grayness bleeding into the blackness of a moonless Noxian night. In less than an hour, their fate would be determined. They had no chance of defeating such a great army with so few numbers of their own. There was no chance of anyone crossing the line to join them now, not since they had witnessed the death of the infamous Ranunculus, the disappearance of the Ancient, the ruthless murder of Murain and the threat, that even in Crofton's death, lingered upon his family – a threat that everyone knew would be carried out in the cruelest of ways.

The fear had taken a stranglehold upon them, and they dared breathe only with its permission. How ironic that in one hour's time, the only light Noxia ever saw would break through the darkness with its intense rays, illuminating the planet's surface for one precious hour before retreating until the following nightfall.

What would its luminescence find when it peeked down from above? A

Pit filled with a host of new eyeless faces that could never return its intense gaze? A rocky terrain littered with the bodies of those who had failed in their attempt to overthrow evil? What message of despair would it carry to the other planets who sought its light? Crofton shuddered at the thought and then repressed it in the deepest recesses of his soul. He had to be strong. He felt not only the weight of Rue beside him, but the weight of the Florenci System resting on his tired shoulders. He wasn't sure how much longer he could bear it.

As they came to the mouth of the Gorge, the others knew their situation was bleak, even before Crofton explained to them all that had happened. Crofton instructed them to rest and ready themselves to stand their ground. Many had scoured the Rocky Ridge for weapons, which Crofton was not opposed to using, given the gravity of their situation. Crofton retreated to a rock to solidify an attack pattern, when he was interrupted by Ky.

"Crofton! Come quick!" Ky shouted across the way. Crofton heard the desperation in his voice, responding at once. Ky was pointing at something in the distance, and Crofton recognized the staggering figure as soon as he spotted it: Ambulia. She was running toward the mouth of the Gorge. Without hesitance, Crofton set out to intercept her. When she saw him approaching, she ran into his arms. He could tell by her tear-streaked face that something had gone terribly wrong. He took the weapons from her hands, which she was gripping so tightly her hands had turned white.

"What's happened?" he asked as he pulled her into an embrace. She was sobbing so hard she could not speak, and her sobs told him that Thor was dead. She had been in danger this entire time, and he hadn't even known it.

"I'm sorry," he whispered as he lifted her up so he could carry her back to camp. "Nothing has gone according to plan. I should have left you on Eudora with Betony."

"No," she said as her crying abated. "I wouldn't have let you leave me behind like you did before."

"What are we going to do with you now? I'll get someone else to protect you - Ky and his brothers."

"No, I will fight by your side. I'm tired of running. I'm tired of being afraid. I'm tired of everyone else thinking they have to take care of me. I will fight by your side - for Thor. His death and his anguish in life by my unknowing hand will not have been in vain."

"Lia, you can't blame yourself for any of this. The blame lies with me and me alone. If I hadn't left you, Thor wouldn't have become attached to you in the way he did. I am solely responsible for that."

"You knew?" Crofton nodded his head at her inquiry. "I was so blind. I never saw it. I would have discouraged him..."

"Lia, look at me," he grabbed her face with his hands. "He wanted you to be happy."

"Then it's settled. I'm fighting with you for Thor. That will make me happy. He was my best friend these last five years, and I will not allow him to be remembered as a traitor. He was the most loyal man I have ever known, and he not only sacrificed his life for me, he sacrificed his own happiness." Crofton knew there was no use arguing. Ambulia's eyes were alight with her stubborn resolve.

"Yes," he conceded. "You will fight by me - all the better for me to keep an eye on you." They walked back to the Free Frats, who had already been discussing a strategy - a last-ditch effort to liberate themselves from tyranny.

Chapter Thirty-Two
A Dark Pit

Betony and Pili came to the entrance of the Pit of Punishment. A putrid mixture of rotting flesh, waste, and vomit stung Betony's nostrils and triggered her gag reflex. Pili grabbed her arm as she stepped forward.

"No goim. Pleasim," he begged her.

"Pili, I have to go. Why don't you just wait for me here?" Pili agreed a little too readily as he leaned to the side and threw up the little he had eaten for lunch. Apparently, he didn't have the stomach for the place either. Betony had only taken a few steps when she heard the symphony of suffering pierce her ears – a moan here, a groan there, wheezing from the corner, a high-pitched shriek to the right – all perfectly orchestrated to convey the pain and anguish of those entombed in the Pit. What was she doing here after all? Who could help her here? And then she remembered Crofton's brother, Pickerel. Pickerel was here, and he was most assuredly alive.

"Pickerel," she called out. "Pickerel! Pick! I'm looking for Crofton's brother, Pick." Mumbled murmurs were her only response as she tried to make her way through the maze of bodies lying in various stages of consciousness and barely clinging to life.

"Pickerel!" She raised her voice in a panicked shout. "Pick!" She was beginning to think she would never find him, when someone responded.

"Who's there?" She heard someone call back from the far corner. She stumbled toward the sound of the voice, uttering apologies along the way as she stepped on people in the darkness. Many were too weak to cry out. When she reached the general vicinity, she asked again, "Pick? Are you here?"

"You must be the Ancient," his voice was gruff. "I was hoping I'd get to meet you."

"How do you know me?" For the first time, Betony was glad she could not see in the dark.

"Your voice. Crofton told me about the sound of your voice – musical is how he described it."

"Have you seen Crofton?" She regretted her word choice the second it left her mouth, but Pick only laughed.

"I haven't *seen* him or anyone for that matter in quite some time as that's pretty much an impossibility. And no, he hasn't come to visit me yet either."

"But you know he's here on Noxia?"

"Of course. He hasn't left me completely in the dark," he laughed again at his own pun. "He had a communicator inserted in my wrist by one of his Free Frats. I hear every communication they make. Tussock doesn't exactly keep an eye on all of us down here. We aren't much of a threat to anyone in our condition."

"You know more than I do about his plans then. I just arrived myself, and I've been left quite out of the loop."

"Yes, I know. You're not supposed to be here at all. You're supposed to be on Eudora with Pili. Where is that big oaf anyway?"

"Waiting for me at the entrance. When we landed, it looked as though fighting had already broken out."

"I'm afraid so. Not a single member of the army had guts enough to turn against Tussock. It's only a matter of time now. Crofton's forces are sorely outnumbered and outgunned. It's too bad he didn't have more resources and more time to organize. I have an arsenal of weaponry hidden down here, courtesy of the Free Frats, but Tussock's army stands between Crofton and us. He can't break the line. I only wish there was more I could do, but I'm too weak to make my way out of here, let alone hold a weapon."

"That's where I come in. Did Crofton ever mention my gift?"

"Yeah, he said you had the power to heal. You healed that Rue fellow just before he was about to die. Said it was the most amazing thing he ever saw, but surely...surely, you can't heal us?"

"There's no harm in trying," she said. She found it disturbing squatting next to him in the pitch black. She couldn't see her hand in front of her face, and she only hoped she had enough energy to tap into her gift.

"Can you guide my hand to your face?" she asked, stretching her hand toward the sound of the voice. It took only a moment before Pick's rough, dry hand found hers. His touch felt more like she was being poked by a stick than touching the flesh of another person. Her hand found its place on what must have been his face, though again, it felt more like touching a withered, dead leaf than living flesh.

"Your hand is quivering," Pick observed, but Betony didn't respond. She had already been overcome by excruciating pain. Her eyes were tightly closed as she tried to concentrate. She pressed her hand more firmly against his face as her mind willed her to release him - to relieve herself of the pain that touching him caused her. Minutes later, the pain subsided. Her body was emitting a soft glow that illuminated the dark cavern. She opened her eyes to find a strong, handsome man staring back at her.

"I can see," he whispered, his deep brown eyes holding her gaze. "You did it! I can see!" he shouted, pulling her into an embrace. "You're trembling. Are you okay?" he asked as he released her.

"I'm okay," she said, weakened by the sudden loss of energy. Pick's cries had awakened the other tortured souls in the Pit. For the first time, Betony could faintly make out her surroundings, and she drew in her breath in horror as she saw the rotting flesh, the scarred faces, the withered bodies – hundreds, even thousands of them. She noticed now that she had never once been walking on the ground because it was covered by bodies, layers of them stacked one on top of the other. Those at the bottom were nothing more than bones, their life force long since succumbing to death's tempting lure.

For the first time, Pick saw the squalor in which he had lived for so long. His large brown eyes filled with tears as he reached out to the person who had been lying beside him.

"Oh, father," he whispered as he looked up with desperation and pleaded with Betony, "You've got to help them. Please help them."

"I don't know if I can. There are so many." She cast her eyes around the Pit again.

"You've got to try," Pick pleaded, rising to his feet. "Look at me." She focused her eyes on his. "You can do this. I know you can. You are the only chance any of us have. You're the only chance Rue has." Rue. The mention of his name brought the last words of his farewell letter to her mind: *because without you there isn't life itself.*

She inhaled deeply, despite the stench that hung in the air. She was sifting through her memories, trying to strengthen herself with the love that emanated from them. She reached her hand into her pocket and turned Rue's seed over in her fingers.

"I can't do it one by one," she finally said. "There are too many, and I won't have the strength, but maybe...just maybe...if we can get them to link hands...It's worth a try." Pickerel called out the instructions, his voice echoing in the gray. One by one, row by row, layer by layer, each man and woman joined hands. Those who were stronger helped those who were weaker until all hands had been joined.

"I think we're ready," Pick announced. Betony sat down by his father who was linked to the man next to him. She knelt in front of him and placed her hand on his disfigured face. The pain surged through her with force, and she withdrew her hand, trying to catch her breath. She turned to Pick.

"You have to hold my hand to his face. I can't do it myself," she told him. He knelt down beside her, resting his right hand over hers and supporting his father's head with his left hand.

"You're going to have to push harder than that," she instructed. "And Pick, whatever happens, do not let go."

"What do you mean, whatever happens?"

"Promise me. Whatever happens you will not let go until it's over."

"But how will I know it's over?"

"You'll know. Now promise me."

"Okay. I promise. I promise," he agreed. She once again focused her attention on the touch of her hand on his father. Another surge of pain jolted through her, followed by another and another. She cried out and felt Pick's hand slacken.

"No. You promised!" she yelled, and the pressure that held her hand in place returned. She felt the intense pain sucking out her very life force. On the verge of surrendering to unconsciousness, she realized her other hand still held the seed. She focused her mind on the seed, pressing it into her palm as she visualized Rue's ocean blue eyes, his touch, his smile, his voice, his kiss. She merged his memory with those she had of her family. She squeezed the seed with all her might, focusing every last bit of strength she had on the love emanating from her memories. And yet, it was not enough. She felt her strength waning, her concentration slipping. At that very moment in her struggle, she heard Clary's voice as clearly as though she were in the Pit with her. She heard her, but she knew that she was not there.

"Betony, I hope you will forgive my intrusion into your thoughts. I've been trying to hone the skill for some years, but have never been successful until now – until I could communicate with another Ancient like myself. I found Bindweed, Betony, so near the verge of death that the only way I could save him was to take him away. I never thought it possible until I felt how strongly he loved me. His love amplified my gift somehow, and we escaped from Tussock, from Noxia, from the Florenci System. We escaped from time, I suppose. We are in a place between time and space, hovering in the interval between past and present. He will remain well as long as we stay, and we are both content to stay here forever, as long as we can be together. This place takes on whatever form we wish, and now we sit underneath a waterfall on Asa-en-Darah. I wanted you to know that I am safe, and I wanted to thank you for giving me the courage to confront my fears. I had only planned to thwart Tussock when I left Asa-en-Darah. I never imagined that I would be reunited with my dear, sweet Bindweed after all these years. Thank you for restoring me to my happiness – for allowing me to tell you my story – to tell it in a way that allowed me to see what course of action I needed to take. I send my love to you and that which you endeavor to do. You are more powerful than you think. Believe me, I've seen it. I am seeing it now."

Betony was left alone again with only her own thoughts in her head, but Clary's words, though she couldn't quite grasp their full meaning, gave her the resolve to press forward, despite the pain. With the resulting jolt of energy, she felt as though she had burst into flames. She did not know how much time had lapsed, but she felt the familiar tingling that signaled the healing was complete. The pressure of Pick's hand on hers disappeared, and she felt her body being lifted from the ground where it had slumped. She tried to move her limbs, but they failed to respond. She tried to open her eyes, but they could not be coaxed open. She was trapped in the darkness once again. She could hear voices, but they seemed so distant. She couldn't understand what they were saying. She was being carried by someone – someone strong. She tried to fight the fatigue, but she did not have the strength. The blanket of unconsciousness was inching closer and closer, until at last it smothered her.

CHAPTER THIRTY-THREE: A HOLY ONE

Prey had watched the entire exchange between Ranunculus and Rue from behind a bush, suddenly overcome with sadness. He had never been sad before, and he didn't like the feeling one bit. His eyes began to itch, as if they too wanted to leak water like those around him. He was annoyed by the sensation. His foreleg glided over his eyes in an effort to wipe away the sudden urge to find a release for this overwhelming feeling that was now gripping tightly onto his heart. His advocate was gone. He was alone on an enemy planet, and - what was the incessant buzzing noise he was hearing? It seemed to be swarming around him, but again he could see nothing. Why did everyone else seem unaffected by it?

He watched as Stephanotis, Galax, Aster, Lisianthus, and Rue retreated with Ranunculus's body. Good riddance to the lot of them! As they got farther away, Prey realized that he was now in enemy territory alone. Tussock was less than a foot away from him, and Prey wasn't really up for combat just yet. His neck was still sore and stiff from its recent reattachment to his head. He backed away slowly and stealthily, crouching low to the ground so as not to be seen. The only place to go was inside the gate to the city, so he sneaked inside. He wasn't sure what to do or where to go. He couldn't make it back to his pod now. He would have to weave through too many Noxian guardsmen. He thought he had seen a pod a ways off – just outside the south border wall when he and Ranunculus had entered the atmosphere. He decided to head in that direction. If he could commandeer a vessel, he would be off.

As he walked, he felt an invisible wall pushing him faster and faster from behind. He felt as though something were trying to run him over. He started to walk at a fast clip, then a jog, and now he was all out sprinting to stay ahead of whatever seemed to be pushing him from behind. He cursed Stephanotis. Surely, he had screwed with his brain. This was beyond a prank. The voice was one thing, but this was quite another. He finally gave up running and took to flying low to the ground. Thankfully, he didn't pass any Noxians along the way. At long last, he reached the south border wall and flew over it. The pod was still there. Curious. It was a pod from Traveriss, not the Noxian pod he had expected. Drats. The Noxian pods were known for their speed, and he was stuck with a clunker. It was an escape vehicle, nonetheless, so he crept inside.

He saw nothing unusual. He sat in the pilot's seat, ready to check the fuel levels, when his legs hit something hard. When he looked under the control panel, he found an empty glass jar. Picking it up, he peered inside suspiciously.

"You have come, O Holy One! Good work my faithful followers. I knew you would not let me down." The voice startled Prey. He could hear it very clearly with his ear, but his eyes had never before deceived him. He could see nothing.

"Is...is someone there? Is this some kind of a joke? Come out wherever you are!"

"Do not be frightened, Holy One. You have been summoned here to rescue me if it be according to your most holy desires."

"Rescue you? But I don't see anyone who needs to be rescued."

"Do not see with your eyes, Holy One. Listen with your ear." Prey concentrated but all he heard was that incessant buzzing amplified a hundredfold within the small compartment of the pod. The buzzing! Of course!

"I hear buzzing."

"Yes, Holy One. That is my convoy. I was captured when relocating to a new planet in a planetary system far from here."

"The Queen! You're the kidnapped Queen?"

"I see my reputation precedes me. I am most honored that your Holiness has heard of me. Now, would you so kindly free me?"

"Why do you call me Holy One?"

"In our planetary system, your species is the Wisest of the Wise. The Holiest of the Holy."

"There are more of my kind where you come from?"

"Many. Now if you would please free me, we will exact our revenge and leave this place to return to our home."

"What revenge?"

"An injustice has been committed. All who inhabit this place must pay recompense."

"You're going to kill everyone?"

"That is our law."

"As a Holy One would you defer to my opinion on the matter?"

"That is our custom. The Holy Ones guide us in our decisions."

"Very well. You are not familiar with this planetary system, and you are not the only kidnapping victim. There is a man who has kidnapped many from his own planetary system. He has murdered a dear friend of mine. It is he who deserves to be punished – he and those who follow him. The others should not pay for his crime. They are as you have been – abducted against their will. If I set you free, will you help me set them free?"

"Those who inhabit this place are lucky to have a Holy One as wise as you. Of course, I would consider it an honor to assist you." Prey had made the connection at last. This was the kidnapped Queen that Tussock and Lamium had been discussing in his first intergalactic interception. The Queen's faithful followers were the Transparencies that had been flying around Traveriss. Run-Dung had told him that story on their way to Noxia. The Transparencies were only searching for their Queen, whom Lamium had instructed Tussock to kidnap. But to what end?

Ah hah! First, they were to serve as a distraction for the Brotherhood as well as the means by which Lamium could poison the Brotherhood. What had he planned to do with them after that? Unless...unless he planned to get rid of the Noxians altogether. He would have lured the convoy to Noxia, and then released the Queen. The Queen would have killed everyone on the planet before returning to her own planetary system, and Lamium would have been unharmed because he had the inoculation. Not a bad plan if it had worked.

But it didn't work because the convoy didn't follow Lamium when he left Traveriss. They didn't take the bait, whatever the bait had been. Instead, they stayed on Traveriss to follow Prey because they saw him as the Holy One who could save the Queen. Him! He was a Holy One, and there were more of his kind in their planetary system! Thank the stars! Female companionship was just around the corner, but first things, first. He would have to save Rue and the others. Stephanotis had saved his life after all.

He opened the jar, though he could still see nothing. Maybe he was delirious, but if delirium gave him this much hope for his future, he was all for it. He may even thank Stephanotis for toying with his brain in the end. Of course, he hoped it was real. He had to believe it was real.

He began formulating his plan with the Queen, who was the only one with whom he could actually communicate. He knew Crofton was set to meet Tussock's army at any moment, so they would have to act fast. He only hoped the others would believe in something they couldn't see. He may have a hard time convincing the others that he wasn't crazy. He was, after all, having a hard time convincing himself of that. But then again, Tussock knew about the Queen. He knew she was invisible as did the Brotherhood, so at least as far as leadership went, he was likely to be believed. Time was of the essence, so there was no point wasting it by worrying about what everyone else would think of him. He knew what he had to do. He was headed for the Rocky Ridge.

"Let's go," he said to the Queen as he exited the pod, his ear abuzz with the excitement of the convoy, which had to number in the hundreds by the noise they were making. At least, that's what he hoped.

Chapter Thirty-Four
A Beginning to the End

"I...I don't think she made it," Pick acknowledged sorrowfully as he gently placed Betony's body into Pili's outstretched arms. "I know you were assigned to protect her, Pili. This is not your fault. This was her choice. She's the most courageous woman I've ever known. I mean, she risked her own life to save all of us - all of us who are strangers to her. Pili, because of her, we can change the outcome of this war. There's hope now, brother. I wonder if you might protect her yet, until she can get a proper burial. Take her to the surface out of this stinking Pit until it's over." Pili nodded, too overcome with emotion to speak. Pick waited reverently as Pili climbed out of the Pit. After carefully handing Betony's lifeless body to Pili and waiting for him to silently retreat, Pick rallied his comrades.

"It's time to join our brothers in battle," he declared to the hundreds that had been healed. He organized them into groups of one hundred and issued them weapons from the pile of arsenal the Free Frats had stored away over the last five years. There were more than enough weapons for all of them - men and women. There were about fifty children present as well, all recent additions to the Pit. Pick was contemplating what to do with them to keep them safe when someone stepped forward.

"We will take them to safety," Calden spoke up. After leaving Betony,

Calden had gone back to the pod fully intending to return to Eudora, but Yerba insisted they stay. She told him that they owed that much to Betony, who had made them whole again. They waited for a while by the pod, but when Betony and Pili did not return, they went in search of them. They reached the Pit's entrance just in time to see Pili carrying Betony's body away.

They felt compelled to help in some way, and Yerba had a longing to be reunited with Bracken, if he had managed to survive these many years. She watched hopefully as each person emerged from the pit, weapon in hand. At long last, the final man surfaced followed by Pick and the children. Bracken was not among them. Yerba cried softly for his loss, knowing that children perished quickly when sent to the Pit. She quietly buried the hope of his survival she had secretly held onto. She then looked at the innocent, scared faces of the fifty children, most likely orphans, who followed Pick, and her heart was softened more. She tugged at Calden's shirt. He did not have to ask what she wanted.

"I said, we will take the children to safety," Calden repeated when Pick failed to acknowledge his offer.

"And you are?" Pick stared at him suspiciously. The man's clothing was foreign, and he did not speak with the Noxian accent, although he looked like a Noxian.

"We came here with Betony and Pili from Eudora, where we defected years ago. Let us help," he tried to explain. At the mention of the familiar names, Pick's face relaxed. He knew they could be trusted. He nodded his agreement, and the children were ushered away by Calden and Yerba.

Pick was surprised at how bright it was on the surface. He waited for his eyes to adjust. The sky was a nothing more than a gray smudge, but compared to the pitch black of the Pit, it was a welcome sight – a shade of hope he never thought he'd see again. He breathed in deeply, relishing the smell of fresh air and allowing it to rush to his extremities. It was the smell of freedom – a smell he would never take for granted again. He walked to the front of the group and led them through the gate on the east border wall to the familiar path that would lead them to the Rocky Ridge.

His plan was simple. Half of his forces would walk to the top of the Rocky Ridge, just above Crofton's position. There, they would have a birds-eye view of the entire battlefield, and they could use their long-range weapons and arrows to their advantage. The other half would align just below the Rocky Ridge, where Tussock's forces could see their faces. He knew that once Tussock's guardsmen recognized their long-lost family members and friends, they would cross the line at last. He had purposely selected only those who had friends and family members in the guard to position themselves on the front lines. Tussock's forces would be greatly diminished when they realized that the Pit was no longer a threat, if only they could hold out until the sunrise so their faces could be clearly seen. He couldn't wait to see the look on Crofton's face when the battle commenced, and he realized he was not alone after all.

Crofton ordered his men into position as the time for the final conflict drew near. Ambulia was armed with a confiscated ray gun, refusing to merely freeze anyone who attacked her. Rue passed by him on his way to join the men under his command.

"I'm afraid we're going to lose this battle. We're too far outnumbered,"

Crofton admitted to Rue.

"We may lose the battle, but we will win the war."

"How can you say that? If we die, it's over."

"Sometime, somewhere, someone will embrace the cause again."

"I hope for the sake of the future of this planetary system you're right, King," Crofton pushed Rue in jest.

"To the fight," he raised his fist to Rue.

"To the death," Rue tapped Crofton's fist one last time.

Crofton waited for every band to report that they were in position. The minutes dragged on before the last band was finally ready, including Pick's forces, though so stealthy was their movement that Crofton was unaware of their presence. Crofton grabbed Ambulia's hand, holding it tightly, as he sent up a flare. The air seemed to chill suddenly with tension and anxiety as each person waited for Tussock's return flare, signaling the commencement of the battle. No one moved. They gripped their weapons, their hearts transforming into war drums in their chests as they beat so loudly no other sound could be heard. Tussock waited, allowing the fear to slither around his opponents before launching its venomous attack. To everyone's surprise, the silence was broken by a strange, high-pitched voice. It was coming from the sky above where Crofton and his men stood. All eyes shifted upward, though they could only make out a strange, lone figure hovering in the air.

"Tussock, I give you an opportunity to surrender," the shrill voice said as laughter erupted from the north border wall.

"What kind of a joke is this, Crofton?" Tussock's response boomed over the low plains.

"This is not Crofton's doing, fool," Prey snickered to himself. He had always wanted to call someone a fool. "I am Prey, the Mantid." He had wanted to say, "I am Prey, the Killer Mantid," but he thought that would be overdoing it, just a little.

"Prey, get down from there. What in the stars do you think you're doing?" Stephanotis called out, fearing that his masterpiece would be obliterated right before his very eyes, but Prey ignored his request.

"The Queen has come to pay her respects," Prey bellowed into the night air. Rue and Crofton drew in deep breaths, knowing full well to whom Prey was referring. *What has he done now?* Rue thought to himself. Surely, the Transparencies would not be the end of them after all.

Tussock had all but forgotten about the Queen, and the mere mention of the invisible insect he had captured unsettled him. He had never really understood the purpose of her abduction, nor the nature of her species. He had merely done as Lamium bid, confident that it would be in his best interest. For the first time since Lamium's arrival, Tussock felt the fear he had so readily unleashed on others, slowly slithering back toward him.

"You're bluffing, creature. The Queen is safe and sound," Tussock spoke with confidence, though he realized that it had been weeks since he had checked on his prisoners. He had no reason to believe she would not still be in her vacuum-sealed container.

"I wouldn't be so sure of myself if I were you, Tussock," Crofton's tone reeked of mockery.

"You will not win this war with trickery, Crofton!" Tussock shouted. The air around him electrified as he spoke, and he knew the lightning storm that ushered in the Noxian sunrise had come at last. He wanted this over before the sun-star rose to its peak. He raised his flare gun into the air, blasting light from it, but the light was lost in a bright strike of lightning within the border wall. While no one saw his flare, they did see the sky light up with a strange yellowish glow. The Transparencies were everywhere, their light brightening the planet's surface as though it were day. It was then that Tussock saw Pick's reinforcements lining the ridges above Crofton and the Low Plains below him. His men saw it too and began to point and shout. Crofton turned to see what all the commotion was about, only to find himself surrounded, but these men and women were not poised to attack him.

Recognition slowly passed by those on the front lines as they recognized brothers, fathers, mothers, and friends who they had long since written off as dead. Tussock's forces broke rank, dropping their weapons and rushing forward to see for themselves if the faces before them were real or part of an elaborate optical illusion set to trap them. At this point, however, they did not care. They had to know.

Prey smiled as he saw the chaos beneath him. He had been just as surprised as everyone else by the sudden light show because the Queen had never told him she could be seen. He breathed a sigh of relief that he had not gone mad. He really was a Holy One. He could scarcely believe his good fortune. He watched as Tussock's loyalists gathered around him. Tussock was at a loss of what to do. There was nowhere for him to go. He could not retreat without being overtaken. Prey watched with delight, and then he gave the Queen the signal. The Transparencies swarmed into a bright yellow fireball, which shot toward Tussock and his followers. So quick was their attack, so thorough their destruction, that there were no remains left of Tussock and the thousand who followed him to their deaths. They simply were no more. Tussock was gone in the blink of an eye. When the fireball had exacted its revenge, it flew higher and higher into the sky until it was no more than a speck. And then it too was gone. All but ten Transparencies remained, and they buzzed around Prey as he descended, his wings tiring from his flight.

"Holy One," the Queen said, "we thank you for your wisdom and guidance. In return for your loyalty, we ask you to join us as we travel back to our home. We would be honored if you would be our Holy One." Prey thought for a moment.

"You say there are more of my kind where you are going?"

"Many more. They, too, would welcome one so valiant as you."

"In that case, I humbly accept your offer. I only ask that I have a few moments to bid farewell to my...friends." It felt good to acknowledge that he truly considered the Brotherhood his friends.

"We will wait, Holy One. Bring your flying machine as it is a long journey, and you seem to tire of flying easily. You will find us orbiting this planet when you are ready." Prey bowed his head, and the Queen departed with her advisors.

Awash with confusion, Crofton was still standing in the same place, holding onto Ambulia's hand. Surely Tussock wasn't gone just like that. What was that creature that had threatened Tussock? Where had the reinforcements come from? He was too stunned to speak when he saw Rue approach.

"Oh, Noxian of little faith! What say you?" Rue asked as he jovially punched him in the arm.

"It can't be over. What has just happened here?" Crofton's confusion amused Rue. He explained who Prey was, though he couldn't explain how he had come to release the Queen, let alone befriend her.

"What of the reinforcements?" Crofton asked, but he did not have to wait for Rue's answer because someone picked him up from behind. Crofton struggled to free himself unsuccessfully. All the while, Ambulia was smiling beside him. The person set him down and turned him around so they could face each other. Crofton stumbled backward as he looked into the face of Pick.

"Pick?"

"Didn't think I'd let you fight a war without me, did you, little brother?" Pick gathered Crofton into a tight embrace and let the tears freely stream down his face.

"Rue," Crofton said when Pick finally released him, "I'd like you to meet my brother, Pick."

"Pick? As in the brother who tried to save my seed-pod? That Pick?" Rue asked as he bumped fists with him.

"The one and only," Pick affirmed.

"But...I thought...are all these people from the Pit?" Rue asked, his face suddenly paling. Pick nodded grimly, the smile vanishing from his face.

Chapter Thirty-Five
An End to a Beginning

Rue didn't need to be told how this had all come about – how an army of healthy, whole individuals had been raised out of the Pit. His heart began to race as he searched the crowd. His wounded arm was pulsing with pain at the acceleration. Where was she? Then, in the sea of faces he did not recognize, one stood out. He was approaching slowly, sadly, his tear-streaked face somber. It was the brawny figure of Pili parting the sea of people as he moved forward, a wave of silence hushing the excited crowd in his wake. Rue looked to Pili's arms to confirm what he dreaded more than anything. There lay the lifeless figure of Betony.

Rue could not move. His body suddenly felt as though it were made of cement, and he could already feel the mallet of grief priming itself to break his heart with one heavy blow. Why had he left her? Why had he denied her only request? The what-could-have-beens swarmed in his mind – those deadly mosquitoes of despair. Had he not once told Datura it was time to leave the maze of what-ifs? Oh, how ignorant and stupid he had been! He had now been sentenced to life in that awful maze himself. If he could just have one chance to do it again – to save Betony – but in the pit of his heart, he knew he could not have saved her nor would she have wanted him to. He had seen the tearful reunions and the shouts of jubilation as those who had suffered in the Pit were reunited. She had saved hundreds – allowed them to see the light again. He could never take that away from them, even if it cost him more than he thought he could bear.

He was so swallowed up in his own torment that he did not notice the crowd bowing down in reverence and respect to the one who had sacrificed her own life so they could live again in freedom. Pili gently laid Betony's body at Rue's feet in a small patch of grass and disappeared into the kneeling crowd without uttering a word. He felt her loss more keenly than most. He had spent the last few weeks basking in her sunlight, and now, she had died at his hand. The weight of his responsibility sunk deep into his heart. He could feel no happiness there. He could not rejoice with the others. Instead, he retreated.

Rue dropped to his knees and gathered Betony's body up in his arms, hugging her close to him as his body gave way to heavy, mournful sobs. Crofton tried to step forward to comfort him, but Ambulia held him back, understanding that comfort would not come easily as she thought of Thor's death. The cheers and shouts of joy and victory had given way to the silence of mourning and grief. The crowd began to disperse to attend to the wounded and dead who had paid the ultimate price for freedom on the battlefield that day. The Noxian, the Oron, the Quamirian, and the Phirunite joined together for the first time to comb the battleground for victims.

It was then that the lightning ceased, and the sun-star reached out a few fingers of sunlight through the dark clouds. Within seconds, the clouds of darkness had dissipated and the full intensity of the Noxian sunrise was bearing down on the planet. Rue was sweating in his solar suit and squinting in the brightness that surrounded him. The Noxians shouted their sun-star chant, a chant they had whispered for centuries unbeknownst to their tyrannical leaders.

A Noxian Sunrise

A star breaking through the night,
A star will one day give us light.
A light bursting through the black.
A light will bring our freedom back.
The sun delivering its ray of hope,
A single, shimmering, golden rope.
Oh, brightness ignite a flame today,
Oh, brightness show us the way.

They repeated the chant over and over until its echo carried through the Gorge of Grief. Rue released Betony's body, laying her gently on the ground. She was glimmering as the sun reflected off her pale green skin. The moon dust had long since faded. Rue watched her dirt-streaked face – the epitome of beauty, goodness, and love. He could not move. He sorrowfully recalled the last time he had seen Betony lie so still for so long just after he had rescued her from a watery grave on Asa-en-Darah. He had never left her side then, and he couldn't make himself do it now. Instead, he took her hand in his, just as he had done then. He sat down beside her, letting the sunshine wash over him, numbing his senses in its heat.

Crofton, Ambulia, Stephanotis, Valerian, and Prey watched, not knowing what to do or say. Crofton held tightly to Ambulia, guiltily grateful that he was not in Rue's position. Valerian thought of Tansy, waiting for him back on Quamir. He relived the pangs of despair he had felt when he thought she would die in the solar flare attack. He turned his head from the scene before him, comprehending Rue's agony to a small extent.

Forty-five minutes passed. Rue finally looked up as the sun-star's beams began their slow retreat. How had death cheated him so? Why did he remain the sole survivor? A few more inches and that spear would have numbed his pain forever. Instead, he had been abandoned again, deserted by death. Those he loved and those for whom he fought had left him: Betony, Ranunculus, the Eudoran people. His thoughts drew back to the present, and he noticed that Betony had been clenching something in the fist of her other hand. He pried it open to find the ancient seed he had left with her. *The Ancient guardian of his heart.* Isn't that what he had told her? She had protected him to the end, and here was the proof. Unfortunately, his heart had stopped beating when she had stopped breathing.

He turned the seed over in his hand. The seed, though it appeared to be dead, was very much alive. He had been like that seed before he met Betony – dormant, hibernating, and unaware of how life could blossom inside of him under the right conditions – her radiant smile, her gentle touch, her endearing wit, her soothing words, her loving embrace. If he buried his heart now it would be in the earthen grave of death rather than the soil of life that prompted a buried seed toward life. There was no light to trigger its growth since Betony's light had been extinguished. What would become of him now? He would be forced to walk among the living though he would be dead inside.

He bent down to kiss Betony's cold lips one last time. As he withdrew, he could have sworn he saw her eyelids flutter. He bent close to her face and ran his hand along her jaw line. Another flutter. He bent closer still, his breath moving the wisps of her hair that framed her face. Another flutter. His heart roared to life. Was she alive? Had she merely been weakened to the point of death and slowly regained her strength with the continued exposure and intensity of the light? She had always been so sensitive to light, and Noxia was so dark – the Pit darker still.

Her eyes fluttered open at long last. She had felt the tugs and pulls dragging her back to reality, but she had clung to the rising shudder of sleep, not allowing it to open for fear of death's dark greeting. She was pleasantly surprised to find Rue's blue eyes welcoming her instead. She stared at his face for a long moment, studying his every feature. Her heart swelled at the sight she now beheld - a sight she never thought she would see again. His hair was matted down in places, his face, dirty and sweaty. His eyes were a pool of emotion - relief, joy, sadness, and pain. Pain. Many kinds of pain, but there was an element of physical pain in the flecks of blue. She had seen it before on Quamir, though it had been much more pronounced then.

She let her eyes wander beyond the features of his face in search of his injury, shocked to find he was wearing no shirt. He had become a true Noxian warrior in her absence. She saw the sheen of the solar suit in the last specks of light that meandered around them, unwilling to surrender to the darkness. He was cradling her head in one of his arms, but the other was carefully obscured from her view. She had found the injury, which he was purposely hiding from her. She reached out for his maimed arm, but he intertwined his fingers in hers before she could touch him, wincing with pain as he did.

"You're hurt, Rue," she observed quietly.

"I'll be fine," he assured her with a smile.

"But you're in pain," she protested.

"Betony, you've healed enough today. Look around you. You've given these people back the things they never dared to hope for - their lives, their families, and their future together. You healed their broken hearts as well, resurrecting them from their shallow graves. You did that, all by yourself. The pain I feel in my arm is nothing compared to what you must have endured, and

I won't allow you to inflict any more pain on yourself - not on my account. I've hurt you enough. My arm will heal, and its scar will be a constant reminder to me of all we've been through - a compass to guide me when I stumble," he smiled subtly. "Yes, I know I must sound more than a little Valerian-esque. Until this very moment, I never truly understood...but now, I know exactly how he feels." A stream of tears rushed down her cheeks as if to wash away his pain. She had known her actions would most likely take her life, but she had not realized the price Rue would pay. Rue lifted a trembling hand to her face, still amazed that when he touched her, she did not vanish, still trying to convince himself that she was really alive.

"Betony...I thought I'd lost you today, and...and...well...please don't ever leave me again," his voice was a gentle pleading.

"I'm not the one who's always leaving," she smiled. He laughed, reality finally sinking in. Then, he found he could not stop himself from laughing - great waves of relief and happiness rolled out of him, clashing with the darkening sky as they echoed.

His onlookers were alarmed, having been too far away to realize what had just taken place. Pick nudged Crofton, who nudged Stephanotis, who nudged Valerian.

"He's gone mad - stark, raving mad!" Stephanotis exclaimed. "We can't lose him now."

"This has gone on long enough. Someone has to do something," Prey urged the others on.

"We'll all go together," Crofton finally said, and they started toward Rue.

"She's alive!" They heard Rue proclaim as he picked Betony up in his arms, ignoring the pain of his wound. "She's alive!" Cheers rose up among them as they came to Betony's side.

"What happened?" Betony asked. The last thing she remembered was hearing Clary's voice in the Pit.

"Now, that is a story," Prey said, clearing his throat. Betony gasped as she turned toward the unfamiliar voice.

"A giant Mantid!" she exclaimed. "This is remarkable! On Unn, the Mantid's were our guardians, well-loved and respected among my people. I never thought I would be so blessed to meet a Mantid myself, especially here."

"I knew I would like this one," Prey said as he tapped her on the head with his foreleg.

"Apparently, the Transparencies share your good opinion of him," Rue explained. "And that's only the beginning of the story."

A Noxian sunrise. No one could have guessed the significance this particular sunrise would have. Before this day, everyone had led separate lives, many unaware of the existence of those with whom they now stood face to face. As the sun rose, all those separate paths converged into one. Even with its brief appearance, this sunrise would forever represent a new dawn of time. Its rays illuminated freedom, peace, sacrifice, healing, and love, but most of all, those rays lit the way home. To each person that home was a different place or a suspension between space and time as in Clary's and Bindweed's case, but it was home nonetheless. For the first time, everyone had been united as each drew strength from the Noxian sunrise. The ancient Noxian chant had been a prophecy - now fulfilled, as hope ignited even in the sun's waning light.

Chapter Thirty-Six
A Planted Seed

They sat down to hear the retelling of the story from the three different perspectives from which it unraveled and entangled itself, mesmerized at the intricate web of connection they had to one another, though just weeks before they had been strangers. The night continued to grow darker, however, and those who had come from Quamir, Phirun, and Oro were anxious to return to their families and bury their dead on their own planets. They were given food and water before boarding the transport vessels to return to their home planets with promises of future communications to arrange trade agreements and spaceway construction. Calden and Yerba stopped by to talk with Betony for a while before returning to care for the children, and the Noxians also dispersed to their homes for a night of revelry. The four remaining members of the Brotherhood, Crofton, Ambulia, Pick, Prey, Rue, and Betony were gathered in a group with several other Free Frats and stragglers hovering around. No one noticed a lone figure advancing toward them.

"What will become of Traveriss?" Ambulia asked.

"I think we should use it as a Florenci System library, so all the knowledge, records, and books that have been accumulated there don't go to waste. Maybe we could even turn it into a school, where anyone from any planet can go to learn," Rue suggested.

"Sounds like a good plan, but who would stay there to run the place?" Ambulia wondered.

"Why not Prey?" Rue offered, surprised by his own suggestion.

"I respectfully decline the offer, Rue. I think my time in this planetary system has come to a climactic close, and with Run-Dung gone, it just wouldn't feel right."

"But where will you go?" Stephanotis asked.

"With the Queen. I've accepted her offer to join her as she returns to her own planetary system. I must admit, it feels good to be worshiped, despite the minor annoyances. Besides, I am told there are more of my kind there, and it's been a while since I've...well...since I've had any female companionship." A sly smile crossed Prey's face as he spoke, and laughter rippled through the small crowd.

"Well, we wish you luck in your journeys then, friend," Rue said, and Prey was happy that he reciprocated his feeling of friendship.

"I must say, this is shocking, Prey. I hadn't thought of life without you," Stephanotis seemed disconcerted.

"I hate to admit it, but I just might miss you a little myself. I guess you'll have to find some other species to torture in my absence," Prey joked. Stephanotis stepped forward to give him another hug.

"Careful, friend," Prey warned as he held him back with his forelegs. "I still haven't forgiven you for tweaking my voice yet." He smiled, and he knew Stephanotis was the only one who could have distinguished the facial expression. He returned the smile, patting Prey's foreleg.

"With that said, I must be on my way. The Queen might be growing impatient by now, and I don't want to miss my chance," Prey turned to go. "Oh, that reminds me, anyone mind if I borrow a pod?"

"Take one of ours," Crofton offered. "We owe you our lives. It's the least we could do." Prey's antennae twitched with excitement. This would be a great journey indeed! Noxian pods were, after all, known for their speed and agility.

"Many thanks," Prey mumbled over his shoulder as he scuttled away toward the Noxian charging stations.

"So, I guess we'll have to go back to the drawing board to find another suitable candidate," Rue said. "Will none of the Brotherhood return?"

"No," Stephanotis spoke up. "We will return to our true homes – our families. If this experience has taught us anything, it's that our family and friends are of the utmost importance, and we've neglected them for far too long as it is."

"I would like the opportunity to establish a school on Traveriss," the voice came from the perimeter of the dwindling crowd. It sounded familiar, but the vernacular didn't match its deep resonance. The owner of the voice stepped forward, and a hush fell over them as they recognized the bulky brawn of the figure.

"Pili?" Crofton could hardly believe that the carefully constructed sentence had come from Pili, who had not been seen since placing Betony at Rue's feet.

"Pili, say something else," Crofton prodded.

"I said I want to go to Traveriss. I'm tired of living in the shadows on this planet. Now that you have been restored to your family and Ambulia, there is no place for me here," Pili reasoned. Crofton was speechless for a moment, captivated by Pili's melodic voice and his ability to speak coherently the words he had been so carefully pondering.

"But you're a part of my family - like a brother to me," Crofton argued when he could speak again.

"Then, set this brother free as Pick has been set free. Let me leave this place of darkness."

"Pili, what's happened to you?" Pili stole a glance in Betony's direction, thankful that she was alive, but she returned his look with a puzzled stare. He decided it was time to give them all an explanation.

"In the Pit, I heard the whispers, 'Join hands if you want to be healed.' I have waited to hear those words all my life. I wanted to ask her myself, but I could not bring myself to do it because I knew healing me would cause her pain. So, I waited, and when I heard the whispers, I too joined hands and received my miracle. I was not born like I was when you found me, Crofton. I tried to tell you over the years, but the words got stuck in my head, and I couldn't release them. I was born with all the abilities of any other Noxian seedling. I was a curious child, and I talked incessantly and asked too many questions. My father was a mean man who valued the quiet I was constantly disrupting. He would threaten to cut my tongue out or beat me senseless, but I knew he'd never harm me as long as my mother was there. Though he was a small man, she was a large woman, and he feared her when she was in a temper.

"One day my mother went out to visit a friend. Foolish as I was, I decided to stay behind as I didn't much care for her friend. My father was carving stone for Tussock's statue garden. I watched quietly, biting my tongue so I could keep quiet though a million questions were fighting to be freed. An hour passed, and still I could not tell what he was carving. Another hour passed in silence, and finally the question broke free. I could contain it no longer, and I hardly knew I said it aloud. I simply whispered, 'What is it you're carving, Father?' That was the last complete question I ever asked, and the last time I spoke to my father. The broken silence startled him, causing the tool to slip, slicing his finger. He beat me until I was barely conscious and was half way through cutting my tongue out when my mother returned. She pulled him off me, grabbed the knife from his hands, and carried him outside. I never saw my father again.

"My mother cradled me in her arms and did her best to sew my tongue back together, but I was never the same. I could understand almost every word she spoke, but when I tried to speak back, the words were all jumbled in my head, and they rearranged themselves before I could get them out. Everyone thought I was slow after that. I withdrew and would probably still be sitting in that alcove if it hadn't been for Crofton. He never treated me as though I were different. He never spoke to me as though I were daft, and eventually I was able to teach myself to communicate in a primitive sort of way.

"But now, I am whole again. The pieces of my head have been set right, and I want nothing more than to learn and to teach and to talk. I would be honored if you would consider me for the position on Traveriss."

The silence stretched on for several minutes after he made his request as everyone processed the story of Pili's childhood, a story no one had ever thought to ask, and even if they had, the story could have never been told until now. At last, Betony bumped Rue with her elbow, prodding him to speak.

"If that is your desire, Pili, the post is yours," Rue finally said. A smile spread across Pili's face, and he winked at Betony. He then walked toward her and presented her with a small token of his appreciation – a stone carving of the Crest of Hope. He gathered her into a long hug and gently kissed her on the cheek.

"You can only go to Traveriss if you promise to visit – often," she whispered to him. He smiled his acceptance of her terms.

"Well, our work here is done. We'll leave you to govern your people," Rue said to Crofton.

"Oh no. I'll not be doing any governing myself. I'm going into retirement to see if I can't make up for the last five years," Crofton shot a glance at Ambulia as he continued, "The people will govern themselves by choosing their own leaders. We've got our work cut out for us, but we're ready and willing. Some have already begun to tear down the border walls. You're witnessing the birth of a new Noxia, thanks in a large part to both of you." Pick stepped up to offer his goodbyes as well.

"If things don't work out between you and Rue," he said to Betony, "you know where to find me." Betony blushed as Crofton pulled Pick away.

"Easy now, big brother," Crofton cautioned, patting Pick's chest. "You're suffering from an acute case of hero-worship, and I'm afraid by the look on Rue's face you may well start a war here. We'll find you a nice Noxian woman."

"So, you're off to Eudora then?" Aster asked.

"First to Asa-en-Darah. Stephanotis has agreed to perform the Grafting Ceremony for us there, so we can officially be unionized. Then, it's off to Eudora," Rue said.

"Alone?" Galax asked.

"Alone for a while yes, until we figure out what to do with ourselves. Calden and Yerba have expressed an interest in returning to Eudora with StarThistle and perhaps some of the orphaned Noxian children after a while. I'm sure we'll be in contact," Rue explained. Before the night was out, the Rocky Ridge and the Low Plains were bathed in a new kind of darkness – the darkness of peace.

Betony sat on the grassy hillside, watching the sun-star descend behind the Eudoran mountain tops. She often came to this spot to breathe in the life around her. She could see the sky melting into the rapids of the river from this very spot. She had come here to watch the stray rays of sunlight dance along the cliffs and glimmer in the river, searching for a place to rest for the night.

She turned a seed over in her palm - the same seed Rue had once given her to protect. She kept it with her always since Rue had permanently unlocked the castle. She stared at that seed, wondering what secrets lay dormant inside its thick shell. She rose to her feet, her long red hair blowing in the gentle breeze that ushered in the night. She caught Rue's fragrance in the wisps of air that circled about her.

"Thought I might find you here," he said as he came up behind her and put his arms around her waist.

"Finished already with your nightly call to Crofton?" she teased. He was smiling when he turned her around to face him. She tucked her hand behind her back.

"What have we here?" He opened her fingers, which were still cradling the ancient seed. He took the seed from her hand and stared out over the horizon for a few moments before turning to face her again. She wrapped her arm around him, her fingers unintentionally coming to rest on the scar he bore on his left arm. A shiver ran through her as she rubbed the mutilated skin – his constant reminder of what he had very nearly lost. He put his hand over her quivering fingers and drew them away from the old wound. He kissed her hand and placed the seed in her palm.

"Do you know what I think we should do with this seed?" he asked. "I think we should bury it and release it from its prison. I once told you that it was the key to my heart, but I know now that you are the only key to my heart. We'll plant it as a symbol of our love." He put her hand over his heart, where her skin had been grafted as part of their unionization. Then, he knelt down and began digging the grass up, and she joined him in his endeavor. They placed the ancient seed in the hole and carefully covered it with dirt, packing it tightly with their hands.

They returned to their spot often to watch the seed transform from a dull, lifeless shell to a green sprout, and they reminisced about their feeble beginnings. They watched as it grew just as their love for each other had grown. They watched as it changed with the seasons just as they had changed over time. And they used it to teach their own seedlings about life, love, loss, happiness and hope.

> One seed
> Dormant, hibernating,
> Unaware of what life has in store
> Until its growth is triggered
> And it is changed
> Forevermore.

Author's Note

Much of my inspiration for this book was drawn from nature. All the characters from the Florenci System were named after flowers, plants, or noxious weeds, and their physical characteristics were based upon the plants from which they were named. *(Drawings by Brinley Mortensen)*

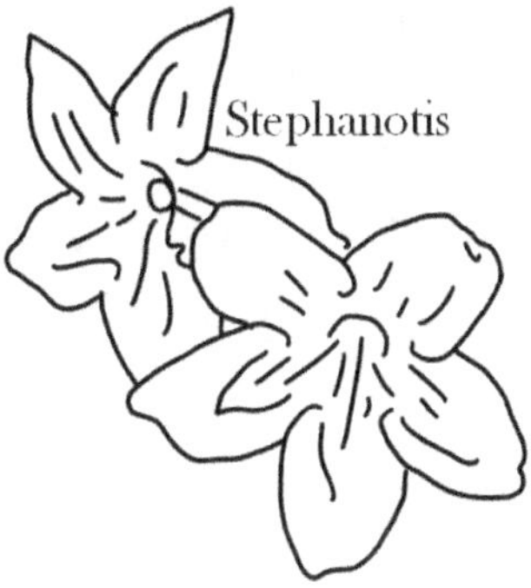

Stephanotis

Ranunculus

Lisianthus

Aster

Galax

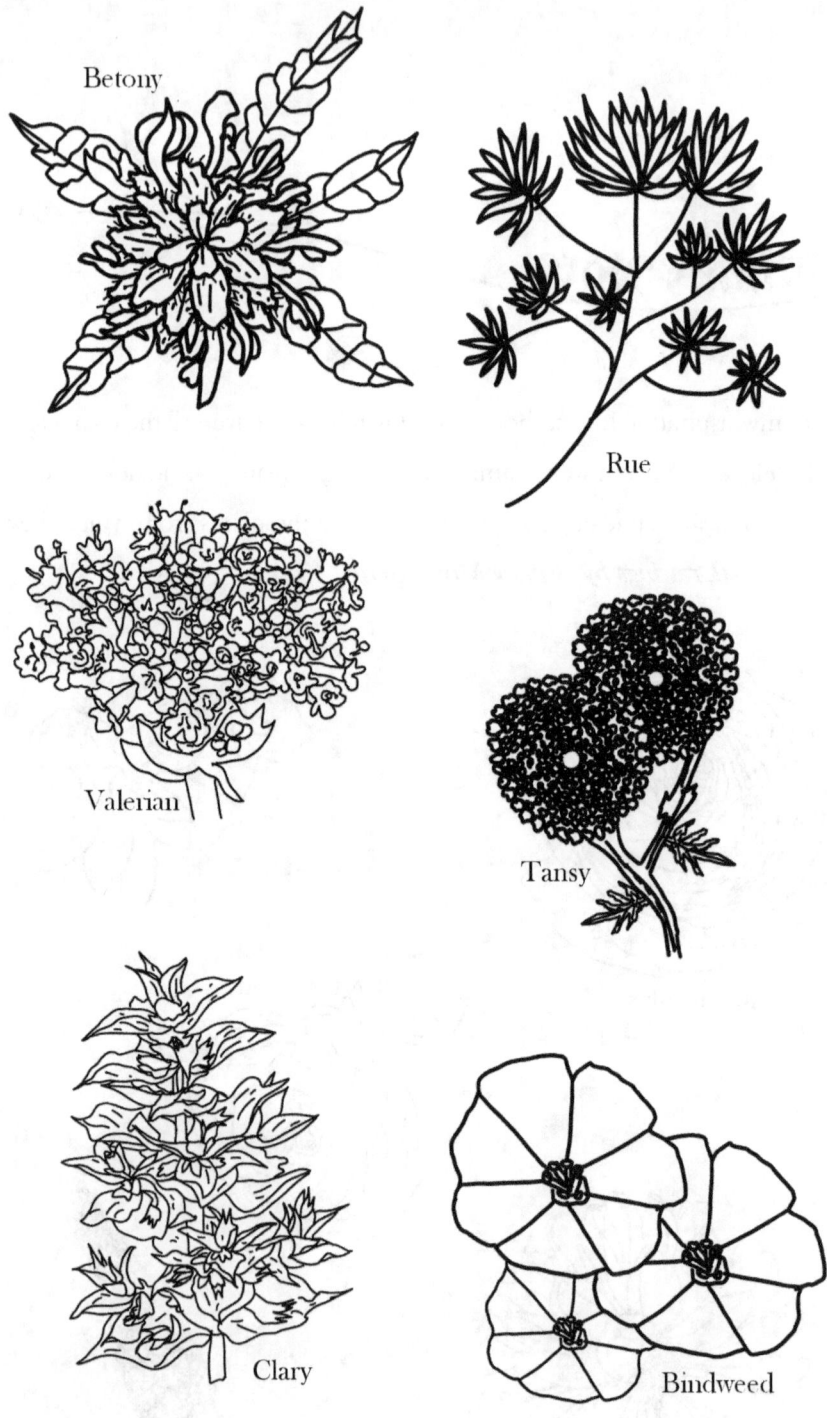

Betony

Rue

Valerian

Tansy

Clary

Bindweed

Kyasuma

Miramar

Boxthorn

Ambulia

Crofton

Pilipiliula

Borreria

Tussock

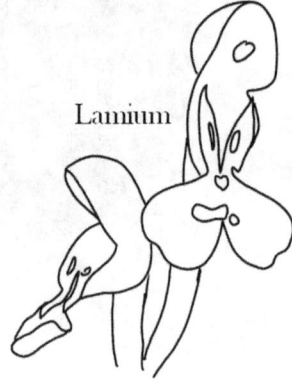

Lamium

About the Author

Tennille Jo Mortensen grew up in rural Idaho where she developed a passion for writing as she began composing poetry and short stories at a young age. After graduating with an MBA from Idaho State University, she became a full-time mother to two daughters. While focusing on her faith and family, she draws inspiration for writing from her everyday life. She enjoys hiking, photographing waterfalls, transforming socks into unique monkeys with needle and thread, and creating memories with her husband, children, and two dogs in Portland, Oregon.

Check out the Spotify playlist that played on repeat during the creation of this adventure:

www.ingramcontent.com/pod-product-compliance
Lightning Source LLC
Chambersburg PA
CBHW071205020726
47502CB00002B/548